**Praise for I**

"This first-clas ... more."

*ro*

"Dangerous, steamy, and full of intrigue."
—*Booklist* on *The Hero*

"Grant's dizzying mix of danger and romance dazzles . . . off-the-charts chemistry and a breath-stealing plot."        —*Publishers Weekly* (starred review) on *The Protector*

"Nonstop thrills and hot romance drive this story at a breakneck speed."        —*BookPage* on *The Protector*

"Grant really packs on the intrigue and non-stop thrills, while the romance is steamy hot."
—*RT Book Reviews* on *The Protector*

### The Dark King series

"Loaded with subtle emotions, sizzling chemistry, and some provocative thoughts on the real choices [Grant's] characters are forced to make as they choose their loves for eternity."        **—*RT Book Reviews* (4 stars)**

"Vivid images, intense details, and enchanting characters grab the reader's attention and [don't] let go."
—*Night Owl Reviews* **(Top Pick)**

## The Dark Warrior series

"The world of the Immortal Warriors is a thoroughly engaging one, blending powerful ancient gods, fiery desire, and touchingly human love, which readers will surely want to revisit."　　　*—RT Book Reviews*

"[Grant] blends ancient gods, love, desire, and evil-doers into a world you will want to revisit over and over again."　　　*—Night Owl Reviews*

"Sizzling love scenes and engaging characters."
　　　*—Publishers Weekly*

"Ms. Grant mixes adventure, magic and sweet love to create the perfect romance[s]." 　*—Single Title Reviews*

## The Dark Sword series

"Grant creates a vivid picture of Britain centuries after the Celts and Druids tried to expel the Romans, deftly merging magic and history. The result is a wonderfully dark, delightfully well-written [series]. Readers will eagerly await the next Dark Sword book."
　　　*—RT Book Reviews*

"Another fantastic series that melds the paranormal with the historical life of the Scottish highlander in this arousing and exciting adventure." 　*—Bitten By Books*

"These are some of the hottest brothers around in paranormal fiction." 　*—Nocturne Romance Reads*

"Will keep readers spellbound."
　　　*—Romance Reviews Today*

# ALSO BY DONNA GRANT

## THE SONS OF TEXAS SERIES
THE HERO
THE PROTECTOR
THE LEGEND

## THE DARK KING SERIES
DARK HEAT
DARKEST FLAME
FIRE RISING
BURNING DESIRE
HOT BLOODED
NIGHT'S BLAZE
SOUL SCORCHED
PASSION IGNITES
SMOLDERING HUNGER
SMOKE AND FIRE
FIRESTORM
BLAZE

## THE DARK WARRIOR SERIES
MIDNIGHT'S MASTER
MIDNIGHT'S LOVER
MIDNIGHT'S SEDUCTION
MIDNIGHT'S WARRIOR
MIDNIGHT'S KISS
MIDNIGHT'S CAPTIVE
MIDNIGHT'S TEMPTATION
MIDNIGHT'S PROMISE
MIDNIGHT'S SURRENDER

## THE DARK SWORD SERIES
DANGEROUS HIGHLANDER
FORBIDDEN HIGHLANDER
WICKED HIGHLANDER
UNTAMED HIGHLANDER
SHADOW HIGHLANDER
DARKEST HIGHLANDER

## THE REAPER E-ORIGINALS
DARK ALPHA'S CLAIM
DARK ALPHA'S DEMAND
DARK ALPA'S LOVER

# THE
# **CHRISTMAS**
# COWBOY HERO

# **DONNA GRANT**

St. Martin's Paperbacks

This is a work of fiction. All of the characters, organizations, and events portrayed in this novel are either products of the author's imagination or are used fictitiously.

THE CHRISTMAS COWBOY HERO

Copyright © 2017 by Donna Grant.

All rights reserved.

For information address St. Martin's Press, 175 Fifth Avenue, New York, NY 10010.

ISBN: 978-1-250-16542-8

Our books may be purchased in bulk for promotional, educational, or business use. Please contact your local bookseller or the Macmillan Corporate and Premium Sales Department at 1-800-221-7945, ext. 5442, or by e-mail at MacmillanSpecialMarkets@macmillan.com.

Printed in the United States of America

St. Martin's Paperbacks edition / November 2017

St. Martin's Paperbacks are published by St. Martin's Press, 175 Fifth Avenue, New York, NY 10010.

10  9  8  7  6  5  4  3  2  1

# Prologue

*South Africa*

*Home.*

The word flashed across the screen of Clayton's cell for the fourth time in three days. He turned the phone over as his way of ignoring it.

It had been over six months since he last spoke to his parents. They hadn't exactly been thrilled when he didn't return home after resigning his commission in the Navy.

How could he? Everyone would expect him to be the guy he'd been when he joined the military. And he wasn't.

Not even close.

There were times he looked at himself in the mirror and didn't recognize the man he saw staring back at him. He wasn't ready to go home and have his family discover just how altered he'd become.

Clayton ran a hand through his hair and glanced out the window. The heat could be seen rising from the ground. A group was already gathering to start patrolling the reserve for the day.

Few of his friends understood why he'd chosen to take the contract job in South Africa guarding the animals instead of the other offers he'd received. Frankly, he was tired of all the killing. Not that it didn't happen in his current job, but they were protecting the animals from poachers. It was different.

He stood from his bed as he pocketed his cell phone and grabbed his baseball hat. Clayton was on his way to the armory to get his weapons for the day when he heard his name. He looked over his shoulder and saw the door to his boss's office open.

Clayton backtracked and poked his head into the room. Jim Collins waved him inside. Apprehension scuttled down Clayton's back when he saw that Jim was on the phone, uttering the occasional "yes" every now and then.

He stared at Jim. A career military man who retired from the Army, Jim was tall and in phenomenal shape for a man in his late fifties. Many took the gray in his black hair to mean that he was slow and weak. It didn't take long for Jim to show them differently.

Finally, his boss held out the phone to Clayton. "Take it."

"Who is it?" Clayton asked without looking at it.

Jim blew out a breath and got to his feet. "Take the goddamn phone," he said in a harsh whisper.

Even as he grasped the receiver and brought it to his ear, Clayton knew it was his family on the other end. There was a second of panic as he realized that it must be dire for them to reach out to his boss.

"Hello," he said.

"Clayton Randall East, I didn't raise you to ignore me," came his mother's commanding words.

He was at once happy to hear her voice and worried, as he perceived the slight tremble in her words. The one thing his mother had always been was strong. He'd grown up believing that she could stop the sun from rising if she had a mind to do it. Justine East was that kind of woman.

So for that tremor to be there concerned him greatly.

"What is it, Mom?" he asked.

"It's your father."

Three words. That's all it took for him to recognize that something had happened. Because his father was the type of man to outlive everyone just because he could. There was no way his mother would call unless things were bad.

"What happened?"

His mother drew in a breath that he heard through the phone. "It'd be better if you came home before I explain it."

"Mom. Tell me now."

"Just like your father," she mumbled. "There was an accident."

Clayton closed his eyes. "Is Dad . . . ?"

He couldn't even finish the sentence.

"No, sweetheart," his mother said in a soft voice. "Your father is very much alive. He had a transient ischemic attack or TIA. It's a mini-stroke. The doctors said it was a warning. There's no permanent damage, and he's recovering now, but I need you home."

This went beyond what had occurred with his father.

And he knew without asking that it involved the ranch. "Tell me all of it."

"We're on the verge of bankruptcy, Clayton. Our last hope rested on Cochise."

He squeezed the bridge of his nose with his thumb and forefinger. The East Ranch had been in operation since 1893 and had passed down through generations of Easts.

There had been times the ranch was in dire straits before, but every time, it managed to survive. When Clayton had left for college and then the Navy, the ranch had been doing more than fine.

Ben East was one of the more frugal owners the ranch had ever seen, so Clayton knew his father wasn't to blame. Which meant something else had occurred, something his mother wasn't ready to share.

"Where's the bull?" he asked.

Cochise had been his choice. Clayton begged his father to purchase the bull years ago, and it had been a wise investment that netted the East Ranch vast profits.

There was a bit of a hesitation from his mother before she said, "Stolen. Along with about a hundred cattle that were set to calf soon."

Clayton couldn't believe all of this had been happening at the ranch and they were just now calling him. Then again, he didn't exactly answer calls, texts, or emails on a regular basis.

"I need you," his mother said.

He opened his eyes and looked at Jim. "I'm on my way."

"Thank you, son."

The fact that he heard tears in her voice only made

him angrier at himself. He ended the call and handed the receiver back to Jim.

"I already got you a flight while you were talking," his boss said. "The chopper will leave in fifteen minutes to take you to the airport."

As Clayton shook Jim's hand, he couldn't dislodge the feeling that he wouldn't be returning. But that was something to deal with later. Right now, he had to help his parents, and figure out who had stolen their cattle.

Though cattle rustling wasn't as prolific as it had been a hundred years before, it still occurred. And it had happened to the East Ranch.

It only took Clayton a few minutes to gather his clothes into his pack. He looked around the small room with the twin bed. Unlike others, he didn't have anything personal to decorate the room with.

He slung his bag over his shoulder and walked from the room to the waiting chopper that would begin his trip back to Texas.

# Chapter 1

This shit couldn't be happening. Abby Harper's heart thumped against her ribs as she turned into the parking lot of the sheriff's department. She parked and opened her car door, only to have her keys drop from her shaking hands. It took her three tries to pick them up because she couldn't get her fingers to listen to what her brain was telling them.

Along with the fact that her brother had been arrested, her mind couldn't stop thinking about the money she was losing for leaving her job early to find out what happened. Which meant that there was a real possibility that she would have to choose between paying for electricity or groceries next week.

She hunkered into her coat, bracing against a blast of cold air as she hurried to the door of the building. As soon as she was inside, the heat engulfed her.

Coming through the speakers overhead was the old

Willie Nelson and Waylon Jennings song *Momma, Don't Let Your Babies Grow Up to be Cowboys*.

The irony wasn't lost on her. The problem was, she'd done everything she could. But Clearview was in cattle country. That meant there were cowboys everywhere— as well as rodeos that happened too frequently to even count.

Abby licked her lips and walked up to the counter and the glass window. A man in a uniform slid back the pane and raised his blond brows in question. His look told her he didn't care what had brought her there or what sad story she might have.

"Hi," she said, her voice squeaking. Abby cleared her throat and tried again. "Hi. I'm here about Brice Harper."

"You don't look old enough to be his mother," the man stated as he reached for a file.

After all these years, Abby should've been used to such a response. But she didn't think a person ever got used to such things.

She forced a half smile. "I'm his sister, but also his legal guardian."

"And your parents?"

If it had been anyone but a sheriff's deputy, Abby would've told them it was none of their business.

"Dad died years ago, and our mother ran off. But not before she gave me legal guardianship of my brothers."

The man's dark eyes widened. "You have another brother?"

"Yes."

As if she needed another reminder that she was failing at raising her siblings.

"Through that door," the deputy said as he pointed to his left.

A loud beep sounded, and Abby dashed to open the door. She walked through it to find another police officer waiting for her. Despite Brice's reckless nature and the rowdy crowd he hung with, this was her first time at a police station.

And, quite frankly, she prayed it was her last.

Nothing could prepare anyone for what awaited them once they entered. The plain white walls, thick doors, locks, and cameras everywhere made her feel as if the building were closing in on her. And that didn't even take into account all the deputies watching her as she walked past.

She wasn't sure if being taken back to see Brice was a good thing or not. Wasn't there supposed to be something about bail? Not that she could pay it.

Her thoughts came to a halt when the deputy stopped by a door and opened it as he stepped aside. Abby glanced inside the room before she looked at him. He jerked his chin toward the door.

She hesitantly stepped to the entrance. Her gaze landed on a familiar figure, and relief swamped her. "Danny."

"Hi, Abby," he said as he rose from his seat at the table in the middle of the room.

His kind, hazel eyes crinkled at the corners with his smile. He walked to her then and guided her to the table. All her apprehension vanished. Not even the fact that he also wore a sheriff's deputy uniform bothered her. Because she'd known Danny Oldman since they were in grade school.

He'd run with the popular crowd at school because he'd been one of the stars of the football team, but Danny never forgot that he'd grown up in the wrong part of town—next door to her.

"I'm so glad you're here," she said.

His smile slipped a little. "What Brice did is serious, Abby."

She pulled out the chair, the metal scraping on the floor like a screech, and sat. "No one has told me anything. Brice refused to speak of it. He just told me to come."

"Perhaps you should be more firm with him."

The deep voice sent a shiver through her. She hadn't realized anyone else was in the room. Abby looked over her shoulder to see a tall, lean man push away from the corner and walk toward her.

His black Stetson was pulled low over his face, but she got a glimpse of a clean-shaven jaw, square chin, and wide, thin lips. It wasn't until he stopped across the table from her and flattened his hands on the surface that she remembered to breathe.

"Abby," Danny said. "This is Clayton East. Clayton, Abby Harper."

It was a good thing she was already sitting because Abby was sure her legs wouldn't have held her. Everyone knew the Easts. Their ranch was the largest in the county. The family was known to be generous and welcoming, but that wasn't the vibe she got from Clayton at the moment.

Then it hit her. Whatever Brice had done involved the East Ranch. Of all the people for her brother to piss off, it had to be them. There was no way she could compete with their wealth or influence. In other words, her family was screwed ten ways from Sunday.

Clayton lifted his head, pushing his hat back with a finger. She glimpsed strands of blond hair beneath the hat. Her gaze clashed with pale green eyes that impaled her with a steely look. No matter what she did, she couldn't look away. She'd never seen so much bottled anger or anguish in someone's stare before.

It stunned her. And she suspected it had nothing to do with her brother or the ranch but something else entirely. She wondered what it could be.

"No," she said.

What should've been internal dialogue came out. Clayton's blond brows snapped together in confusion. She glanced at Danny, hoping that her outburst would be ignored. It wasn't as if Clayton needed to know that her history with men was . . . well, it was best left forgotten.

When she looked back at Clayton, she was arrested by his rugged features. He wasn't just handsome. He was gorgeous. Skin tanned a deep brown from the sun only highlighted his eyes more. His angular features shouldn't be appealing, but they were oh, so attractive.

She decided to look away from his face to gather herself but realized that was a mistake when her gaze dropped to the denim shirt that hugged his wide, thick shoulders. The sleeves were rolled up to his forearms, showcasing the edge of a tattoo that she almost asked to see.

Abby leaned back in her chair, which allowed her to get a better glimpse of Clayton East's lower half. Tan-colored denim hung low on his trim hips and encased his long legs.

He was every inch the cowboy, and yet the vibe he gave off said he wasn't entirely comfortable in such attire. Which couldn't be right. He'd been raised on the ranch. If anyone could wear such clothes with authority, it was Clayton East.

Danny cleared his throat loudly. Her gaze darted to him, and she saw his pointed look. Wanting to kick herself, Abby drew in a deep breath. Just as she was about to start talking, Clayton spoke.

"Cattle rustling is a serious offense."

Abby's purse dropped from her hand to the floor. She couldn't have heard right. "Cattle rustling?"

"We picked up Brice trying to load cattle with the East brand on them into a trailer," Danny said. "Those with him ran off."

She was going to be sick. Abby glanced around for a garbage can. This couldn't be happening. Brice was a little reckless, but weren't most sixteen-year-olds?

Though she knew that for the lie it was. She'd known from the moment their mother walked out on them that it would be a miracle if Brice graduated high school. He acted out, which was his way of dealing with things.

"I . . . I . . . ." She shook her head.

What did one say in response to such a statement? Sorry? I don't know what's wrong with him?

Danny propped himself on the edge of the table and looked down at her, his hazel eyes filled with concern. "You should've come to me if Brice was out of control."

"He hasn't been, though," she argued. And that wasn't a lie. "Brice's grades have improved, and he's really straightened up."

Danny blew out a long breath. "Is there anyone new he's been hanging around with?"

"No," she assured him. "Not that I've seen."

After the last incident when Brice was about to enter a house that his friends had broken into, he'd sworn he wouldn't get into any more trouble. Abby truly believed that the brush with the law had set him straight.

Her heart sank as she realized that her brother could very well go to jail. She knew she was a poor substitute for their mother, but she'd done the best she could.

"What happens now?" she asked, racking her brain to come up with memories of past shows she'd seen to indicate what would happen next. "Is there a bail hearing or something?"

"That depends on Clayton."

Just what she needed.

But Abby was willing to do anything for her brothers. She sat up straight and looked Clayton in the eye. "My brother is young and stupid. I'm not making excuses for him, but he's had a hard time since our mother left. I'm doing everything I can to—"

"You're raising him?"

She halted at his interruption before nodding. "Both Brice and Caleb."

He stared at her for a long, silent minute.

Abby wasn't too proud to beg. And she'd even get on her knees if that was what it took. "Please don't press charges. I'll pay back whatever it is you've lost with the theft."

"Abby," Danny said in a harsh whisper.

"Is that so?" Clayton asked as he crossed his arms over his chest. "You're really going to repay my family?"

Abby looked between Clayton and Danny before returning her gaze to Clayton and nodding. Her throat clogged because she knew the amount would be enormous, but if it meant her brother wouldn't go to jail, she'd gladly pay it.

"There were a hundred cows stolen. Thirty of them were recovered when your brother was arrested, which leaves seventy unaccounted for. Let's round it to $2000 each. That's $140,000. Not to mention that each of them is about to calf. Each calf will go for a minimum of $500 each. That's an additional $35,000."

Oh, God. She would be paying for the rest of her life. And she was fairly certain Clayton wanted the payment now. How in the world was she ever going to come up with that kind of money?

But Clayton East wasn't finished. He had yet to deliver the killing blow.

"Then there's Cochise, one of our prized bulls. He's worth $100,000."

She put a hand over her mouth as her stomach rebelled. She really was going to be sick, and at the moment, the idea of vomiting on Clayton East sounded tempting.

There was no way she could come up with $275, much less $275,000. Worse, Clayton knew it. It was written all over his face.

Danny rose to his feet and stood at the end of the table. "Abby, you need to get Brice to tell you where the rest of the cattle are."

The words barely penetrated her mind. She stared at the metal table, her mind blank. Usually, she was able to think up some way to get her brothers out of whatever mess they'd gotten into—and there had been some real doozies.

She'd toiled through various jobs until she landed a position at the CPA company where she was currently employed. Despite the fact that she worked sixty hours a week, they wouldn't put her on salary because that would mean they'd have to give her health insurance.

Even with those hours and every cent she scraped together, it still didn't cover their monthly bills. But the one thing she'd promised her brothers was that she would take care of them.

And she had.

Up until today.

She scooped up her purse and stood before facing Danny. "I'd like to see my brother now."

It took everything within her to walk out of the room without giving the high and mighty Clayton East a piece of her mind.

# Chapter 2

Stunning. It was the only word that came to Clayton's mind when Abby Harper walked into the room at the sheriff's station.

He was glad he'd been in the corner so he could take his time looking her over. She was of medium height, but there was nothing ordinary about her. Her big blue eyes seemed to suck his very soul away. Her lips were supple and generous with a pale pink shade of lip gloss that gave them shine. He had a ridiculous urge to wipe away the color—not with his fingers, but with his mouth.

Her brunette hair was pulled back in a ponytail to fall in a queue of deep brown with the occasional caramel lock in the mix. It had him wondering just how long her hair was. And how the length might feel if he ran his fingers through it.

The fawn-colored coat she wore hung past her hips. It was frayed at the hem in several places, and there were buttons missing at the cuffs and one at her waist, which kept it hanging open. That allowed him to glimpse the cotton candy pink sweater beneath.

His need to see more of her was what brought him from his position in the corner of the room to stand opposite her at the table. And when he saw the ample breasts that not even her sweater could hide, his cock went hard. Her long, black pencil skirt and tall boots hid her legs, but the material of the skirt molded to her amazing curves like a second skin.

He hadn't reacted like this toward a woman since . . . well, since high school. Clayton hadn't cared to listen to the things Danny tried to explain to him about the Harpers. Until she walked in. Then, he couldn't take his eyes off her. And he wanted to know every detail.

Abby had a delightful mix of strength and vulnerability that made him instantly want to protect her.

Not that he would carry through with that thought. He had his hands full at the ranch trying to find the CPA who had stolen their money, as well as the missing cattle.

Clayton had intended to press charges against Brice. Yet, the longer he stared at Abby, the less that mattered. Especially when she declared that she would pay back everything.

Her eyes had gone wide, and her already pale complexion had whitened further when he'd told her the final price. She hadn't cried or begged. Her shoulders had slumped, but she'd lifted her chin, the steel in her spine keeping her focused on her family.

Clayton had watched her demand to see her brother before walking out of the room. But he didn't move. He couldn't. He was too mixed up about the entire meeting.

"I tried to warn you," Danny said when he returned a few minutes later. "Abby is a good person who is doing her best with Brice."

Clayton dropped his arms and hooked a thumb in his belt loop. "The boy needs a male in his life."

"I agree."

"Is she dating anyone?" But why did the thought of that anger him so?

Danny flattened his lips as he shook his head slowly. "I've several friends who asked her out. Hell, I was even interested, but ever since their mom left when Abby was just eighteen, she's put her entire focus on her brothers."

"Why didn't you ask her out?" Clayton didn't know why his mind stuck on the fact that Danny was interested in her.

"Because she needs a friend," Danny replied. "And if I ask her out, she'll no longer consider me a friend."

She'd think of him as someone who wanted in her pants. As pretty as Abby was, Clayton thought for sure she'd have someone steady or even be married. But there hadn't been a ring on her finger. In fact, the only jewelry she wore was a pair of gold star studs in her ears.

Clayton didn't want to admire Abby Harper. And he certainly didn't want to like her, but he found himself doing both against his better judgment.

"Are you going to press charges?" Danny asked.

Clayton walked to the door and looked in the direction Abby had disappeared. There was no sign of her, but it wasn't difficult to imagine how the reunion with her brother was going. He rubbed his jaw and listened as Danny continued to sing her praises. It was during

Danny's speech about how Abby always carried through with her promises that he had an idea.

"She won't have the money to bail Brice out, will she?"

"No," Danny said.

With his decision made, Clayton turned his head to Danny. "I want to talk to Brice."

"What do you plan?"

"I'm going to make him work off his debt at the ranch. If he won't tell me who the other rustlers are, perhaps I can convince him to take me to the cattle before they're sold or slaughtered."

Danny rocked back on his heels. "That's a good idea. Besides, everyone around here knows the East brand. No one in their right mind would buy any of your cattle without your family being there, but especially not now that the word has spread about the theft."

"That's what I'm hoping."

It was a long shot, but Clayton knew he'd get nothing if Brice were prosecuted. And, for some odd reason, he wanted to help the boy. Or perhaps he wanted to help Abby.

Danny motioned for him to follow as they left the room and moved through the hallways, turning left and right several times "Brice will agree. He's thoughtless and rash, but deep down, he's a good kid. He adores Abby. The three of them are tight, leaning on each other to get through each day."

"Then Brice should stay out of trouble." Clayton winced as he heard his father in his words.

Danny glanced at him over his shoulder, as if he too were shocked at what he'd said.

Of all the people Clayton had encountered since his return to Texas three days ago, Danny had been the only one who hadn't pressed to know about the years he had been away. And Clayton was thankful for that. It had begun to get difficult dodging the questions or changing the subject.

They came to stand in front of a jail cell. It was the first time Clayton had seen Brice, but the moment he laid eyes on the teenager, he could see the resemblance to Abby in the teen's blue eyes and dark hair.

The fear in the boy's gaze reminded Clayton of himself when he'd had that rowdy period in his life after his brother died. Someone had given him a second chance. Maybe that's why he was feeling generous with Brice.

The youth's mouth went slack as he recognized Clayton. Brice slowly got to his feet while nervous energy had him picking at the hem of his shirt.

"Mr. East," Brice said.

Clayton bowed his head. "Mr. Harper."

The boy seemed stunned at the response for a moment, but Clayton decided to treat him like an adult and see how things went.

"Abby said you're pressing charges," Brice continued.

Clayton inhaled deeply and crossed his arms over his chest. Beside him, Danny remained silent and still. "Your sister offered to pay back what the ranch is losing because of the stolen cattle and the bull."

"Really?" Brice asked with a grin forming.

"It's $275,000."

The magnitude of it seemed to hit Brice as he collapsed onto the bench. His gaze dropped to the floor. "Abby can do a lot. She manages to pay our bills and put food on the table while seeing that we always have clothes. But she goes without. The only thing she does for herself is take a night class from the university every now and again if she can scrape together the money. There's no way she can repay that."

While he spoke, something occurred to Clayton. "Why did you steal the cattle?"

There was a slight hesitation as Brice looked up at him. "The money I was promised would've helped Abby so she didn't have to work or worry so much. I wanted her to buy something for herself just once."

After hearing that, Clayton knew he'd made the right decision about Brice. What the kid had done was wrong, but he'd been doing it to help his sister, not just for the thrill of breaking the law.

"Will you tell me who is behind the theft?"

Brice's Adam's apple bobbed as he shook his head.

Clayton let that go. For now. "I have a proposition for you, Brice. It's quite a tidy sum the ranch is out. You're the only one who got caught, so it all falls on your shoulders."

"I know," Brice said, lifting his chin in much the same manner as Abby had not so long ago.

Clayton was impressed that the teen hadn't tried to shake off the responsibility. He was shouldering it like a man, which was proof that Abby had done a good job raising him. "I won't press charges, and you can walk out of this cell today."

"What's the catch?"

"You'll work it off at the ranch. During the week, you'll arrive straight from school and do your homework. Once that's done, you'll work until dinner. Then

I'll drive you home. On the weekends and any time you're not in school, you'll arrive at six a.m. and work the entire day, returning home at dinner. If you miss one day for anything other than an illness—that I'll have to confirm—I'll have Danny pick you up and bring you right back to this cell."

"Deal," Brice said as he stood and walked to Clayton, sticking his hand through the bars.

Clayton hesitated. "Don't you want to talk to Abby first?"

"It's my mess. I'm going to fix this myself for once."

There was hope for the boy yet. Clayton clasped his hand, and they shook. As soon as they stepped apart, Danny opened the jail cell, and Brice walked out.

The teen was tall, nearly as tall as Clayton. He had a good head on his shoulders, but he needed guidance. Clayton didn't exactly want the job. Yet, somehow, he found that it was his—and it felt right.

As they walked from the station, Clayton motioned to the black Chevrolet truck parked in front of the building. "Get in. I'll take you home."

Once they were on the road, Clayton noticed how Brice tried to look around at the interior of the vehicle without making it obvious.

"Do you drive?"

Bryon shook his head. "We only have the one car. Abby taught me, and I have my permit, but I haven't gotten my license yet. It's fine. I don't need to drive."

"Sure you do. You could share the car and help her out by getting groceries and the like."

"I didn't think of that," he murmured.

Clayton glanced at Brice, who ran his hand through

his cropped hair. "You seem like a good kid. Don't make me regret giving you a second chance."

"I won't," he said as he turned his head to Clayton. "I may act stupid sometimes, but I'm not a fool. I know what you're doing for me, Mr. East."

"My father is Mr. East. Call me Clayton."

"Thank you, Clayton," Brice said. "I won't let you down."

Clayton nodded as they turned onto a road. "You should have that same dedication to your family."

"I know," Brice murmured and looked out the windshield. "I was angry for so long, and I took it out on Abby. She didn't complain. Not once. She doesn't deserve to be stuck with us."

"Son, I don't know your family, but I can guarantee that your sister doesn't feel stuck with you."

That brought a hint of a smile to Brice's lips. The silence of the rest of the ride was only broken by the teen telling him how to get to the house.

When Clayton pulled into the driveway, he saw the age of the small residence in its peeling paint and the sway of the roof. But everything was clean, and the small yard mowed.

"Abby says just because we're poor doesn't mean we have to live in filth."

"She has a point," Clayton said as he noticed there was no other car in the drive. "I'd hoped to talk to her."

Brice unbuckled his seatbelt and shrugged. "Knowing her, she went back to the office and tried to work a little longer to make up for the hour she missed. I'll see you tomorrow afternoon, Mr . . . Clayton."

"Tomorrow," he replied.

He watched as Brice walked to the door and was greeted by a younger brother. Once they were inside, Clayton drove off, wondering at the regret he felt for not getting a chance to talk to Abby once more.

# Chapter 3

"The universe is against me," Abby said as she pulled the stuttering car onto the side of the road and put it in park.

She felt tears threaten. They rushed forward, burning her eyes, but she refused to let them fall. If she gave in now, she might very well cry for the next week with all the things trying to crush her.

Blinking several times, she got a hold of herself and swallowed. Then she popped the hood and climbed out of the car. The wind whipped around her, sending a gust straight up her skirt against her bare legs.

She shivered and hurried around to the front of the 1990 white Honda Accord. The only reason her mother hadn't taken it with her when she left was because Abby had removed one of the tires to change it the night before. Otherwise, Abby and her brothers would have been left with no vehicle.

The car had been a blessing, but lately, it was breaking down more and more. The fact that it had done it after her horrendous encounter with Clayton East at the sheriff's office and had decided to attempt to strand her on the lonely stretch of road was the last straw.

"You're going to run," she told the car while lifting the hood.

Her hands were so cold that she could barely grip anything. Gloves were a luxury she literally couldn't afford, but what she wouldn't give to have something warm against her hands.

With her teeth chattering, she leaned over the hood and began checking the usual suspects—converter and ignition switch. Everything seemed in order.

If it weren't so cold, she might actually be able to think. Give her a hundred degree heat, and she was fine. But let the temps drop below sixty, and she couldn't function. Since it was now forty-two degrees out, all she could think about was a warm shower, sweats, and two pairs of socks as she snuggled beneath a mound of blankets.

But in order to get all of that, she had to fix the stupid car.

"Think, Abby," she admonished herself.

She'd repaired the Accord more times than she could remember. She should be able to do this. After doing a couple of jumping jacks to get her blood flowing while holding her arms against herself—partly for the heat, partly to hold her boobs—she once more leaned over.

The sound of an approaching vehicle reached her. No doubt it was a sheriff's deputy since they patrolled the road often. The roar of the engine grew louder as it pulled up behind her and stopped.

She glanced over her shoulder and saw a black truck. Mentally groaning because no doubt it was some manly man who thought she was a damsel in distress, she went back to looking at the engine

"I'm fine, thanks," she hollered, hoping they'd hear her instead of getting out of the vehicle.

She checked a couple of other parts. With Christmas only a few weeks away, the very last thing she needed was to spend more money on the Accord.

Tears welled again as she tried to imagine Christmas morning without Brice. While they couldn't afford decadent Christmases, they had always been together—through tough periods, and even rougher times.

The sound of the truck door closing made her roll her eyes. She turned as she said, "Really, I'm fi—"

The rest of the words lodged in her throat as her gaze landed on none other than Clayton East. He was like a bad penny that kept turning up.

She began to open her mouth, but he quickly spoke over her. "If you tell me you're fine one more time, I'm going to throw you over my shoulder and toss you into the bed of my truck."

The thought of all those muscles beneath her palms was intriguing. Part of her wanted to call his bluff. Yet she kept silent, because she wasn't sure she wanted to be anywhere near that hard body of his. Mostly because she knew she'd like it entirely too much. And she didn't have time for anything like that.

Once Brice and Caleb had graduated with jobs and—hopefully—going to college, then maybe she'd consider it. But not until then.

Clayton removed his cowboy hat, showing off a wealth

of golden hair that hung long and wavy. He raked a hand through the thick length, shoving a portion of the top over to one side.

She swallowed hard, all too aware of the way her body warmed just looking at him. Her nipples puckered—and it had nothing to do with the cold. And just like in the sheriff's office, she found herself drowning in his green eyes.

"What happened?" he asked.

She blinked, confused. What was he talking about? Her bewilderment must have shown because he pointed behind her. Abby turned and looked at the car. The fact that it took her a second or two to remember why the hood was up, let her know just what kind of effect Clayton had on her.

"I don't know. I thought it might be the ignition switch or converter, but both look good."

He came up beside her and gazed down at the exposed engine. His eyes met hers. "May I?" he asked, pointing to the car.

She shrugged and wrapped her arms around her waist. She didn't want help from the man who was sending her brother to jail. Never mind that Brice had broken the law. But she knew Clayton wouldn't be able to fix the vehicle. No one knew her car like she did.

"Be my guest."

He bent at the waist, and Lord help her, her eyes went straight to his ass and the way the Wranglers molded to him. She pressed her lips together and looked away, but that lasted only a moment before she glanced back. She was pretty sure there wasn't a part of Clayton that didn't look superb.

He tinkered with a few things. Then his voice reached her. "I don't remember you from school."

"I'm five years younger than you."

A grunt was his response. It made her roll her eyes. She was thinking of all the ways she might try to earn extra money to pay off Brice's debt so he wouldn't go to jail when Clayton straightened, grease covering his fingers.

"Try her out," he urged.

It would get her out of the wind. And that was the only reason Abby did it. She opened the car door and sank behind the wheel. She twisted the key, fully expecting nothing to happen, but the car roared to life.

"Your open mouth tells me that you were sure I'd fail."

She turned her head to find him standing at her open door. Damn, but he moved fast. "I was."

"You're still angry with me."

She glared at him in surprise and anger. "Of course, I am. He's my brother, and I don't want his life ruined because he's stupid. Haven't you ever been that dumb? Don't you believe in second chances?"

"Yes. And yes."

He caught her off guard with his response. She was so taken aback, that for a moment, she couldn't reply. Then it hit her. If he believed in giving someone another chance, why hadn't he with her brother? Before she could form the words, he was talking again.

"Brice is at home," he said and closed her door before moving to the front of her car and lowering the hood.

She stared at him as he got into his truck and drove

off. For long minutes, she sat there, letting his words sink in. Then she drove like a maniac to get home.

Once there, she ran from the car and through the front door to find Brice in the kitchen starting dinner as Caleb set the table. She dropped her purse and slammed the door behind her as she rushed to her brothers, and the three of them hugged in the middle of the small kitchen.

"It's going to be okay, Abby," Brice said.

She squeezed her eyes closed in an attempt to stop the tears for the third time that day. Leaning back, she kissed Caleb's forehead before looking at Brice. "What happened?"

"Clayton went to see him," Caleb said, not wanting to be left out. At fourteen, everything Brice did was something to be copied.

Brice motioned to the table. "Sit."

Not once had either of her brothers ever cooked dinner, no matter how many times she'd asked them. They would cook for themselves, but not for her. So she wasn't going to argue the point.

Abby walked to the table and shrugged out of her coat before she sat and looked at Brice. "Clayton came to see you?"

"Yeah. After you left. I was scared shitless, to be honest."

She watched as he continued to brown the meat while Caleb got out the pasta and the tomato sauce for spaghetti. The waiting to discover what had been said was killing her, but she'd already asked twice.

Finally, the pasta was boiling in the water, and the ground meat and sauce were simmering, which allowed Brice to turn to her. "He offered me a second chance."

"There's a catch in there somewhere," she said.

Caleb paused beside her while placing napkins on the table, "That's what I said."

"There is," Brice replied. "I'm to work off the debt at the ranch beginning tomorrow. I'll arrive after school and do any homework. Then I'll work until dinner. For the weekends and anytime I'm not in school, I have to be there at six in the morning and work until dinner."

Abby wanted to find some kind of flaw in it—mostly because she was still irked with Clayton. He could've told her all of this at the sheriff's offices instead of remaining silent.

But the truth was that this would be good for Brice. She'd wanted him to get a job for months now. Not to bring home money, but to teach him responsibility and keep him from the group of friends who were constantly getting into trouble.

"I think I had that same reaction," Brice said. "I kept waiting for him to demand something else, but they released me, and he drove me home."

Abby leaned back in the chair. "That's good." Wasn't it? Yes, it was good. Actually, it was great.

Suddenly, Caleb's face was before her, his brown eyes twinkling as he smiled at her, something he rarely did since getting his braces. "He asked about you."

The thrill that went through Abby was unwanted, but there was no stopping it. Then she found herself asking Brice, "Did he really?"

"Yep," Brice said with a grin as he stirred the meat sauce.

"I'm sure he just wanted to fill me in on things. But he didn't say anything when I just saw him."

"You just saw him?" her brothers asked in unison.

Abby nodded, looking between the two. "The Accord broke down."

"And it's cold," Caleb said, wrinkling his nose.

Her brothers knew her so well.

"I guess he was driving by," she said with a shrug. "Anyway, he stopped and got it fixed before telling me you were home. Then he drove off."

A frown marred Brice's young features. "I wonder why he didn't tell you."

It was because she was being bitchy. It was his way of getting back at her—and it had been a smooth hit.

"The work is going to be rough," she warned Brice.

His blue eyes met hers. "I'm actually looking forward to it. Oh, I know I'll complain, but I've always been curious about what goes on at a ranch. Then when we took the cattle, I was fascinated with them."

"Where are the rest of the cattle?" she pressed. "And the bull? Do you know that animal is worth $100,000 by himself?"

By the regret on Brice's face, he'd known the animal was worth a pretty penny. "I can't say."

"Can't or won't?" she demanded.

He refused to look at her. "Can't."

"You could save everyone a lot of trouble if you just tell Clayton where the cattle are and who was involved."

Caleb pulled out the chair beside hers and sat sideways, throwing his arm over the back of the seat. "He's got that look, Ab. Brice isn't going to say anything."

Yeah. She knew that look all too well. Brice was one

of the most honorable people she knew. If he gave his word, he kept it. That would serve him well in later years, but right now, it irritated her.

"I'm fixing my mess this time," Brice said. "You've done enough for me. It's time for me to be a man."

She wondered if it was her brother's hours in jail or the time he'd spent with Clayton made him chance, because when he spoke, she could actually picture Clayton's face as if the words were coming out of his mouth.

# Chapter 4

Anger simmered and boiled in his gut. Clayton rubbed his tired eyes as he looked through the paperwork from their last CPA while in his father's office. If felt strange to be sitting there. When his eyes began to cross, he rose and poured himself a shot of bourbon.

He stood, looking out the window into the night. His mind should be on figuring out the mess the accountant left them, but he couldn't stop thinking about Abby Harper. He really wished he could've seen her face when Brice told her the news.

"You're smiling. That must be a good sign."

He turned at the sound of his mother's voice. Looking into her soft brown eyes, he shrugged. "I wasn't smiling."

"I know a smile when I see one," she admonished.

She walked to him and wrapped her arms around her thin frame. The thick navy robe she wore was one of her favorites that she'd had for years. In many ways, his parents had been born in the wrong century. His mother kept her hair long, the blond strands now showing some white, and it was always either in a bun or braided as it was now.

"I'm guessing you haven't solved the shit storm of the books?"

He gave a shake of his head before finishing off the bourbon. "What happened?"

"Bill retired," she replied with a sigh. "He was our CPA for almost forty years, and his father worked for your grandfather, and his before that."

"Family business." Clayton knew all about that.

His mother walked to the couch and sat, tucking her legs beside her so that her robe covered her bare feet. "Nathan took over for his father as Bill had done with his. Nathan had been working with Bill for the past five years. We had no misgivings about allowing Nathan to continue on as every Gilroy has done for nearly two hundred years."

"Mom, I only took a few accounting classes in college, and as soon as I finished, I promptly forgot everything. We need to take this to Bill."

The remorse on his mother's face said he wasn't going to like what he heard next.

"When the bank called because there were no funds to pay the bills, we went up there to figure out what was going on." His mother rubbed her hands up and down her arms. "I thought it was some computer glitch that would be straightened out soon."

Clayton went back to the desk and sat in the chair. When he returned home, he'd immediately set about trying to find the cattle. It wasn't until this evening that he attempted to look at the books—or talk about the disaster before them.

"And?" he prompted when she paused.

"They showed us how the money had been moved out of our accounts."

Clayton laced his hands over his stomach. "What about the investments? What about the savings account and the other business accounts?"

"Gone."

There had been a part of him that thought—hoped, really—maybe his mother had exaggerated the family's financial difficulties. Now, he knew she hadn't.

"How?" he demanded.

Her shoulders slumped as the worry settled around her face. "Nathan had full access to our accounts to work our investments and move money as he saw fit. Just as his father and grandfather before him."

"Yeah," Clayton said tightly. "I get that, but things have changed, Mom. Why would you give someone that kind of control of your money?"

"It's how we've always done things. We had no reason to think Nathan wouldn't be honorable."

Clayton was having difficulty reining in his fury. He'd always thought his parents were smart and safe with their money. It never dawned on him to see for himself.

As if reading his mind, his mother said, "I know you don't want to be here. You haven't since Landon died."

God. Why did everything always have to circle back around to his brother's death? "No, I don't want to be here, but it has nothing to do with Landon, and everything to do with me not being ready to return.

Regardless, I'm here now, and we're going to get this figured out."

"It was the thought that your father might be the one to lose the ranch that caused his stroke. He won't admit it, but I know that's the reason."

Clayton did, too, but Ben East was as obstinate as a mule. "I saved a lot over the years, and did some questionable investing that lost me a lot of money but netted me more. I've transferred money into the main business account and made sure all the bills that bounced have been paid. I also made sure Nathan was taken off all the accounts, so he no longer has any access." He glanced at the stack of invoices on the corner of the desk. "I suppose those were things Nathan was supposed to take care of, as well?"

His mother nodded slowly. "I pay our credit cards and things like that, but the Gilroys have always taken care of the ranch's bills."

Based on the amount his family had been paying the Gilroys, it was no wonder the East Ranch was their one and only client. While most CPAs only handled taxes for LLCs and corporations and the occasional individual, the Gilroys had also handled Accounts Payable and Accounts Receivable for the East Ranch. That meant they knew everything there was to know about the Easts and the ranch.

"Your father liked the invoices to come to him, and then he'd bring them to Bill and Nathan," his mother went on to explain.

Clayton ran a hand down his face. Much of his aggravation stemmed from the fact that these were things he would've known had he returned after college.

They were things his brother would've made sure to learn before he graduated high school. Because Landon had wanted nothing more than to take over the ranch one day.

Clayton shoved aside those thoughts and leaned forward to rest his forearms on his knees. "Here's what's going to happen. All the bills will get paid. We're going to find the stolen cattle and Cochise. We're also going to find Nathan. I've already put a call in to the FBI. One way or another, everything is going to work out. There's no way we're going to lose the ranch."

"Don't use all your money on us, son," she said, her brow furrowed deeply.

"I've got more than enough."

The silence stretched between them. He knew what she was thinking even before the words left her mouth. Still, he held his breath, hoping that she'd let it go.

He should've known better.

His father was stubborn, but he had nothing on his mother. She was like a dog with a bone. Determined. Persistent. Tenacious. All of those words described his mother to a T.

"Clayton," she began.

He sat up. "Don't," he warned.

"My heart hurts that the first conversation you and your father have had in years ended in an argument."

It hadn't exactly been a fight. More like a disagreement because there had been explicit instructions by the doctor once his father had been released from the hospital that nothing should upset him.

"Dad needs to rest."

His mother pursed her lips. "Sweetheart, he's been

in charge of the ranch for so long that he doesn't know any other way to be. He needs to feel as if he's still part of it."

"He is."

She paused, her face falling. "So Ben's right. You will leave."

"Let's focus on what's happening right now and all the problems facing us." He wasn't in the mood to talk about the future or why he couldn't remain at the ranch.

To his parents, it would always be about Landon. And his brother's death did play a part in it, but it had gone beyond that. War had changed Clayton in too many ways to even try and explain.

There wasn't a night that he slept through. Each time he closed his eyes, he was assaulted by nightmares of the brothers in arms that he'd lost—and the men he'd killed in order to stay alive.

"I won't apologize for enjoying you being here," his mother said. "Whether you want to believe it or not, the ranch is in your blood. It's always passed down through family."

And it probably would have already had Landon not been killed.

Two years older, his brother had been the one capable of doing anything he set his mind to whether it was academics, football, or ranching. Landon had been fearless in everything he did. And he'd excelled at all of it.

He'd shone as brightly as the sun in Clearview. But there had never been any jealousy between the brothers. Clayton had been content to let Landon shoulder the responsibilities of the eldest who would one day take over the ranch because it allowed Clayton to goof off.

But it had all come screeching to a halt one cloudless summer night.

Unable to sit still any longer, Clayton rose and returned to stare out the window. "The Harper boy will be here tomorrow."

"You think he'll show?" she asked.

Grateful that she'd allowed him to change the subject, Clayton nodded without looking in her direction. "I'm hoping I can earn his trust so he'll tell me where the rest of the cattle and Cochise are."

"If they haven't already been sold off."

"Not around here, they haven't. That means they'd have to haul them somewhere. All the roads are being watched for just such activity."

He observed his mother in the reflection of the glass as she played with the end of her braid that fell over her shoulder. "So you believe the cattle are still here?"

"I do," he replied.

"Then let's hope it works. Those calves could go a long way to helping us pay you back."

His gaze shifted toward one of the barns and beyond. "I've set up men to watch the other herds. No more cattle are going to be stolen from the East Ranch."

"You can't stop the thieves if it's something they want badly enough."

He turned to his mother. "This ranch has pretty much stayed with the times, but there are other things that should be implemented right away."

"Like?"

"Surveillance equipment."

Her soft brown eyes went wide. "We can't afford that."

"The first thing I did when I arrived was ride around the ranch and mark the spots where someone could get onto the property undetected. Before I saw Dad, I ordered everything that is needed. Installation begins tomorrow."

His mother brightened. "So there will be people to cook for?"

He'd never understood why his mother felt the need to cook for the masses, but it made her happy. And she was phenomenal at it. Then there was her baking, which was even better.

"Yes, ma'am."

She jumped up, mumbling about items she would need from the grocery store. It didn't take much to bring a smile to his mother's face.

His gaze drifted upward as his thoughts turned to his father. Things weren't so simple there. In the four years since he'd last seen his parents, his father had aged greatly. The worry and stress of the ranch had taken its toll.

This was the time when Landon would've begun to take more responsibility, allowing their father to ease into retirement—not that men like Ben East ever retired. He'd always have his hand mixed in with the ranch because it's all he knew.

Clayton looked at the computer once more. The ranch wasn't exactly bankrupt. There was still revenue coming in with the sales of cattle, but it wasn't enough to cover expenses.

When he got his hands on Nathan—because he would—he was going to take great pleasure in wringing his neck.

And for some reason, that made him think of Abby. He was fairly certain she'd wanted to do that and more to him when he stopped to help her earlier.

There was something about the spitfire that intrigued him. Perhaps it was her valiant attempt to rein in her brothers. She had a steady head on her shoulders, but the weight of responsibility was taking its toll on her.

And why the hell did he even care? He had to save the ranch, which was why he needed to concentrate instead of thinking about blue eyes and a wealth of curves that begged to be touched.

# Chapter 5

*Everything was going to be all right.*

Abby went to bed repeating that line, and it was the first thought when she opened her eyes the next morning. While she got ready for work, she kept thinking of all the ways Brice being at the East Ranch could go wrong.

Then she had to stop herself and say her mantra again. It helped. Some. The truth was, nothing had ever come easily for her or her brothers. They'd been clawing and scraping by since they came into the world. And she knew it would never change.

Her stomach was a bundle of nerves when she walked into the kitchen to find Caleb munching on a waffle as he tried to hide a can of Coke from her.

"Juice," she said.

Caleb rolled his eyes, but he went to get a cup and poured some orange juice. There wasn't a lot in the glass, but it was better than nothing.

"Thank you." She took the carton from him and poured half a glass before downing it.

"This is one of those things where I'll thank you when I get older, right?" he asked.

She nodded as she finished her last swallow. "That's right."

"Yeah, well, I'm not liking it now."

She smiled. "That's the point, kiddo."

The toaster went off with two more waffles that her brother quickly grabbed and gripped with his teeth as he put on his jacket.

That's when she looked around for Brice. "Where's your brother?"

"He caught a ride with the Millers down the street."

Brice, up early? Something was wrong. "Where did he go?"

Caleb gave another dramatic eye roll. "School."

"What? Why?"

"How the hell should I know?" Caleb shrugged as he bent and retrieved his backpack, slinging it over his shoulder. He then put the unopened can of Coke into his coat pocket and started for the door. "I'll see you after school, sis."

She opened the freezer to grab a waffle for herself but found an empty box instead. "Of course," she mumbled and tossed it into the trash.

With two teenage boys, it was difficult to keep any food in the house. She walked to the front room when she heard the squeal of brakes from the bus and watched Caleb climb up the steps.

There was a time she'd counted down the years until she was free from raising her brothers. Now, she was nearly there, and she wasn't sure what to do. Her life had been nothing but raising her siblings. What would she do with herself once they were gone?

Date?

That made her snort. She hadn't been on a date in forever. She'd tried it once not long after their mother had left, and both of her brothers had freaked out. So, it hadn't happened again.

Abby sighed and walked back to the kitchen where she started the coffee. She didn't want to think about how quiet the house would be when her brothers were gone. After a cup of java, she gathered her coat and purse and drove into work.

The day alternately crawled and rushed by before slowing again. When she glanced up and saw that it was four o'clock, her stomach clenched nervously.

Brice should be at the ranch by now. Had he actually shown up? She prayed that he had, otherwise, he was back in jail. The next hour moved at the speed of molasses. When the clock struck five, she hurried to get her things and drove to the East Ranch to make sure Brice was there.

Halfway to the ranch, she pulled over. This was when she wished her best friend, Jill, was still around because she really wanted another woman to talk to. Yet a once-in-a-lifetime job had come Jill's way, sending her to California. The time difference made it hard for them to catch up on Skype, but Abby was never more aware of the absence of her long-time friend than at that moment.

"What am I doing?" she asked herself. "Brice will be pissed if I show up."

He'd assured her the night before that he was done screwing up. He'd kept talking about taking responsibility and being a man. She didn't know where any of that had come from, but the change had been refreshing.

Brice was smart, but the anger he carried about their mother leaving was something he'd never dealt with, much less spoke of. It was like a chip on his shoulder that never let up.

Abby pulled out her cell phone and checked how many minutes she had left for the month before she called the house. There were precious few, but she needed to talk to someone. Caleb answered on the second ring. "Hey," she said. "Everything okay?"

"You're at the ranch, aren't you?"

Where had the time gone when she could ask a question and her youngest brother didn't know she was hiding something? It had happened without her even knowing it. Which sucked.

"I stopped on the way there," she admitted.

Caleb made a noise. "How long have you been sitting on the side of the road?"

"Long enough to know that I should come home."

"You do know I'm fourteen, right? I'm no longer a kid you need to worry over."

"I'll always worry."

"I know, but you shouldn't have to. That's our mother's job."

She closed her eyes, hating when their mother was brought up. Caleb didn't remember much about her, but Abby suspected he kept a lot of things to himself. "Well, you've got a sister who loves you as both a sister and a mother. Two for the price of one. You can't beat that."

"I wouldn't change anything, Abby. You know that, right?"

She felt the damn tears again. What was wrong with her? "I love you, too."

"Go check on Brice. I'll start dinner."

"Is there even any food to cook?"

He chuckled, his voice deepening every week. "We're having my favorite."

"Sausage rice," she guessed, smiling.

"That's right. And it's gonna be spiiiicy. Now stop using the minutes. Love you. Bye."

The line disconnected. She put the phone back in her purse and found herself chuckling. Sausage rise was nothing more than frying sausage in a pan with garlic and onions before adding in some rice and other seasoning.

It was a dish she turned to often because it was fairly cheap, and it had quickly become Caleb's favorite. He'd have it every night if he could. Brice, on the other hand, wasn't as fond of it.

Abby looked at the clock on the dashboard. It was now 5:30. She had no idea what time Clayton considered dinner, but at her house, it was between 6:00 and 6:30.

"Screw it," she said and pulled back out onto the road, heading toward the ranch.

Ten minutes later, she was turning onto the long drive. A massive, whitewashed brick wall sat on either side. A wide, black, wrought iron gate hung open, but her gaze was drawn upward to the wooden beams that came out of the brick and held up an even thicker beam with a simple black iron sign that said *East Ranch*.

She drove beneath the sign and was shocked that the winding drive was not only calming, but also beautiful. She'd never had cause to come to the ranch, so she hadn't known what to expect. This was . . . well, it was stunning.

The fence seemed to go on forever. The horses and cattle she spied lazily gathered together made her want to stop and stare.

She finally made it to the house and was glad she was alone because her eyes were bugged out and her mouth hung open. The dwelling was massive. It had a very Spanish-style feel with the stucco walls, sweeping archways, and a red clay tile roof, but the architecture and layout of the residence was what made her breathless.

The areas around the house were impeccably manicured. As she pulled to a stop at the front of the house in the curving drive, she had the urge to just keep going and pretend as if she'd never come. But the front door opened, and a woman came out wearing a smile.

Abby reluctantly put the car in park and shut off the engine. She opened her door and stood, getting a better look at the lady who had blond hair with only a few white strands interwoven throughout. She was tiny and thin, but she wasn't frail. If anything, the woman appeared as if she could face any challenge thrown at her.

"Hi. I'm Abby Harper. I'm here to pick up my brother, Brice. If you could let him know I'm waiting once he's finished, that would be fantastic."

When the woman frowned and cocked her head, Abby gaped. "Oh, God. Do I need to move? Should I go somewhere else? I'm so sorry. I didn't mean to come to the front. I just didn't know where else to go."

The woman let out a laugh. "You're fine, dear. Please, come inside."

"Thank you, but I don't want to intrude."

The woman put her hand on a hip and raised a brow, but the smile never waivered. "I've never let a visitor sit outside my house, and I'm not about to start now. If you don't come inside, I'll come out there with you."

Good God. This was Justine East. Abby wanted to crawl beneath the car and bury her head. But she knew the tone. Justine wasn't going to take no for an answer. Abby looped her hand through the handles of her purse and closed the car door behind her as she walked up the few wide-spaced steps to the front door.

"Welcome, Abby Harper," the woman said and held out her hand. "I'm Justine East."

Abby shook her hand and smiled, feeling instantly welcome. "Hello, Mrs. East."

"Justine, please. Let's get you warmed up," she said and motioned Abby inside before shutting the door behind them. They walked through the large foyer and hung up Abby's coat before Justine pointed to the left. "If you go straight through there, you'll come to the living area. There's a fire waiting. Would you like some coffee?"

"Yes, please," Abby replied as her gaze took in the high ceilings and antler chandelier.

Abby made her way into the living room and found her mouth hanging open once more. Her entire house could easily fit inside this single room.

The walls were painted dark beige while the cathedral

ceiling had braces of dark-stained, wooden beams. It was at once grand and homey. The floors were tile in an off-white marble that she knew had to be expensive.

There were six arched windows—three on either side—that were easily ten feet wide. Every one of them had double door entries. In the corner was a Christmas tree that was easily twelve feet tall and dripping with champagne-colored ornaments.

And, at the center of the room, on the far wall, was the grandest fireplace Abby had ever seen. It had thick garland laced with white lights and an array of more champagne-colored ornaments on the mantel. The brick went all the way up to the point of the ceiling.

The furnishings were just as gorgeous. Everything was arranged to focus on the fireplace. There were two cream sofas facing each other while a massive curved sofa faced the fireplace. Sitting in the middle of the floor atop a gorgeous rug with various whites, beiges, and browns, was a huge square coffee table. An ivy plant sat atop the table on one side with its vines spilling over the pot. On the other side were various antlers turned upside down to make a work of art that she liked.

"Here you go," Justine said as she walked into the room.

Abby gratefully took the coffee and wrapped her cold hands around the mug. She took a sip, letting the warmth spread through her. Everywhere she looked in the house, there was Christmas. Trees, garland, Santas, bells, and sleighs.

"Oh," Justine said with a gasp. "Do you need cream or sugar? I'm so used to my men taking it black."

Abby smiled, she couldn't help it. There was something about Justine that she immediately liked. The woman wasn't at all what she had expected. "I'll take coffee any way I can get it."

"I feel the same," Justine confided as she sank onto one of the smaller sofas. "Have a seat. I don't think Clayton and Brice will be done for another hour or so."

Abby wasn't comfortable drinking in the living room, so the thought of sitting down where she could stain something made her nervous.

"It's just furniture, dear. It can be cleaned if there's a spill. Trust me, I've had them cleaned countless times. There was nothing clean in this house with two boys running around."

"Oh, I know," she said as she sat on the other couch. "I swear I think my two brothers have some kind of magnetic energy that attracts dirt. It's gotten better, but there was a time when I didn't think anything would ever be clean again."

They shared a laugh, and then Abby found Justine's dark eyes staring intently at her.

"I like you," Justine said. "Clayton told me some of your story. So, you're raising your brothers? That's amazing."

For a moment, Abby couldn't answer. All she could think about was what horrendous things Clayton had told his mother about her. "Yes, that's right."

"Tell me about them," Justine urged.

This was safe territory. Abby was always happy to talk about her siblings. So, after a deep breath, she began singing her brothers' praises.

# Chapter 6

There was no denying the calmness that fell around him as quiet as snowfall. Clayton had been apprehensive about saddling the horse and riding around the ranch all day.

Yet it didn't take long for him to settle into a nice rhythm with the other hands as well as the company he hired to set up the surveillance system that was costing him a fortune. But it was something that should've been done years ago.

Time had gotten away from him, so Clayton was surprised when his mother phoned for him to return to the house for Brice.

By the time he arrived, his mother had already given the teen a sandwich and cookies. Brice was downing a bottle of water when Clayton walked into the kitchen. As soon as Brice saw him, he stood up.

"Thank you for the snack, Mrs. East," the teen said with a bow of his head.

Clayton watched the way his mother's eyes crinkled at the corners as a bright smile filled her face. "It was my pleasure."

The teen then turned to him. "I'm ready."

"Did you finish any homework?" Clayton asked.

"I finished it at school."

"Then let's get started."

They walked out together. As soon as Brice saw the bay Clayton had ridden, he went to it, softly stroking the animal's neck.

Clayton watched the easy way the teen was around the horse. "Do you ride?"

"I've never been around a horse," Brice replied, a wide smile pulling at his lips when the animal rubbed his head against him.

"You're a natural." Clayton should know. He'd seen enough people claim to know how to ride and know nothing.

Brice's blue eyes met his. "I've always loved horses."

"There are a lot of things around the ranch that we do on horseback, so you'll have to learn." Just as he expected, the teen's eyes lit up at the prospect. "Until then, you'll use this," Clayton said and tossed a set of keys Brice's way before walking away.

Brice caught them easily. After looking longingly at the horse, he followed Clayton. "You'll really teach me to ride?"

"If you want. My father bought the SxS for my mom when she broke her ankle a few years ago. Many ranches use them instead of horses."

"I can see why, but I'd prefer the horse."

Clayton hid his smile as they reached the dark green,

two-seat Side by Side that had a small bed in the back for tack. Brice walked around the all-wheel-drive, off-road vehicle, running his hands over the top and inspecting the windshield.

"This is nice," he said.

"Follow me, but don't get too close because you'll spook the horse."

Brice look affronted that he'd even mention such a thing. "I won't."

Clayton turned on his heel and headed back to his gelding. He put his foot in the stirrup and swung his right leg over the saddle before settling in.

"Let's go, boy," he murmured to the horse as he moved his hand to the side, guiding the animal to turn to the right.

As he started out, Clayton heard the SxS roar to life. He didn't look back. Brice was a smart kid. He'd figure it out. Sure enough, moments later, the sound of the engine grew louder as the teen followed.

Clayton took them back out to the team setting up the security system. The way Brice fidgeted nervously was just what Clayton wanted.

"Show me where you got in," he ordered.

Brice swallowed hard and turned up the collar of his fleece-lined denim jacket. "Yes, sir."

Clayton mentally added gloves to the list of things he needed to get for Brice. The kid had shown up, but if he wanted Brice to do the work, he would have to supply the accessories.

"Look under the seat of the UTV. There're some gloves. Find a pair that fits. You won't be able to use your hands if your fingers are frozen," Clayton said.

Without a word, Brice did as instructed. He returned, rubbing his gloved hands together. "Thanks. I won't lose them."

For some reason, Clayton believed him. "Which direction?"

Since they were on the west side of the property where Clayton saw many opportunities for someone to sneak onto the ranch, he wasn't surprised when Brice pointed north.

Every ranch had blind spots. And with the various roads in and out of the property leading to various pastures, it would've been easy for anyone to get in. Clayton was just surprised it hadn't happened sooner.

Instead of getting back on the horse, he walked to the UTV and slid into the passenger seat. Brice hesitated for a second before hurrying to follow. The teen's hands were steady as he drove them to the spot about four miles away.

Clayton got out of the vehicle and stood, staring at the repaired wooden fence. He walked closer and inspected the dirt road that ran parallel to the pasture. There were still some tracks visible, but nothing that stood out.

Still, he jumped the fence and went to take a closer look. Some of the tread marks he recognized as those from the ranch. Too many vehicles had run over the area since the theft for Clayton to be sure of anything.

He walked the space before turning toward the fence and squatting down to look closer at some tracks. Then he lifted his head and pinned Brice with a look. The youth's blue eyes caused him to think of Abby. The bold, sassy woman had plagued Clayton's thoughts during the night. It was really irritating that he couldn't shake her.

"How many were involved?"

Brice glanced away as he put his hands into the pockets of his coat. "I don't know."

Clayton slowly straightened. "The one thing you've not done is lie to me. Why start now?"

"Don't ask me anything about it," Brice said, his head hanging.

"Why?"

"I can't say."

"Can't or won't?"

"Both. Please. I'm begging you, leave it."

There was no denying the distress that colored the teen's words. It didn't take a great deal of thinking to conclude that the man or men had threatened Brice.

As much as Clayton wanted answers, it was useless to press Brice now. He'd keep with his original plan and earn the kid's trust. Once Brice knew Clayton would look after him, then all the secrets would be spilled.

The only snag was that time was of the essence. The cows would start calving soon. And the longer the cattle were away from the ranch, the harder it would be to find them.

Clayton jumped the fence again and walked back to the SxS. They returned to the others, and he put Brice with a few of the older hands that worked the ranch, doing the chores no one wanted to do.

As the UTV disappeared on the way back to the barns, Clayton's thoughts turned to Abby. Would he see her tonight when he dropped off Brice? He hoped so. Perhaps he'd get out of the truck and go inside the house to make sure he got some face time with the spitfire.

Another hour and a half later, he called it a day. While the workers got into their trucks and drove off, and the ranch hands raced each other back to the barns, Clayton took a leisurely ride.

On the way back, he detoured to a ravine that had been a favorite of his and his brother's. They'd spent countless hours swimming and fishing and talking.

Clayton stopped the gelding and looked down at the ravine. The last time he'd been there was the day of Landon's funeral. He hadn't returned because it was too painful. And instead of facing things, as soon as Clayton was able, he'd run away.

There was no more running for him.

He turned the horse around and headed back to the ranch as rain began to drizzle. It gathered and dripped from the brim of his cowboy hat. The gelding shook his head to dislodge the drops that fell into his ears.

Clayton didn't mind the cold or the rain. His russet-colored suede coat was lined with thick wool, as were his gloves. Though he'd fought returning home, he couldn't deny that he'd always loved the land.

Hard work was as ingrained in him as saying grace before a meal. Taking care of the land, the horses, the cattle, and even the people who worked there was something he relished.

But it was never meant to be his.

It had been meant for Landon.

Yet everything that stretched around him would

someday be his. Clayton wasn't sure how he felt about that. He didn't want to let his parents down—or Landon, for that matter—but it didn't feel right.

By the time he reached the barn, the drizzle had turned into a shower. He heard Brice in the tack room, asking the older hands questions as he worked.

Clayton dismounted and walked the gelding to his stall. He removed the saddle and the bridle before dumping feed into a feeder. Then he began to brush the horse down with long, slow strokes.

He glanced over when he heard Brice walk up. "How's it been going?"

"It's awesome," the youth said with a bright smile.

Clayton knew the older men had given Brice the dirtiest, toughest jobs, and if the teen was still smiling after, then there was hope for him. "Glad to hear it."

"I can't imagine growing up with all of this."

"It's beautiful, I'll grant you that. But it's work. Lots of work."

Brice lifted his head to look at the top of the barn. Then he sighed as he lowered his face to Clayton. "I know I screwed up, and I know you're giving me a second chance. I could say thank you ever day, but Abby taught me that actions speak louder than words. I'm going to prove to you that I'm worth that second chance."

"Good," Clayton said and walked from the stall, closing the door behind him before sliding the bolt in place to lock it.

Brice cleared his throat and shifted his feet nervously. "I'm hoping that after I've worked off my debt—which I fully understand will be years—that you might hire me."

Now that surprised Clayton. He cocked an eyebrow at the teen. "You've worked here one day. Not even a full day, I might add. You may very well change your mind after a weekend."

"No way," Brice said with a shake of his head "Abby always said that if you find an occupation that makes you happy, you should hold onto it with both hands, regardless of what it is. This," Brice said, waving his arms around to encompass the ranch, "makes me happier than I've ever been."

There was a lot about his words and actions while speaking of the ranch that reminded Clayton of Landon. "Abby is a smart woman."

"Oh, you've no idea," Brice said with a chuckle.

Clayton could see the love the teen had for his sister. The siblings might have endured hardships, but they were close, their love holding them together.

"Abby has always been there for me and Caleb. Whatever we needed, she somehow found a way to get it for us." The smile faded. "I wanted to do something for her. Instead, I screwed it all up."

"Nothing illegal is good. Remember that. Abby just wants you safe, happy, and loved. She doesn't strike me as the kind of woman who wants things."

Brice shrugged. "Everyone wants things. Abby keeps it hidden, but I wanted her to be able to open a present this Christmas that wasn't something from around the house we wrapped just so she'd have something to open."

Coming from wealth, Clayton couldn't imagine what the three siblings went through. Though he should just let it go, something within him refused to.

"Neither you or Caleb will have to do that this year.

You'll make your sister something right here on the ranch."

Brice's blue eyes widened. "That would be awesome, Clayton. Thank you."

He slapped the boy on the back. "Come on. The day is over. Abby will no doubt want you back home."

# Chapter 7

Rich colors met Abby's gaze when Justine brought her into the large office to await Clayton. Hand-scraped, dark wood floors set the tone. The walls were a deep gray, which warmed the space. The ceiling was coffered so that it was set in a grid of recessed, square panels in a soft gray tint that were accented by dropped beams stained a deep, opulent color. Another chandelier of antlers hung above her, though it was much smaller in size than the one in the living room.

The desk looked old, and she had a feeling it had come from the first East who began the ranch. She ran her hand along the wood, trying to imagine what it was like to grow up with such a family.

The connection, the history, the love.

They were things she recognized but didn't have a concept of for herself. She saw them in others and dearly wished them for her brothers.

Movement outside the window grabbed her attention.

She walked around the desk, stepping behind the tall, dark leather office chair when she spotted her brother in the rain. He was smiling.

She let loose a deep breath of relief. There had been a slight fear that he wouldn't show up, but she should've known better. As she tried to remember the last time she had seen him smile so freely, she realized it had been years.

When he'd grown old enough to recognize their situation and began to listen in on her conversations with creditors when they called, his boyish smile was wiped from him. He'd aged overnight, it seemed.

Their hardship was something she wished neither of her brothers knew, but she also didn't believe in lying to them. Although she kept the major concerns to herself so they didn't get bogged down with things they couldn't change. It wasn't their fault that she didn't have a better-paying job or that things cost too much for them to ever get ahead.

But being here on the ranch, Brice was getting a glimpse of another life, one that could be his if he worked hard enough and got a degree.

Her spine straightened when she saw Clayton. Somehow, he looked even better than he had the day before. Maybe it was because he was in his element, or maybe it was just the man himself.

He held all the control when it came to her brother, which left her beholden to him. While Abby liked Justine, she wasn't comfortable owing Clayton in any way. Yet, here she was.

Without meaning to, her eyes lowered to his hips. He walked with the long, sure strides of a man who knew exactly who he was and how he fit into the world. Clayton wore an easy half-smile as he listened to her brother, and it made her breath catch.

When was the last time a male had taken an interest in Brice? Never. And here was a man who Abby was more than happy to have showing her brother attention. Whatever she might think of Clayton, he was honorable and dependable. Brice could learn a lot from him.

Because no matter how hard she tried to be sister, mother, and father, she couldn't be all things.

As the duo approached the house, Abby was pulled out of her thoughts. She turned to retrace her steps and accidentally bumped the computer mouse.

The screensaver vanished, and accounting pages popped up. She knew she should walk away, but there was a line item that caught her eye. While she tried to figure out where the money had been allocated, she forgot all about being in someone else's house.

"Find something of interest," came a deep voice.

Her head jerked up as embarrassment consumed her when her gaze clashed with pale green ones. Clayton stood just on the other side of the desk in a black button-down and jeans. Had she been so involved that she hadn't seen him? Apparently.

Clayton's face was lacking in either anger or irritation. In fact, he was unreadable. But his stony expression sent a chilled warning down her spine to never piss him off. She might not know Clayton, but she recognized a man who kept a tight leash on himself—until he let loose.

"Oh, God. I'm so sorry. I know what this looks like, but I swear I wasn't snooping." She glanced over her shoulder at the window. "Your mother told me to wait in here, and I saw you and Brice. I wanted a closer look, and when I turned around, I hit the mouse," she hurried to say, her words coming out in a jumbled rush.

His hat was gone, leaving her once more to look at his long, blond hair. It was plastered to his head by the hat, rain, sweat, or all three

Slowly, he raised a brow. "Indeed."

"I'm so sorry," she repeated and came around the desk.

He blocked her retreat. "You were frowning."

His words took her aback. Then she remembered what she'd been looking at. "Yeah."

"Why?"

"I noticed one of the line items was coded weirdly."

His closed-off expression switched on a dime to one of intrigue. "You know accounting?"

"I'm taking night classes to get my accounting degree. To help things along, I work for a CPA company."

"So you know accounting."

Isn't that what she'd just said? Instead of letting those words fall from her mouth, she nodded. "Yep. That's right."

"If I let you look through the books, you'd be able to figure things out?"

She took an involuntary step back. "I think you should hire someone to do that. Someone with a degree."

"I'm not trying to trick you," he replied smoothly. His green eyes pinned her. "Our CPA embezzled nearly every cent from my parents and the ranch. And he's run off."

"That's horrible, but not surprising."

Both brows rose this time. "Why is that?"

"Everyone knew that Nathan Gilroy was bad news, but I never would've thought he'd do something like this."

Clayton merely stared at her.

Right. "Um . . . did you call the state board? Every CPA is required to keep up their license. You need to file a complaint so he can't set up shop somewhere else."

"With the funds he stole, I don't think he plans on working again."

"Of course." She nodded, trying to think. "Oh. Did he have malpractice insurance? It's something that CPAs get in case they get sued. I don't know if it'll apply to him embezzling, but you could check." Then, for some reason, she said, "Or I can do that for you."

Clayton's head tilted to the side. "That would be helpful. Thank you."

"Sure. I'll do it tomorrow."

Wow. She was shocked. They were being cordial to each other. She smelled leather and horse on him—and liked it.

"You didn't have to pick up Brice. I planned to bring him home."

She found herself picking at her thumbnail. "You're letting him work off his debt. The least I can do is drive him home."

Clayton's chest expanded as he inhaled a deep breath. "Brice is eating again, which makes my mother ecstatic."

"He's a bottomless pit, as is Caleb," she said with a laugh.

"Abby, my having him work here is two-fold. Yes, he's working off his debt, but I'm hoping he'll tell me who stole the cattle or at least let on where they're being held."

She nodded and cast a glance to the door to make sure her brother wasn't there. She lowered her voice and said, "I thought that might be the case. I asked him, but he won't tell me."

"I also asked today. He became agitated. I believe whoever it is has threatened him."

Abby's stomach soured at the thought. She wrapped her arms around her middle, suddenly chilled again. "There's a possibility that with him working here, they'll think he talked."

"Yes. But as long as I don't come for the cattle, he's safe."

"My one goal was to have both my brothers graduate high school without a record. I've been so diligent about keeping track of who he was hanging out with."

A shadow passed over Clayton's face. "Sometimes, boys don't listen to reason no matter who says the words."

There was a story there. She wanted to know what it was, but she refrained from asking. "I'll try to talk to Brice. I'll even ask Caleb. Sometimes, they share things that they don't tell me."

"Boys," Clayton said with a slight tilt of his lips.

Abby knew she should leave so the Easts could get ready for dinner, but she was finding it difficult to walk away from Clayton.

She pulled her gaze away from his to look at the floor for a heartbeat. "Thank you. That smile on Brice's face earlier, I've not seen it in years. I know this job is supposed to be tough, but he's happy. I can never repay you for that."

"Yes, you can."

"How?"

"Take a look at the books with me. Teach me."

She was wary of his proposal because she wasn't licensed and she didn't want to make a mistake that could cost the ranch more money.

"I need to try and figure out where Nathan hid the money," Clayton continued. "It's somewhere, because he wouldn't have taken it all in cash. The bank wouldn't have let him. That means it's traceable if it was sent via wire transfer."

He was right. But she still wasn't sure about getting involved. Yet, what would it hurt to help? "Okay."

"You don't negotiate well, do you?" he asked with a grin. "You should've asked me to pay you or take off some of the debt your brother owes."

She frowned at him. "Why would I do that? You didn't press charges against Brice."

"Is that why you're willing to help?"

The little twinkle in his eyes was gone, and that made her sad. "In part, yes. I'd still help even if Brice weren't involved. And I wouldn't ask for money then either."

"Even if you need it?"

"It's called Karma. You did a good thing for us. I'm doing a good thing in return. We've always found a way, and we'll continue."

He gave a small shake of his head. "I can't quite figure you out, Abby Harper."

She looked away as she began smiling. His words

pleased her immensely. Mostly because he'd half whispered them, looking at her as if she were a puzzle he wanted to decipher.

"Shall we start tomorrow?" he asked.

Before she could respond, Justine spoke from the doorway. "And I can cook for all of you."

"Even Caleb?" Brice asked as he walked up beside her, another huge chocolate chip cookie in his hand.

"Brice," Abby ground out in embarrassment.

But Justine was already looking at her brother. "Of course. I want to meet the youngest Harper. Tell me what your favorite thing is to eat?"

"Pretty much anything," Brice said.

That was the truth. Abby grinned as she watched Justine wrap an arm around him and walk him away before she winked at Abby over her shoulder.

"I'm going to apologize in advance," she said as she looked at Clayton. "My brothers will no doubt gorge themselves."

"You said you've not seen your brother smile in a while. Well, I don't think my mother has either. With my father's mini-stroke—"

"Oh, I'm so sorry," she interjected.

He shrugged. "Things happen."

"Was this recently?"

"Yeah."

That's when Abby realized it must have happened when the cattle were stolen. "Clayton, I'm sorry."

"You don't have to keep saying that," he said and turned away.

She walked to him and put a hand on his arm. "I do.

My brother's involvement means that my family is to blame."

He looked down at her hand. She snatched it away, but he reached over and gave it a little squeeze. "It seems like our families are intertwined."

Yes, it did. And Abby wondered how much the Easts were going to change them all.

Or perhaps she was more worried about the heat Clayton's touch caused.

# Chapter 8

Impatience. It ruled Clayton the next day. He'd spent hours on the phone with the Texas State Board of Public Accountancy, filing a complaint against Nathan Gilroy, before he found himself once more atop the bay gelding riding across the land.

The surveillance system was coming along nicely. Clayton had chosen one of the small offices in the front barn that hadn't been used for anything in years to set up the monitors. Alerts were set up, and everyone who worked at the ranch would be notified if anyone tried to cross the property barriers again.

While cameras could only do so much—and could be disconnected—only Clayton, his parents, and the small crew installing the system knew that another line was being run around every inch of fencing throughout the property. If another fence were torn down, they'd know about it.

It would take another week before all the line was run

and the computers were set up, but Clayton already felt better about the security of the ranch.

If only his father felt the same. The man was maddening, but he was slowly coming around. Clayton knew a large part of it was that his father believed everything was his fault—when it wasn't. Though Ben should be resting, he kept demanding to know everything Clayton was doing. To keep his father from becoming more agitated, Clayton began giving him nightly reports.

But Ben East wasn't the type of man to remain off his feet for long—no matter what the doctors said. Not that Clayton could blame him. He'd do the same.

Yet, Clayton knew it would give his mother some relief if his father continued to rest. Every day, his father pushed himself. He was out of bed and already going down stairs while threatening to get back on a horse. So far, Justine had kept Ben in check, but how much longer could that last?

It made Clayton wonder about leaving her alone with his father. His parents, while tough and resilient, were getting older. What if something happened to them that could've been avoided if he remained?

He pushed that thought out of his mind for now. There were countless other things that needed to be taken care of before he went down that road. Thanks to Shane, the manager of the ranch for the past twenty-five years, things were still running smoothly with the day-to-day business. At least that was one area Clayton didn't need to worry over.

It felt like years before he spotted Brice driving the UTV to the west pasture. Clayton knew it was only a little longer until Abby arrived.

"Well, your attitude changed quickly," Shane said.

Clayton's head whipped around to the ranch manager. He didn't know how long Shane had been beside him, but by the twinkle in his dark brown eyes, it was some time. "What do you mean?"

"You were scowling like a bear with his paw caught. Why do you think everyone is keeping their distance?"

Clayton looked around at the others, but the security team was busy working. "They're doing their jobs."

"Not anywhere near you like they were yesterday," Shane pointed out.

He shrugged. "There's a lot I have to see to."

"About that." Shane removed his cowboy hat and scratched his head of brown hair before replacing it. "I already spoke with your folks, but I wanted to apologize to you as well."

"For what?" Clayton asked, confused.

Shane's face crinkled into a frown. The very epitome of a cowboy, he spent more time out in the sun than in his office. Shane was very hands-on, which was what made him so valuable to the ranch.

"I should've known something was up with Nathan."

Clayton put his hand on the man's shoulder. "It wasn't your job to notice."

"I still feel responsible."

He looked into Shane's brown eyes and nodded as he dropped his hand. It had been the ranch manager who'd found him holding the broken body of his brother all those years ago.

Clayton would never forget how Shane had gently taken Landon's body and set him aside before holding

Clayton as he cried tears of remorse and shame. While Shane was a valued employee, he was also a close family friend.

"It wasn't for you to control," Clayton repeated the words Shane had once said to him.

The man's eyes watered before he hastily looked away, clearing his throat. "You've turned into a damn fine man, Clay."

Coming from Shane, that was quite a compliment.

Before he fought emotions himself, Clayton asked, "What do you have planned for Brice today?"

"Saddles need to be cleaned."

Clayton winced. That was one chore he detested— and one his father always gave him when he was young and being punished. Clayton absently rubbed his shoulder because he knew Brice would be hurting in the morning.

"You'll have to go easy on him tomorrow," Clayton said.

Shane grinned. "You told me to make sure I made a man of the boy. And you said he was working off his debt."

"He asked me if I'd hire him once he's that debt is paid up."

Shane's brown eyes widened in his tanned face. "A cowboy in the making, huh?"

"A teen who has romanticized ranch life."

"He asked you this yesterday after we worked him to the bone, right?"

Clayton nodded. "He did."

"You and I both know this life isn't for everyone.

Those who live it do it because it's in our soul. A love for the land and animals that gives us comfort we can't get anywhere else. Perhaps the boy is meant for it."

Shane's words made Clayton frown. Mostly because he believed them. He'd been certain he would spend his life right here on the ranch working for his brother. But things always changed when you least expected it.

"I didn't mean to open old wounds," Shane said softly.

Clayton glanced at the overcast sky. "You did nothing, old friend."

After a few minutes of silence, Shane lightly slapped him on the shoulder and turned away to mount his horse and ride away.

It wasn't much longer before Clayton whistled to the gelding, who munched on grass about thirty yards away. The horse jerked up his head before galloping to him.

Clayton unhooked the reins from the saddle horn and grasped it before he mounted and pointed the animal in the direction of the house. Then he clicked twice. The bay jumped into a run. The lower Clayton bent over the horse, the faster he ran.

The wind rushing over his face was icy and roared in his ears. The ground was a blur beneath him, but it was the vibrations of the hooves meeting the earth that made him smile. The power of the animal could be felt in every movement as he ran over the terrain.

He became one with the horse, their bodies moving in unison—symbiotic even. Adrenaline spiked, coursing through his body like lightning. All his worries disappeared, and he began to relax.

How could he have forgotten how good it felt to let a

horse have its head and run? Clayton felt truly alive for the first time in a very long while.

When he sat up and slightly tugged on the reins, the gelding slowed his pace. By the time they reached the first barn, everything looked more vibrant, more brilliant than it had when he'd first arrived.

Then again, riding had always cleared his head and helped him sort his emotions. Now that he remembered how good it felt, he planned to ride like that every day.

After giving his horse a nice rubdown and a carrot as a treat, Clayton found himself glancing toward the house and then at his watch. When would Abby get there? If she got off at five o'clock, it would take her about ten minutes to get home. Give her another ten minutes to collect Caleb and change if she needed. That would make it 5:20.

She'd need twenty minutes to get to the ranch. So he'd allot five extra minutes for anything else that might come up. Which meant that she should be there around 5:45.

It was now 5:43, and she wasn't there.

Clayton closed his eyes and told himself to be patient, that Abby would get the information they needed.

But the truth was that it was more than what she could find in regards to Nathan and their money that had him so antsy. It was Abby.

He hadn't been looking—and God knew he didn't need a woman in his life—but there was no denying that she had caught his attention. He could usually forget women easily enough, so it said something that he couldn't stop thinking about her.

When his mother had told him that Abby was at the ranch last night, his stomach had fallen to his feet in nervousness and excitement. He'd thought he would have the entire drive to her house to think about what to say to her, but instead, she had come to him.

He'd taken his time gazing at her in the office. Her brunette locks hung down about her like silky waves he yearned to touch. And her eyes!

Each time she looked at him, he felt as if she pierced his soul. Her gaze was direct, unflinching. In her blue eyes, he saw her strength, her determination, her worry, and her fears. Above all else, he saw how much she cared about her family.

He understood that. Perhaps it was that connection that had prompted him to give Brice a second chance. Every time he saw Abby, she impressed him.

5:52.

He ran a hand down his face. She should be here. Did she get a flat? Or worse, have an accident? Maybe he should drive to see if he could find her.

As he walked to his truck, thinking of all the ways she could've crashed now that it was dusk, he saw a slim body run around the house, making a beeline for the pasture where some of the horses grazed.

"Caleb, wait!"

Two words were all it took for the tightness in his chest to fall away. The sound of her voice was music to his ears. A few moments later, Abby rounded the house.

Even in just the light of the lamps hanging from the house she sparkled. She shoved a hand through her luxurious, dark tresses, pushing them away from her face. The same coat she had worn the other day was buttoned up the front, preventing him from seeing her shirt. But he smiled when he saw the faded denim that encased her legs. Since he'd only seen her in office attire, he'd wondered what she looked like in jeans.

Though she didn't have cowboy boots on, the black boots that her jeans were tucked into came up past her calves and were laced up the side.

On her way to follow Caleb, her gaze clashed with his, and she came to a halt. Clayton wasn't sure what to make of the way his stomach quivered with excitement or the way his balls tightened with need.

He knew lust well, and this wasn't it.

Need, yes.

Desire, definitely.

But the hunger within him was raw, visceral.

Primal.

How could he experience such a thing with someone he just met? He wanted to be near her, and when an opportunity had presented itself, he'd jumped at the chance.

It was a mistake. Every instinct he'd honed through the years told him not to mix business with pleasure. Yet he hadn't listened. He couldn't.

Abby glanced at Caleb before changing course and heading to Clayton. His palms started to sweat, and his heart pounded against his ribs. Damn, this woman was beautiful. He couldn't believe someone hadn't snatched her up and claimed her heart, but it was their loss and his gain.

"Hi," she said with a shy smile when she reached him.

He returned her grin. "Hey."

There was a beat of silence as they both tried to find something to say. He wondered if she was attracted to him. Both hoping that she was and that she wasn't.

"I'm sorry about Caleb. He's excited to be here."

"Come. I'll give you a tour," he said.

Her brows snapped together. "Not on a horse."

"Not this time," he teased.

Her lips curved into a smile. "You won't get me on a horse."

She'd learn soon enough never to place such a dare before him—because he never lost.

# Chapter 9

Abby finally understood what it meant when someone's mind was in a whirlwind. After the tour of the barns and paddocks closest to the house, she'd been staggered by everything—and couldn't wait to see it all in the light of day. She'd had an idea of what the ranch did, but seeing it up close and personal was another matter entirely.

And she'd just gotten a peek at a slice of it.

Remembering to look at the things Clayton was showing her instead of staring at him had been the hardest part. But what had she expected when she arrived and saw him standing there with the wooden fence behind him and cattle grazing beyond?

She'd seen numerous photos of hot cowboys in front of such a landscape, and he blew them all away. Even if his hair wasn't styled, and his shirt wasn't half unbuttoned. In many ways, he was sexier because of it.

His black hat had been pulled low so she couldn't see his eyes. He'd stood as still as stone, but she'd known he was watching her. There was a particular heat that came over her whenever his gaze touched her.

His suede coat was unbuttoned, allowing her to see the beige button-down beneath that was tucked into denim. He carried gloves in one hand as if he'd removed them and had stopped what he was doing when he saw her.

As handsome as Clayton was, it was his quiet stillness that she saw first and foremost. He appeared unmovable, but not rigid. He reminded her of a great oak—steady and strong.

She hadn't expected calmness, knowing some of what the ranch was going through, but she suspected that everything would methodically be taken in hand and set to rights because of his composure.

She was introduced to Shane, who then asked if Caleb wanted to see more of the ranch. Her brother's exuberant response brought a smile to her face. As the two got in the SxS and drove off, Clayton had beckoned her into one of the other barns.

The smell of hay, manure, leather, and horse filled her senses. She paused to stroke a white mare, who hung her head over the stall door. The velvety nose and the way the horse blew against her arm kept her petting.

Clayton leaned against the stall a few paces down, watching her while rubbing the neck of another horse. His pale green orbs studied her so intently that she felt as if he were reading her actions and facial expressions.

She met his gaze, wishing she knew what he was thinking. While he belonged to this wonderful, intimidating world, she was never more aware that she knew nothing of ranching than at that moment.

Yet, it didn't bother her. She was being given a glimpse into a way of life that used to dominate Texas. Now, as more and more ranches went under, it almost seemed as if men like Clayton were a dying breed.

"I take it from your earlier comment that you don't ride," he drawled.

She laughed and looked into the mare's dark, fathomless eyes. "No. Horses don't frighten me, I've just never been atop one."

"Want to change that?"

His query had her sliding her eyes back to him to see if he were joking. The seriousness of his expression said he wasn't. She was about to decline, but something stopped her.

Why couldn't she have some fun? She'd worked hard for so long that she wasn't sure she knew what having fun meant. Besides, hadn't she just reminded herself that it wasn't going to be long before her brothers graduated and were gone? She needed to think about the future and discover things that she might like to do.

While she'd never be able to pay for horseback riding lessons herself, this was an opportunity only an idiot would pass up. And Abby stopped being stupid in eighth grade after she'd let Joey Ashworth take her to the homecoming football game.

"Say yes," Clayton urged.

She licked her lips and grinned. "Okay."

One side of his mouth tilted up in a charming smile that made her weak in the knees. "Good."

"Why are you being so nice?" It probably wasn't something she should ask, but she couldn't help it.

He pulled something small and white from his pocket

before offering it to the horse, who quickly gobbled it up. Then he sauntered over to her and took her hand.

The contact of his large, warm palm on hers was like being shocked. Her stomach trembled, and she couldn't catch her breath. When he set something on her palm, she looked down to find a sugar cube.

"Keep your fingers flat, so the horse doesn't accidentally bite them," he warned as he moved her hand closer to the mare's mouth.

Abby held her breath as the animal's lips nibbled at her hand before taking the cube. She laughed at the tickle, and instantly wanted to do it again.

No wonder both of her brothers wanted to be around horses. They were amazing. Sweet, gentle, beautifully powerful creatures that spoke volumes with their eyes.

"I'm being nice because I want to be," Clayton said.

Abby had forgotten her question. Now, as she looked at him, she felt like a fool. "The people I know are only nice when they want something in return. After what Brice has done to your family—"

"He's working it off," Clayton interrupted. "And you're helping, as well. Unless you offered your assistance in exchange for something," he asked with narrowed eyes.

"No," she hastily assured him. "I'm just not used to this sort of kindness."

He didn't say anything else, simply kept a hold of her hand and pulled her after him as he walked away. Abby looked longingly at the white mare as she silently promised herself that she would come back with a box of her own sugar cubes.

It wasn't long before she heard voices and picked out

Brice's. Clayton slowed his steps until they stopped outside of an open door. She halted beside Clayton and peered around the door to see Brice sitting in a tack room, vigorously rubbing something into the leather of a saddle.

"Then what?" Brice asked.

A man of indiscernible age due in part to his wrinkles and weathered face continued his instruction on how to approach horses both broken and wild. Brice ate it up as if it were air that would sustain him. All the while, he kept working.

She'd never seen him so dedicated to anything before. He'd gone to bed with a smile on his face the night before and had woken up with it still in place. Abby was beginning to think it was a permanent fixture now.

She looked up at Clayton to thank him and realized their bodies were touching. His eyes seemed to swallow her whole, as if he stopped looking at her he might die.

And she was fairly certain she'd perish if he did.

The moment suspended as time slowed. It held them, seizing them both in a world all their own. Her senses came alive with Clayton. The warmth of his body swallowed her while she dragged in a deep breath of his spicy, earthy scent. His breathing was ragged, his eyes dilated. His fingers slid sensuously from her hand to her wrist.

The desire she saw in his gaze made her stomach drop to her feet—and her body to shiver eagerly in response. Every fiber of her being was focused on Clayton, on the need pulsing through her.

The sound of Justine calling Clayton's name broke them apart. He gave her a look full of longing and promise before turning on his heel. Abby fisted her hands, which were suddenly cold again now that he'd released her, and followed him to the entrance of the barn.

"I suppose we'd better get started," he said.

She smiled and waved when she saw Justine. "I suppose."

There was much she needed to do, but she hadn't wanted her tour to end. It had been all too short, but magical all the same.

They walked into the darkness side by side until they met up with Justine. Abby glanced around for Caleb.

As if reading her mind, Clayton leaned close and said, "Shane won't let anything happen to him. He'll keep Caleb busy for a while."

Once inside the warmth of the house, Justine took her coat and ushered Abby into the kitchen. Abby found herself looking at all the garland hung around the house that she longed to have. It made things feel so much more like Christmas than the pitiful four-foot artificial tree they had.

"Mom is a nut for Christmas," Clayton said in a flat tone.

Justine turned and swatted him with the towel she picked up from the kitchen counter. "Hush, you. He only hates it because he and his father are the ones who have to carry all of the boxes up and down the stairs."

Clayton barked in laughter. "You make it sound like you only have a few boxes." Then he turned to Abby. "Do you know how many trees are in the house? Five."

"I can't choose what color to use each year," Justine stated with a shrug.

Abby smiled at the banter. While Clayton griped, it

was done in a loving manner, because it was obvious he'd do anything for his mother.

"Let me give you a hint about how many boxes there are," he told Abby as he leaned an arm on the island. "She has red, silver, gold, burgundy, champagne, black, pink, copper, and purple. Each of those colors has about five huge boxes of ornaments and other decorations."

Justine rolled her eyes. "We host a lot of parties, and the decorations need to match whatever color I use in each room."

"Abby, she even changes out the comforters in the bedrooms to Christmas ones."

She turned her wide eyes to Justine. "No way! I've always wanted to do that."

"Finally," Justine said and looked Heavenward. "Someone who understands a love of Christmas decorating."

Clayton let out a sound that was something between a groan and snort. "You're supposed to be on my side, Abby."

"No, no, no," his mother said with a wag of her finger. "This one, I win. You've always had your father on your side. Now, I have someone," she declared proudly.

Never had Abby felt so . . . included. For the first time, she wasn't just watching families interact, she was a part of it. It was an amazing feeling.

And a reminder of everything her brothers didn't have.

Justine opened the oven and took out some freshly baked bread that Abby knew she'd made herself. "Abby, please don't think I'm overstepping, but I'd love if you and your brothers joined us for Christmas dinner."

Abby hesitated, unsure how to respond. Was Justine giving the invitation out of pity or because she really wanted them here.

"We have a big party the night before," Clayton said. "Christmas is our private dinner. Say you'll come."

How was she expected to refuse now that he was staring at her with those gorgeous green eyes and that crooked grin? "We'd be delighted."

"Oh, good," Justine said with a clap of her hands. "And Ben will be feeling so much better by then. He's dying to meet you. In fact, he's coming down to dinner tonight."

"Mom," Clayton replied, worry filling his face and voice.

Justine put her hand on Clayton's arm. "Leave your father to me. He's promised to return to bed when I tell him."

Abby glanced around the massive kitchen. "How can I help with dinner?"

"No need," Justine said with a grin. "I love to feed people. It's my thing, sweetheart. Clayton, why don't you get her settled before you take your shower? You're not sitting at my table smelling like that."

He chuckled and put his hand on Abby's back as he led her from the kitchen and down a hallway toward the office.

"Your mother is wonderful."

He glanced her way and nodded. "She is pretty special."

"You've no idea how lucky you are."

"Do you miss your mom?"

Abby paused inside the doorway to the office. "At

times, though they are less and less as the years go on. Why should I care about someone who didn't think twice about leaving her children behind without money or food?"

"Did you ever grieve?"

She felt those damn tears again. What was it about Clayton that he could bring them forth so easily? "I didn't have time. I had to help my brothers deal with things, find a job, and handle all the legal papers making me their guardian."

"You've been doing things for everyone but yourself. When are you going to let someone do something for you?"

Abby was certain he didn't mean him, but she really wished he did. Because if there was ever someone who made her want to forget her responsibilities and do something selfish, it was Clayton East.

# Chapter 10

"I don't know," she replied.

Not even talk of her mother could ruin the flutter in her stomach. Abby liked the way she felt around Clayton, but she knew to be careful. It wouldn't do her any good to go searching for something that wasn't there. The Easts were being generous despite the situation Brice had put them in.

Some might be suspicious, thinking Clayton was using her for his own gain. And he might be. She wasn't naïve enough to fall for his charm.

Well, not too much.

It was damned difficult to shut him out completely. Mostly because he was so gorgeous and dark and . . . wounded. Then he'd look at her with his stunning pale green eyes and flash her that crooked grin. How was anyone supposed to withstand that? Besides, it had been a long time since anyone had paid any attention to her. It didn't hurt that she enjoyed the interest.

Then there was Justine East. The woman was everything a mother should be—loving, devoted, strong, and determined. Abby had blocked so much about her own mother that it was rather wonderful to be around someone like Justine.

And with Jill now living so far away where the time difference made it difficult for them to talk, it was nice to have another female to bond with.

"You should think about letting others do for you," Clayton said.

She wasn't sure what to say. The concept was foreign to her, but she wouldn't pass up the chance if something came along.

Clayton walked to the desk and pulled out the chair for her. Once she sat, he put a finger on a stack of papers. "I printed everything from the last year. I like to look through papers rather than at the computer, but the files are all open and ready if you'd rather."

"I like paper, too, but I'm sure I'll still need the computer."

"Then I'll let you get started. I need to get washed up before Mom has my ass."

They shared a smile. And then he walked away. Abby let her gaze drop to his fine ass. Until Clayton, she hadn't realized how good Wranglers looked on a man. When he disappeared around the corner, she took a deep breath and pulled the papers to her. They were stacked with the most recent month on top.

In order for her to get her bearings, she would have to go through the financials line by line, month by month. It was going to take days, weeks even, but she would gladly do it since she owed the Easts.

* * *

Clayton braced his hands on the shower wall and let the hot water beat upon his back. His palms still tingled from touching Abby.

There had been a moment in the barn when he'd wanted to pull her against him and kiss her. And had his mother not said his name, he probably would have.

Would Abby have kissed him back? While she seemed to like being around him, he also sensed that she was leery. Then again, frightened might be a better term. Not that he could blame her. She had the world upon her narrow shoulders, but she carried it without complaint.

He straightened and hurriedly washed the day from his body before rinsing. After quickly toweling dry, he walked naked to his closet. As he looked inside, he shook his head. His mother had gone shopping again. She'd been shocked at his lack of clothes when he'd returned home, but it wasn't like he'd needed a lot while in the Navy or for his job in South Africa.

Clayton chose a cream-colored, long-sleeve Henley that he left untucked over his jeans. He combed his hair and made his way downstairs without shoes or socks.

Ever since he'd gotten the call from his mother, he'd been going through the motions of a dutiful son. It wasn't that he wasn't happy to see his parents—or the ranch. But, coming home had been just as hard as he'd thought it would be. Luckily, he had something to occupy his mind.

Now, he rushed down the stairs just to get back to Abby. While he didn't want to think too hard about the *why* of it, he recognized—and accepted—the emotion.

He stopped at the office door, leaning a shoulder against it as he watched her work. She had a pencil in hand and scribbled on a legal pad in between rummaging through the papers and mumbling to herself.

She lifted her head of glossy, dark hair to look at the computer screen. She put down the pencil, and as her right hand clicked on the mouse, her left twirled a strand of hair around a finger.

Suddenly, her eyes jerked to him. Having those blue orbs directed on him was like a punch in the gut—a wonderful, amazing punch. There was no bitterness or animosity in her eyes, no resentment or cynicism. It was so different than what he saw in the mirror each day. Perhaps that was why he was drawn to her.

"Checking up on me?" she asked with a grin.

He pushed away from the door and walked to her. "I didn't want to interrupt you. You looked deep into it."

She blew out a breath and spread her hands, palm up as if taking in everything. "I was. Oh," she said as she swiveled the chair to face him. "I forgot to tell you earlier that I called about the malpractice insurance. Turns out, Bill Gilroy's father had the company surety bonded. Bill kept that going, and so did Nathan."

"Which means what?"

Abby's smile grew. "It means that you can get the money back. Malpractice insurance won't cover embezzlement, but the bond will. I already began the paperwork for the ranch during my lunch break today."

She hadn't needed to go that far. The fact that she had told him just what kind of person she was.

"Thank you."

Abby shrugged and moved the pencil to align with the legal pad. "It was nothing. Just a few phone calls and a couple pieces of paper."

"That you didn't have to do. I appreciate it."

"Someone would've figured out the Gilroys were bonded sooner or later."

He rested his fingers atop the desk. "Perhaps. But probably months down the road. You saved us a lot of trouble."

They stared at each other for a long time. Something ignited within him. In truth, that something had sparked the moment he laid eyes on Abby at the sheriff's station. There was chaos all around him, but she was the center of the storm. Calm, serene, exquisite. She was like a glimmer of hope that everything was going to work out.

He might tell his parents that every day, but in the back of his mind, Clayton had been coming up with different plans to save the ranch.

Abby was the first to look away. She licked her lips and fidgeted nervously, which he thought was adorable. Everything about her intrigued him. He wanted to know what she was thinking and feeling, but more than anything, he wanted her to be comfortable in his home.

Lights flashed through the office windows, signaling that Shane was back with Caleb. It wasn't long after that, the voices of the two boys could be heard.

Abby rose and went to the window to watch her brothers beneath the lights of the barn. She wrapped her arms around herself. "The ranch is the best thing that's happened to my brothers in a long time."

"They're always welcome here. So are you."

She looked over her shoulder at him. "After what we've done? Why would you say that?"

"Everyone makes mistakes, Abby. The ranch has been in trouble before, but it's going to be fine because of you. Some might call that Fate."

"You believe in such things?" she asked as she turned to him.

He walked until they stood less than a foot apart. "Look at all the connected things that occurred that brought you to my door. None of the authorities I've spoken to—including the FBI—asked anything about Gilroy being bonded."

"You make it sound like I did something amazing."

"You did in my book," he said before she could continue. "I'm saying thank you. Please accept that."

She gazed at him a long moment before she softly said, "You're welcome."

His eyes dropped to her lips. Blood surged to his cock at the thought of taking her mouth and tasting her sweetness. Just before he was about to lean forward, Brice and Caleb came into the house with Shane.

The sound of her brothers had Abby looking away. Clayton stopped her before she turned from him. When her gaze once again met his, he said, "Your brothers are fine. Mom and Shane are with them. You can take some time for yourself."

"I know," she said in a low voice. "I'm just so used to being the only one to watch over them. Brice seems to have grown up overnight. I think you're the cause of that."

He held back a frown at the sadness in her voice. "Are you happy about that?"

"Yes," she said with a small smile. "You're a good example for both of my brothers."

"So are you."

"Abby," Caleb said as he came into the office, his hair windblown and his brown eyes alight with joy. "Oh, my God. This place is so awesome. It's so much more than Brice described. I mean it's . . . wow."

She smiled, laughing at Caleb's enthusiasm. "I'm glad you think so."

Caleb then turned to Clayton. "I know Brice is working off a debt, but is there any way I can come work with him this weekend? I promise I'll pull my weight."

Clayton was surprised at the boy's request. "Did you ask your sister first?"

"Abby, please," Caleb begged. "You can have an entire weekend to yourself."

"I wouldn't know what to do with myself," she said with a wink. "Actually, I think I'll be here going over the books anyway. I'm fine with it, but the ultimate decision is Clayton's."

Caleb turned his dark gaze back to him, silently pleading. As if Clayton could hold out against such fervor. He gave a nod, which had Caleb yelping in excitement before running back to the kitchen to Brice.

"I hope you don't regret that," Abby said, chuckling.

But all Clayton could think about was that she would at the ranch. With him. He swallowed, his gaze lowering to her lips as he thought of kissing her. Hell, it was all he'd been thinking about for days.

Then he had a thought. "Why don't the three of you stay the entire weekend? Come Friday night."

A small frown furrowed her brow. "I don't know."

"Why not? We have plenty of room. The boys can bunk with the other workers if they don't want to stay in the house. Consider it a little vacation for you. You don't even have to work."

She shook her head while she smiled. "I'll be working."

"Not the entire time. Say yes, Abby."

"Why?"

"Why not?" he countered. He didn't want to tell her that the thought of her staying at the ranch pleased him more than anything had in years.

Abby blew out a breath as she contemplated his offer. "I don't know."

"What are you afraid of? Having a good time? Enjoying this place? Or letting someone do something for you?" he challenged.

"I knew you were going to bring that up."

He shrugged, knowing that she was the one doing him a favor by looking through the books, but he intended to make sure she had some fun, as well.

"Don't make me go to the boys," Clayton said. "If I mention it to them, they won't let up until you give in."

Her gaze narrowed on him as she tried to hide her smile. "Oh, that was sneaky."

"I do what must be done to get what I want." And he wanted her there.

She gave a single nod. "All right."

It was all Clayton could do not to give a shout just like Caleb had earlier.

# Chapter 11

Home. He'd been back less than a week, but it finally felt as if he'd truly come home. Why now? Was it because he realized he missed his parents? Was it because he recalled his love for the ranch?

Or was it because of Abby?

He waited until she was in the kitchen with the others before Clayton took the stairs two at a time. He knocked softly on the master bedroom door that was cracked open and looked inside.

"Dad?"

"I'm here, son."

Clayton pushed the door open to find his father standing before the window. Ben East stood tall and straight. His light brown hair now had a streak of gray on each side at his temples, but he was still fit. He was fastening the last button on his shirt.

"Mom is going to kill you."

His father chuckled and slowly turned around. "Why

do you think I waited until she was involved with the cooking to get dressed? Besides, I feel great."

He looked into his father's green eyes that were still bright. "You could've remained in your robe."

"I know, but I wanted to dress. I'm tired of sitting in here feeling like an invalid. Oh, don't worry," he hurried to say when Clayton opened his mouth. "I'm not going to get back on a horse anytime soon. I know all about making sure I don't have an actual stroke. I'm not ready to leave you or your mother, so I'm not going to be stupid."

Clayton nodded. "Good. Because I'm not ready to lose you."

His father's face, which now carried more worry lines, softened in understanding. "It's good to have you home."

"By the way," Clayton said as he waited for his father to meet him at the door. "Abby just told me that the Gilroys were bonded."

"CPAs can do that?"

"Apparently."

Ben grunted, his brows raised. "I take it to mean that's good for us."

"It means that they were insured against theft. Abby already started the paperwork to get us back the money."

His father paused and cocked his head to the side. "I think I'm in love with this girl."

"Don't let Mom hear you say that."

Ben laughed as he reached the door. "Perhaps it was fortunate that Brice was caught, and you gave him a second chance. It brought us Abby."

Clayton had been thinking the same thing. "I hope

tonight isn't going to be too much for you. The boys are young and loud."

"Just what this big ol' house needs," his father said as he walked out the door and down the hall.

Clayton kept pace with his father down the hall and as they descended the stairs. Ben was recovering nicely, but rest was playing a big part in it. Clayton was relieved that his father was taking the mini-stroke seriously. Ben had been given a chance to change things to prevent an actual stroke—not many people were that lucky.

"I invited the three of them for the weekend," Clayton said before they reached the bottom stair.

His father glanced at him, a grin in place. "Good. Now take me to meet Abby."

Clayton found her setting the silverware on the table as her brothers brought in bowls of food, his mother directing them where to place each. The scene reminded him so much of his younger years with Landon that he had to stop and catch his breath at the sense of loss that assaulted him.

His father placed a hand upon his shoulder and squeezed. When Clayton looked over, Ben was rapidly blinking back tears as he watched Brice and Caleb. The silence from the kitchen warned that Justine had seen her husband. A moment later, she was standing before him, wiping away her own tears.

Clayton drew in a shuddering breath. He hadn't thought about how his parents would feel about Caleb and Brice—or how he'd react to seeing them inside his house. He certainly hadn't expected to feel the loss of Landon so acutely after all these years.

"Did we do something wrong?" Caleb asked.

Clayton turned his head to Abby, who was watching him with silent concern. "No," he answered.

His mother and father shared a kiss and private words before she turned to the others, a smile in place. "Not at all, dear. It just reminded us of the past when our other son, Landon, was alive."

Without meaning to, Clayton studied Abby's face as his mother broke the news. Abby's eyes widened with sorrow and regret.

"Who's hungry?" his mother asked.

Just as expected, Brice and Caleb were the first to reply. While they got seated, Clayton motioned Abby over to him and his father.

"Hello, Mr. East," Abby said with one of her sweet smiles as she held out her hand.

His father took it and covered it with his other hand, squeezing it before releasing her. "Ben, please. It's so nice to meet you, Abby. You're a blessing this house needed."

Her gaze darted to Clayton. "Uh . . . thank you."

"Clayton told me that you discovered the Gilroys were bonded."

"Oh." Abby put a hand to her chest as she laughed. "Yes. It was my pleasure."

Ben grinned. "I'm glad Clayton convinced you to look at the books. Otherwise, we'd never have known. Why don't you come sit beside me."

Clayton watched Abby take the seat on his father's right while Brice took the one on the left. Caleb sat beside Abby, much to Clayton's disappointment. He then helped his mother into her chair at the other end of the table and sat to her right next to Brice.

He took his mother's hand, and soon, everyone joined hands. They bowed their heads as his father began to pray over the veritable feast. After a subdued chorus of "Amens," the food was passed around while they each filled their plates.

Clayton saw the many looks and smiles exchanged between his parents. He hadn't realized how lonely they must have been over the last several years. Even though there were always people coming and going from the ranch, once he'd left, the huge house must have been awfully quiet with just the two of them. It struck Clayton how selfish he'd been to stay away.

It was another reason for him to remain. And the longer he was at the ranch, the more he wanted to do just that.

The boys kept the conversation going as they told each other all that had happened to them while at the ranch. As for Abby, she ate slowly as she looked between her two brothers with so much love shining in her eyes that Clayton was left speechless.

No one but his parents had ever looked at him that way. He hadn't cared about such things in the middle of war—or when he'd run from his responsibilities. But now, suddenly, he ached for something that solid and beautiful.

It wasn't long before Ben shared the news about the Gilroys being bonded with Justine. Clayton couldn't take his eyes from Abby when she beamed with pride as she handled the praise from both his parents and her brothers.

It had Clayton wondering just how long it had been since anyone had told Abby that she'd done something good. She had been taken for granted for too long, and it was time that changed.

Her blue eyes met his, and they exchanged a smile before Brice asked her a question. Clayton was glad that the Harpers fit in so well with his family. It was just what his parents needed.

And perhaps it was what he needed, as well.

"Did Clayton share the news with you, dear?" Ben asked his wife.

Justine raised a blond brow as she pierced Clayton with her gaze. "You have more news?"

"Well, it came so suddenly that I've not had a chance to share it," Clayton said. He glanced at Abby to find she was holding her breath until his dad patted her hand. Clayton then said, "We're going to have three guests staying with us for the weekend, starting Friday night."

Without missing a beat, his mother looked at the boys and said, "I know exactly what I'm cooking for you two."

Caleb and Brice exchanged looks before they turned to Abby. A slow smile spread over her face before she shrugged at them.

"No way!" Caleb yelled. "Christmas has come early."

Brice turned to Ben and began asking question after question about the ranch.

Clayton set down his fork and put a hand on the back of Brice's chair, taking it all in. He'd wanted Abby to stay over for purely selfish reasons, but he'd known the boys would be ecstatic about it.

Now, he had to wait three more days to have Abby under the same roof.

Once dinner was finished and the dishes were done,

Clayton carried a cup of coffee into the living room to Abby. She stood before the roaring fire, looking at the array of family pictures on the mantel.

"The boys are having hot chocolate around the fire pit outside with my folks," he said.

She turned and accepted the mug. "I didn't know you had a brother."

He nodded. "He died a long time ago when we were just kids."

"I'm sorry."

He never knew how to respond when someone said that, so he drank his coffee instead.

Abby turned back to the pictures, looking at one where he and Landon had been swimming in the river. Their hair was flattened against their heads, still wet. They stuck out their tongues, showing the camera they had turned the colors of the popsicles each of them had had. Landon's was purple, while Clayton's was blue.

"That was taken a year before Landon died," he said.

Abby grinned. "He has your mother's eyes and your dad's hair."

"While I have my dad's eyes and my mother's hair."

She looked at him, a soft smile still in place. "You miss him."

"Every damn day."

"Tell me about him. If you want."

Clayton looked back at the array of pictures. There were ones of him and his brother together, one of just him roping a calf, one of Landon branding a steer, but his favorite was from when he and his brother had raced their horses, as they did every year. His mother had been standing at the finish line, camera in hand. She'd snapped it as the noses of their horses crossed in unison.

He took down the picture and stared at it. "Landon was an amazing brother. He was my best friend and someone I looked up to. All he wanted was to run the ranch and make my parents proud."

"I would've liked to meet him."

Clayton moved his gaze to her. "He would've liked your spunk. And he would've asked you out."

Abby threw back her head and laughed. "You don't know that."

"Yes, I do," he replied with a smile. "I knew my brother as well as I know myself. We thought alike."

Her smile slowly melted away as their gazes locked. The only sounds were the crackle of the fire and the distant voices of her brothers.

Heat simmered through Clayton. It would be so easy to put his hand on her waist and draw her near, to inhale her clean, alluring scent, and perhaps slide his fingers through her thick locks. The fierce, unrelenting need to taste her lips surged through him, making him burn. Making him ache.

Her pulse beat rapidly at her throat. Dear God, he wanted to feel her against him. His hands shook with the force of it. But it wasn't the right time.

He replaced the picture. "How much longer do you have before you earn your accounting degree?"

"Too long. The fact that I can do it online makes it easier, but I can't take as many classes as I should."

Because of money. She didn't say it, but it hung between them. Clayton wondered what her life would be like if she'd been able to go to college like he had. Most likely, she'd be running her own CPA firm and kicking ass while doing it.

"It's getting late," she said. "I should take the boys home."

The happiness Clayton felt disappeared as quickly as if someone had let the air out of a balloon. It was only then that he fully comprehended the change Abby brought out in him. She made the ghosts that haunted him vanish. She made him feel whole again. He wanted to call her back, to beg her to stay. Instead, he got her coat as she called her brothers in.

His feet felt sunken in lead as he watched her drive away. Now, he had to count down the hours until she returned tomorrow evening.

"It's going to be a long damn night," he murmured.

# Chapter 12

*I feel like a woman.*

Abby stared at herself in the mirror as she played with her hair. She reached for a pink lipstick and applied it before rubbing her lips together. Then she added a light layer of lip gloss.

"Whoa," Caleb said as he came up behind her. "You look good."

She looked at him in the mirror. "Thanks."

"Does it mean something that you've changed out of your work clothes and put on makeup?"

"I . . ." She sighed. "The Easts are doing our family a huge favor. They're nice people, and I want to make a good impression."

Caleb crossed his arms over his chest and widened his stance. "You've already done that."

In the last few days, both of her brothers had seemed to age overnight. Brice acted more like a man than a rowdy teenager. Caleb had begun to notice things other than himself. And she saw that his jeans were getting too short again and his shirts weren't fitting properly over his widening shoulders.

"You need to start wearing some of Brice's clothes until I can get you new ones."

He raised a brow. "You're not changing the subject, and my clothes are fine. I saw you last night, sis. You like the Easts. Or more importantly, you like Clayton."

"He's nice," she admitted.

Caleb snorted. "And good-looking."

Abby hesitated. She didn't want her brother to get his hopes up about anything, but she didn't want to lie either. "Yes, Clayton is handsome."

"He was staring at you."

Her stomach clutched at the revelation. "Was he?" she asked, trying to sound uninterested while checking her makeup in the mirror once more.

"It's okay, you know. Have some fun. It's not like you don't deserve it."

Abby turned to face her brother. "You and Brice mean the world to me. I don't regret anything."

"I know, but I want to see you happy."

"I am," she said, shaking her head as a frown formed. "What makes you think I'm not?"

Caleb dropped his arms and gave her a flat look. "Abby, you never go out. Not with guys, not with friends. Not even when Jill was still here. All you do is look after us. You fill your days with work and stuff around the house so you don't notice you're lonely."

She put her hands on the sink behind her to help steady herself. All this time, she thought she'd been hiding things so well from her brothers. Apparently she'd been wrong.

"I like Clayton," Caleb continued. "I like Mr. and Mrs. East, and I love the ranch. Flirt with Clayton. Let him flirt with you. Hell, kiss him, Abby. It doesn't have to go anywhere. But remember, you're pretty and should have guys falling all over you."

Abby glanced at the ceiling as the tears gathered. Then she pushed away from the sink and pulled Caleb to her for a hug. She squeezed her eyes closed. "I have the best brothers."

"You're damn straight, you do."

They shared a laugh as they pulled apart. "Get your coat."

"You look great. Just smile at him. That's all it'll take."

She thought about Caleb's words as they drove to the ranch. Her heart was pounding so hard when they pulled up to the house that she thought it might burst from her chest.

Her brother was out of the car before the vehicle had come to a full stop. She watched him go with a smile. At least here, she knew her brothers weren't getting into trouble. But that thought led to why Brice was working at the ranch to begin with.

She needed to mention the people who'd gotten him involved with the rustling again. Maybe this time, he'd tell her something, anything. Even though the Easts would get the money back that their CPA had embezzled, they should have their cattle and the bull returned, as well.

Abby frowned as she sat in her still-running car. Was it a coincidence that the money had been stolen at almost the same time as the cattle? Something told her it was connected. But how? When she'd mentioned Nathan Gilroy to her brothers, neither had shown any kind of recognition.

She jumped, grabbing her throat when someone knocked on her window. Abby found herself looking at a familiar silhouette in the darkness. She turned off her car as Clayton opened her door.

"Everything all right?" he asked worriedly.

She reached for her purse as she stood. "Just thinking about things."

He closed the car door behind her and walked her to the front of the house. "Like what?"

"The embezzlement and the theft of the cattle. It all happened very close together, right?"

"Within a day, yes. You think it could be tied together?"

She nodded as they entered the house.

He put a hand on her back and maneuvered her toward the back of the house. As he did, he leaned close and said, "I came to the same conclusion."

Once inside the office, she turned to face him when he closed the door. "Do you have anything that will link the two crimes?"

"Nothing. It's why I need some clue from Brice."

"I know." She flattened her lips. "I'll talk to him again."

Clayton removed his hat and raked his hands through his blond locks. "Just to warn you, Mom already plans for you three to stay for dinner again."

"Oh, we couldn't."

"You'll break her heart if you decline," he stated with a solemn face.

She knew she was being played, but she liked being with the Easts—especially Clayton. "We wouldn't want that, now would we?"

"I certainly don't."

"Then we'd be delighted to stay."

The smile he flashed her could've lit up a room. He replaced his hat and bowed his head. "I'll let her know. Is there anything you need?"

Why was the first response that sprang to mind "you?"

It was all Caleb's fault. If he hadn't told her about Clayton staring at her the night before, she wouldn't be a nervous wreck around him. Now, she was very aware of him.

Actually, that was a lie. She'd been aware of him from the moment she realized he was in that room with her at the sheriff's station.

Clayton's raised brow reminded her that she hadn't answered him. She jerked, embarrassed to find herself gawking at him. But, my God, the man was so damn gorgeous he was lickable.

And that made her think of tangled limbs, sighs of contentment, and moans of pleasure. Her body heated instantly, while her sex clenched.

"I'm fine," she finally said.

But it came out like a needy whisper.

Damn her body for revealing what she was trying so desperately to keep hidden from everyone—including herself. She was lonely. Extremely so.

To have someone hold her, comfort her, was something she dreamed about every night. She didn't remember what it felt like to have a man's arms around her, much less the taste and feel of a kiss.

Was kissing like riding a bike? Would she remember how to do it? Or would she need to relearn all over again? The thought made her groan inwardly.

She was pathetic. On an epic scale.

"I should get to work," she said and turned to the desk.

She walked to the chair and soon realized that Clayton had moved with her. Her head lifted as she met his gaze. He was standing so close, she could lean to the side and rub her shoulder against him. And it was such a tempting thought.

"Let me move this out of your way," he said.

Abby looked down to see him reaching for a stack of papers. And here she thought he'd wanted to be beside her. She quickly moved out of the way, her embarrassment growing by the second.

"You've worked a long day," Clayton said. "Maybe it's too much asking you to come every night."

She shook her head, forcing a smile. "It's not that, but thank you all the same. I want to do this for you and your family."

"Because you feel like you owe me?"

He wore a smile, but she couldn't help but suspect there was more to his words than he let on. "There is that, yes. It's also nice to test myself and put what I know from work and what I'm learning in college into action. I'm making lots of notes for you to then take to the next CPA you hire."

"Right. Another CPA." Clayton glanced away and blew out a breath. "I'm not in a hurry to do that after what happened with Gilroy."

"But I'm not licensed. I don't even have my degree. This is the kind of work I do every day, but my boss, the CPA, looks over things after me to make sure I caught everything."

Clayton's head cocked to the side. "You mean you do her work and she takes credit for it?"

"Well . . . yeah. She's the one with the degree and certification."

He grunted, which could mean anything. She didn't know him well enough to understand all his intricacies. But she wished she did.

"You should have your degree," he said.

She shrugged, trying to look as nonchalant as possibly. "I wish I did, but I'm making do. I'll get there eventually."

"I've no doubt."

He held her gaze for a long minute before he tipped his hat to her, said her name in a low murmur, and walked out.

A shiver went through her. The man was perfection.

"Damn," she whispered.

He reminded her of a placid tiger who watched everything with belied interest. But if anyone stirred the animal, then there would be a lethal show of force.

Abby sat and managed to focus her mind on the books. She'd only been studying them for half an hour before there was a knock on the open door. She looked up to find Justine.

"Hi," Abby said, waving her inside. "I should've come to say hello, but Clayton led me straight here."

Justine smiled and set a mug of hot chocolate near her. "He is very bossy. He gets it from his father."

Abby chuckled. "I want to thank you for the dinner invitation again, but you don't need to do that."

"Why not?" Justine asked. "You're here, your brothers are here, and it'll be dinner time when they finish their chores. I have to cook for my two men anyway so there will be plenty of food. This way, you don't have to worry about cooking after working all day and then coming here to work some more."

Abby had a feeling that there weren't many arguments that Justine lost. "We appreciate it. And if there's anything I can do to help, let me know."

"Sweetheart, you're doing it already," Justine said with a smile. "And, I confess, I'm almost glad all this happened. I'm not happy that my husband was hospitalized, but it's made him slow down. It brought my son home, and it's brought you and your brothers here."

Unable to help herself, Abby asked, "Where was Clayton?"

"South Africa." Justine sighed and walked to the sofa. She sat and crossed one leg over the other. "Clayton fought for his country. Although he won't tell me much of anything about it, I've read enough in the news and seen movies to know that, as a SEAL, he did some dangerous things."

Abby was so shocked, she barely found the words to ask, "He's a SEAL?"

"Was. He resigned from the Navy after many tours. Hell, I don't even know all the places he was stationed.

I just know that somehow, my son survived. And when we thought he'd return home, he chose instead to take a job guarding wildlife in South Africa." Justine paused, her eyes filling up with tears. "The day we lost Landon, we lost Clayton in another way entirely."

Abby rose and walked to Justine. She took the older woman's hands in her own. "I'm so sorry."

"Clayton didn't smile for the first three days he was here. Then you arrived. He's different around you. Almost the way he used to be."

Abby wasn't sure what to say to that declaration. "I haven't done anything."

"That's the blessing, my dear. It's not what you've done or said. It's you. All you."

# Chapter 13

The haunting, gentle melody of the fiddle in the distance filled the air. How many times had Clayton sat on the back porch and listened to the ranch hands playing after dinner?

"It's beautiful. But sad."

He turned his head at the sound of Abby's voice as she walked from the house. "Haven't you heard? All country songs are sad. Even when they're upbeat."

She grinned and moved to stand beside him with her hands in her coat pockets. "I suppose you're right. Do they always play?"

"Nearly every night."

"How many live on the ranch?"

He shrugged and looped a thumb through his belt loop. "Only a handful now. Most have families they return to. Those who stay are the ones who are divorced or never got married."

"And Shane?" she asked.

"Never married." Clayton looked into the distance. "That's him playing."

She was silent for a long while as she listened to the music. "He seems like a nice guy."

"One of the best. It's not right that he's alone."

Abby turned to lean back against one of the columns to face him. "You can't say that and leave me hanging," she replied with a quick grin.

Clayton chuckled softly. "No, I don't suppose I can." He ran a hand over his jaw. "Shane fell in love once. Hell, I bet he's still in love with Irene."

"Why didn't they marry?"

"She was already married. To his brother."

Abby's face paled. "Oh, God."

Clayton nodded slowly. "She wanted to leave Shane's brother, Paul, but Shane wouldn't have it. Paul was madly in love with Irene, as well, and Shane didn't want to come between them."

"So they're still together?"

"That's how it should've ended. But she couldn't let go of Shane. It wasn't long before Paul discovered what was going on, and he confronted Shane right here on the ranch."

Abby's blue eyes widened. "You saw it?"

"All of it. Shane was trying to tell his brother he hadn't touched her, but Paul was beyond listening to reason. It didn't help that Irene had run away from Paul and come here to Shane. There was a fight, which was bad enough, but Paul also brought a gun. He got the upper hand because Shane wouldn't defend himself. Then Paul went to shoot Shane. Instead, Irene stepped between them and took the bullet. She died in Shane's arms. That was twenty years ago. Shane and Paul haven't spoken since."

"That's so tragic."

"I don't think Shane has ever recovered from it."

Abby looked toward the bunkhouse where the music came from. "I don't think many people would."

Clayton glanced behind him through the wall of windows to see his mother in the kitchen. "Mom has tried to set Shane up multiple times. She thinks he should find someone and be happy."

"I agree with her. Don't you?"

"I do, actually." At Abby's raised brows, Clayton found himself grinning. "Did I surprise you?"

She laughed and nodded. "You did. I was expecting you to say something like 'perhaps the past won't let go of Shane.'"

Clayton knew for a fact that the past never let go, but he didn't tell her that. Abby had her own worries. There was no need to drag her into the mire with his.

"Did you make a lot of headway tonight with the books?" he asked, wanting to change the subject.

She wrinkled her nose as she lifted her shoulders to her ears. "I wish I could say yes, but your mom came into the office."

"No need to say more," he interrupted her. "Mom loves to talk."

"We had a nice chat until she went to cook dinner. I did get to work some then. I'm sorry it's taking so long."

He wasn't. The longer it took her, the more he got to see her. He probably shouldn't ask her to come every day so she could rest, but Clayton couldn't quite get the words out. "Don't think twice about it."

"I'll work harder this weekend."

He grinned in response because he didn't intend to let her work all weekend. But there was no need to tell her that. Abby would just argue.

"Walk with me?" he said as he stepped down from the porch. He held her gaze, silently daring her to find a reason to object.

To his surprise, she said, "Okay."

He waited until she stepped from the porch, and then they leisurely strolled the grounds in comfortable silence. They stopped beside a paddock and watched some yearlings that were being sold to fill other rancher's stock.

"Your mom told me you were working in South Africa before you returned," Abby said. "Do you plan to go back?"

If she'd asked him three days ago, his answer would've been a firm yes. Now, he wasn't sure what he wanted to do. "The longer I'm here, the more I remember how much I love this place."

"Then maybe you're meant to stay," she said, looking up at him.

"Maybe."

She tucked her hair behind her ear and swallowed. "I might be out of line for saying this, but you look as if you belong here."

He shot her a smile and motioned for her to follow him into one of the barns. Clayton took her back to the white mare she'd petted the day before. He'd seen the way Abby had connected with the animal, and he wanted to build on that bond.

As soon as Abby saw the mare, the smile that pulled

at her lips displayed her joy. She oohed and ahhed over the horse.

"Her name is Diamond."

"Diamond," Abby repeated as she stroked the horse's neck. "It fits you."

The mare had fallen for Abby almost immediately, and Clayton could understand why. There was something about the woman that drew people and animals. She was quiet and unassuming. He suspected that might be because so many people overlooked her. That was their loss because there was so much about Abby that was intriguing.

"You're staring," she said as she cut her eyes to him.

Clayton lifted one shoulder in a shrug. "I like what I see."

She paused in her caress of the mare. Then she took a step back, and then another and another before she turned and walked away.

He frowned as anger spiked through him. He'd moved too fast. Abby was like a spooked mare. He should've trodden slowly. Earned her trust first.

When Abby reached the back of the barn, she stopped and looked at him over her shoulder. It was the seductive curve of her lips that halted his thoughts. As soon as she turned the corner, he started after her.

His blood rushed through him in a frenzy before pooling in his cock. With his heart beating furiously, he found her leaning back against the barn.

Clayton stood before her. His palms ached to feel her skin, to hold her glorious curves against him. He couldn't seem to catch his breath, and as he took a step closer to her, he realized that it had been years since he'd hungered to kiss anyone as he did Abby.

Her lips parted, drawing his attention to her mouth. The longing he'd suppressed for days consumed him. He took the final step that brought their bodies close. The soft light from over the barn couldn't reach them in the shadows.

He held her gaze and put a hand on her waist before slowly pulling her against him. Her palms landed on his upper arms. Then she lifted her face to him. That was all it took to push him over the edge.

Clayton lowered his head, her eyes drifting shut right before their lips met. He softly plied her mouth with light kisses until her hands moved up his arms and twined around his neck. When she sighed, he slid his tongue against her lips.

As her mouth opened, and their tongues met, need coursed through him. The desire, the yearning to have her seized him, overwhelmed him as the kiss deepened. He wound one hand into her long hair while his other splayed over her back. With each lick, each sigh, each moan, the hunger grew. Without a doubt, he had to have her. Not because he was in need, but because he ached for her.

But now wasn't the time. He wouldn't have their first time together be against the back of the barn in the shadows so no one saw them. He wasn't ashamed of Abby, and he wanted her to know that. He cared about her.

That in and of itself shocked him, but he accepted it. What choice did he have, really?

Clayton knew he had to end the kiss now before he

was past the point of no return. Already he was circling down that drain. He forced himself to pull back. Then he saw her heavy-lidded eyes and the way her chest heaved.

He ran his thumb over her swollen lips and briefly thought of picking her up and riding somewhere where no one could find them. Luckily, there was enough sanity left in him that he was able to keep dominion over his desire.

"Why did you stop?" she asked.

He was glad she didn't know how easily she could've broken through his restraint by simply pulling his head down for another kiss. That was all it would've taken. He wanted her so badly he shook with it.

"I'm already walking a tightrope, Abby," he confessed. "If I keep kissing you, I won't stop."

"I don't want you to stop."

He groaned at her husky words. If he wanted to stay in control, he had to reason with her, and he knew just the thing to say.

"You don't want your brothers finding us, do you?"

Just as he expected, it was as if she were doused with cold water. "Or your parents."

He forced a smile even as he missed the sexy woman who had been begging for more kisses a moment before. But he'd find her again soon enough. "Exactly."

"It's been a long time since I've kissed anyone."

"Their loss. My gain." And damn if he didn't feel male pride at having her in his arms.

She glanced at the ground as she smiled. Then her gaze met his as she pulled her hands down to rest on his chest. "Be careful, Clayton East, I might realize you're a good guy."

"I can promise you that I'm not."

Her grin widened. "You're wrong."

He drew in a breath and took a step back, separating their bodies. There were no more words needed as they began their walk back to the house. No sooner had they reached the porch than her brothers opened the back door to look for her.

"I'm so full my stomach hurts," Caleb said, looking a bit green.

Brice rolled his eyes. "You shouldn't have eaten that slice of cake after the pie and the four cookies."

"Caleb," Abby admonished with a roll of her eyes.

Her youngest brother put one hand over his stomach as he raised the other, palm out. "Give me five minutes, and I can eat the ice cream Mrs. Justine offered."

"Oh, no you're not," Abby said. "You've had more than enough."

Caleb's face crumbled in a frown. "Abby, that's not fair. Brice ate just as much as I did. And he had the ice cream."

Clayton hid his smile as Abby swung her perturbed gaze to Brice.

The teen merely grinned and shrugged. "What? I can hold my food better."

"Oh, my God, you two," Abby mumbled. "Grab your coats. We need to get going."

When the boys went back into the house, Clayton grabbed her hand before she could follow them. Abby turned to him. As her big blue eyes met his, he grinned.

She gave him a wink in return. He reluctantly re-leased her hand as they entered the house. There was a round of good-byes with his parents before he walked her to the door.

Right before she closed the car door, he said, "Be careful."

"Always," she replied.

# Chapter 14

Kissing had never felt so good before. Abby looked at her lips in the bathroom mirror at work. Or maybe it was that it had been more years than she wanted to think about since her last kiss.

Or it could be because Clayton East kissed like a god.

She really couldn't say which was the reason. All Abby knew was that the kiss had seriously rocked her world. Her knees had gone weak, and her toes had actually curled.

Her eyes closed as she pulled up the memory of the night before. Clayton's harsh breaths, the moan that had rumbled in his chest. His hands—one holding her as if she were the most precious thing in the world, and the other fisted in her hair as if to make sure she wouldn't get away.

She snorted while opening her eyes. As if that would happen. She'd wanted that kiss probably more than he had. There were no words to describe how it had felt to be held again. For just a few minutes, she'd stopped being Abby the sister/mom, the one having to make all the decisions.

She'd been able to be Abby, a woman being kissed by a handsome, charming cowboy. And it had been glorious.

Her body hadn't felt like her own. Desire and heat had coursed through her, making every nerve ending come alive. Making her sizzle with awareness and . . . need.

Even now, that yearning drummed through her, a reminder that she was still very much alive and aching for more of Clayton's touch.

There was a pounding on the door that caused Abby to jump, twisting her ankle in her heels. She gripped the sink, biting back a string of cuss words. "Yeah?"

"You've been in there forever, Abby, and this is the only bathroom in the office."

She rolled her eyes at the sound of Jada's high-pitched voice. It was like nails on a chalkboard, only made worse by the fact that Jada loved to hear herself talk. And she was pregnant, which meant that every conversation started with, "If you can't tell, I'm having a baby." Then she'd flash a wide, fake smile with her over-whitened teeth.

Abby flushed the toilet so Jada wouldn't know she'd been standing in front of the mirror the whole time. Then she opened the door to find the receptionist with her hand on her hip, and her head cocked.

"It smells," Jada said testily.

It was all Abby could do not to call her a liar. Instead, she grinned and walked out, forcing Jada to move out of the way. There was a loud huff behind her before Jada and her barely there baby bump sauntered into the bathroom.

Abby returned to her desk and tried once more to focus on the file before her. Every night she spent with Clayton at the ranch, the harder it became for her to concentrate at work the next day. If only a few hours with Clayton did this to her, what would she be like come Monday morning after the weekend with him?

She shivered just thinking about it. That weekend started in a few hours. She was so looking forward to it that she'd been packed for two nights. Except she'd unpacked everything last night, reevaluating what she'd planned to bring and then repacked. Twice.

Her brothers had put their bags in her car that morning. The entire week, there had been no griping about homework, teachers, or any drama going on at school. There'd been no fighting, no back talk when she had reminded them of chores, and they'd been getting up on time each morning without her having to yell at them to get ready.

She knew the cause—Clayton. Or the ranch. Or both. Clayton and the ranch were one and the same in her brothers' eyes. The change in them eased the worry around her heart some.

For the first time in a long while, she saw a bright future for Brice and Caleb. And that made her happy.

Abby mentally shook away thoughts of the weekend, Clayton, and her brothers as she read over the paper in her hand. It was a registration at the county clerk's office for a new brand. Since this was ranching country, it wasn't the first time such a piece of paper had come across her desk.

She pulled up the company on the computer and noted it was a fairly new one, as in just a few weeks old. She keyed in the license payment as well as the payment for the company who made the brand.

Just as she was setting the paper aside, she saw a picture of the brand attached. The 4B brand was simple, but not as simple as the Easts' brand, which was a single E. That made her think of Clayton.

Then again, everything made her think of Clayton.

She moved on to the rest of the invoices. When she looked up at the clock on her computer, only twenty minutes had passed. At this rate, the day would never end.

With the daily invoices entered, she moved on to the next assignment. Abby found a stack of papers very much like the ones she was working on for Clayton within a green file folder. She settled in to work when she heard Gloria, the owner of the firm, raise her voice.

Abby looked over her monitor and through the windows of Gloria's office to see her boss standing tensely beside her desk with her cell phone pressed to her ear. Gloria was in her late forties with no kids and three ex-husbands. She worked hard to maintain a slender figure, often wearing slim-fitting clothes that showed off her svelte body.

And that wasn't the only thing Gloria showed off. Her nails were always manicured and painted. Abby hadn't seen a single chip on Gloria's nails in the four years she'd worked there.

Gloria's makeup was always immaculate, as was her long, dark length of hair. Today, Gloria had a small plait on the right side of her head that fed into the side bun on the left. Tendrils of hair were pulled free to frame her square face to soften it.

By the fire shooting from Gloria's black eyes, someone had crossed a line. Her lips were pinched, her chest heaving in anger as she talked low into the phone. That apparently had no effect because whatever the person on the other end of the line said shattered what little control Gloria was struggling to keep hold of.

"You wouldn't have done it without my help!" Gloria bellowed.

Then she looked up, her gaze clashing with Abby. Gloria stomped over to her door and slammed it before she shut the blinds so no one could see into her office.

This wasn't the first time Abby had seen or heard such a call, but in truth, they were rare. Gloria was well known and respected in Clearview. Her CPA firm thrived because she got the majority of the business in the town and its surrounding areas.

Why then did Abby get the feeling that there was something about that conversation Gloria hadn't wanted her to hear? Abby gave a shake of her head.

It was silly to let her thoughts go down that road. Gloria didn't want *anyone* hearing that conversation, not just her. Abby was just cranky because she wanted the day to end so she could start her weekend.

Fifteen minutes later, she caught sight of someone beside her desk. She looked up with a smile that froze when she saw it was Jada. "Yes?"

While rubbing her belly, Jada gave an overly sweet cat-that-got-into-the-cream smile. "I heard your brother was arrested for cattle rustling. From the East Ranch," she finished, her eyes widening.

The glee on Jada's face made Abby want to punch her. This was one of those times she wished Jill was still in town. "How did you hear that?" Because Abby knew Danny would never tell a soul.

"Oh, please," Jada said with a roll of her blue eyes. "Something like that doesn't stay silent for long. So, it's true?"

"It's true that Brice was mixed up with the wrong people."

"I knew it," Jada said with a little clap of her hands. "I always said those brothers of yours were destined for prison."

Abby sat back in her chair. It was time for her to smile now. "Obviously, whoever gave you that information didn't tell you all of it. Brice was never charged with anything. As a matter of fact, he's now working after school at the East Ranch."

And just like that, Jada's smile vanished. The satisfaction Abby felt was euphoric. There were only five of them working at the firm, and no one really liked Jada, but because she was one of Clearview's gossip queens, no one wanted to get on her bad side.

It had been the same in high school where Jada had been two years older than Abby. While Jada liked to make fun of the fact that Abby didn't have a degree, Abby didn't point out that Jada had married the high school quarterback who had peaked in school but couldn't hold down a job anywhere now, while Jada was merely a receptionist.

Because, hey, Abby had her own problems, and she didn't want to get caught up in anyone else's drama.

"Anything else?" Abby asked sweetly.

Jada's face soured, her cheeks sucking inward as she puckered her lips. "No."

"You might want to watch making that face. Wrinkles form early."

Abby wasn't sure why she'd given that parting remark. It was definitely something Jill would've said, and after so many years as friends, her friend must have rubbed off on her. But seeing the horror in Jada's eyes as she began smoothing out her face with her hands was too good.

The next few hours were uneventful. Abby kept her head down and plugged away at her pile of work. She had a sandwich, chips, and water for lunch that she'd brought from home and ate at her desk while working. So she was surprised when Gloria called her into her office.

No matter the occasion, Abby always felt as if she were being called into the principal's office when she had to go see Gloria.

"Yes?" she said as she stood in the doorway.

Gloria smiled and motioned to a chair before signing a paper and setting it aside. "How's it going, Abby?"

Instantly on alert, Abby shrugged as she sat. "Good."

"I just wanted to say I'm sorry I gave you a hard time on Monday when you asked to leave. I had no idea your brother had been arrested."

Abby wanted to tell Gloria that when she'd said it was an emergency, she hadn't lied. And it shouldn't matter if Brice had been arrested or brought to the hospital. An emergency was an emergency.

"Thanks," she said tightly.

Gloria rested her arms on the desk. "Is everything all right now?"

"Yep. Right as rain."

"Good. That's good." Gloria sat back and crossed one slim leg over the other before folding her hands in her lap. "Jada told me that Brice wasn't charged with anything."

Abby tensed. "He wasn't. May I ask why you're questioning me about this?"

Gloria laughed, the sound light and airy. But Abby wasn't fooled.

"I'm sorry. I should've said that I was worried about you. I didn't want to say anything earlier this week when I heard about Brice. No one said he'd been released, so I assumed he was going to jail."

Wow. They might have to scrape together pennies every month, and yes, her brothers weren't perfect. But not once had either of them been in trouble with the law. This was the first time, and yet Gloria made it sound as if it were a common occurrence.

Abby merely looked at her, waiting to see what it was that Gloria really wanted.

And she didn't have to wait long.

Gloria licked her bright pink lips. "Jada told me that Brice now works at the East Ranch."

"He does." And that's what Abby would continue to say. None of those bitches needed to know that it was to pay off his debt.

"Well," Gloria said with a smile. "I know for a fact that the Easts need a new CPA. How about helping me get them into the firm?"

In the past, Abby would've nodded, and that would've been it. But something had changed in her. She wasn't sure when or where or even how, but it was there.

"And what's in it for me?" Abby asked with a lift of her chin. Jill would've been so proud of her.

Gloria raised a brow, her smile growing. "Now that's what I like to hear." She leaned an elbow on the arm of her chair. "How about a five-percent raise."

"Fifteen," Abby countered.

Gloria's black eyes narrowed shrewdly. "Ten."

"Deal," Abby said and stuck out her hand.

She should've felt giddy at the negotiation, but as she shook Gloria's hand, she just felt dirty.

# Chapter 15

Clayton learned the hard way that he hadn't mastered the art of patience as he'd believed. Waiting for Friday evening to come was the slowest, most cruel type of torture.

But when he spotted the lights of Abby's car, he was both nervous and excited. By the time he walked to the front of the house from the corral, Abby and the boys were out of the Accord and standing by the opened trunk.

"Are you sure?" Caleb asked, his brow furrowed deeply.

Clayton stopped behind them. "Something wrong?"

All three Harpers whirled around. Both Brice and Caleb briefly met his gaze. Clayton turned his attention to Abby and raised a brow.

"Um," she hesitated, glancing at her brothers. "We wanted to make sure the invitation still stands."

Clayton knew she'd included herself so the boys

weren't singled out. And that gesture made him want to kiss her. Abby always knew what to say and how to handle her brothers.

"Of course," he replied. "I think my mother would chase you down if you tried to leave."

Caleb elbowed Brice, a huge smile on his face. Brice looked at Clayton and gave a nod before he took his and Abby's bags from the trunk. Once Caleb removed his bag, and the trunk was closed, Clayton led them into the house.

As usual, his mother had George Strait's Christmas CD playing, the music flowing from the speakers throughout the house. When she heard the front door close, she hollered for the boys, who rushed to the kitchen.

"She's been baking all day," Clayton said.

Abby closed her eyes and inhaled. "It's amazing. Just what Christmas should smell like."

He wondered what her Christmases had been like, but decided not to ask then. He wanted her laughing and smiling, not thinking of the past with her mother—or without.

"I'll take you to your room," he said. "Have Brice and Caleb decided where they want to sleep?"

She laughed as they made their way to the stairs. "Really? You must have known they would choose the bunkhouse. Both have officially declared that they're going to be cowboys and work on the ranch."

He looked back at her as they climbed the steps. "How do you feel about that?"

"If it keeps them out of trouble, I'm fine with it."

He brought her down the same hall as his bedroom.

His gaze was on her face when he opened the door to the guest room and showed her inside.

"Oh," she murmured softly as she walked in and ran her hand over the red bedspread with a white reindeer and snowflakes. Half of the coverlet was folded down to show white sheets with red snowflakes.

She picked up a rectangular shaped pillow with a white background and four stockings and held it briefly. She replaced it and smiled down at another square pillow that was white with *Merry Christmas* scrawled across it.

Clayton knew Abby would probably love any of the bedrooms, but for some reason, he'd thought of her when he looked at this room. He'd assumed from the comments that she and her brothers had made that none of them had had a Christmas in the traditional sense. At least not in quite some time.

It had been something he'd never been denied, and something he'd taken for granted. Now, he wanted to give Abby and the boys what he'd always had just so he could see their smiles.

Not to show off his family's wealth, but to share the love he'd always felt. The Harpers deserved it, needed it even. Especially Abby.

She stood in the middle of the room and turned in a slow circle, taking it all in. She laughed when she saw the two-foot, white Christmas tree decorated with tiny red ornaments sitting on a table. Then Abby faced him. "This is amazing."

"Enjoy it," he said as he set her bag on the bench before the bed.

"Oh, I plan to," she replied with a laugh.

He moved closer to her, staring into her bright blue eyes. All he'd thought about all day was kissing her again. With his hands settled on her hips, he drew her close as his head began to lower.

It was the pounding of feet up the stairs that pulled them apart seconds before Brice came into the room, followed soon after by Caleb.

Brice let out a long whistle as he looked around.

"Damn," Caleb said.

"Caleb," Abby admonished.

Her youngest brother widened his eyes as he shrugged his shoulders. "Seriously? Look at this room!"

"I know," she said in a conspiratorial whisper.

Brice walked up beside Abby and put his arm around her shoulders. He gave her a smile and a squeeze before his gaze slid to Clayton.

In that moment, Clayton saw that Brice was aware of his interest in his sister. Which meant there would need to be a conversation later. It was the least he owed Brice as the man of the house.

"Mr. Ben is downstairs," Caleb said. "Mrs. Justine says he's been stealing cookies all day."

Clayton laughed as he thought back over the years. "They have a tradition that goes back to their very first Christmas together after they were married. He tries to see how many cookies he can steal while she tries to either catch him or stop him."

"Who wins?" Brice asked.

Clayton found his gaze on Abby. "Mom lets him steal them, and Dad does it to be with her."

"So they both win," Caleb said with a nod.

The boys then walked out of the room, talking about the weekend out on the ranch. As they left, Clayton watched Abby's gaze follow them.

"All Brice has ever known was the revolving door of men our mother brought into the house after our father died. I shielded my brothers as best I could, but Brice saw them. Caleb did, too, but he was so young that it didn't really register. Neither of them remembers our father, so they don't know what it means to have a true relationship." Her eyes swung to him. "Your parents are showing them that."

His brows snapped together when he saw tears well in her eyes. As he moved toward her, she hastily blinked to hold them back.

"I'm sorry," she said with a sniff. "It's just that my telling them how two people are supposed to be together fell on deaf ears. They didn't get it until your parents. And I can't tell you how much that means to me. Maybe now, they'll have the right kind of relationships."

That was one aspect that he hadn't thought about with the boys, but it had obviously weighed heavily upon Abby's mind. And it brought forth another question.

"Is that why you didn't date?"

She glanced away and took a deep breath. "Partly. I wasn't sure their young minds would understand dating after what my mother did. And they were so scared I was going to leave them, that it became easier not to think about it."

"And now?" It probably wasn't the right thing to ask, but Clayton had to know.

"Is different."

That's just what he wanted to hear.

When they walked back down the stairs, Abby tried to go to the office, but he grabbed her hand and led her into the living room where all the lights were off except for the Christmas tree.

With the twinkling of the soft white lights and the red-orange glow of the fire, the room looked inviting and cozy. Abby didn't even hesitate to walk to the tree.

"This one is my favorite," she declared.

He raised a brow. "The champagne-colored ornaments?"

"Nope," she said and glanced at him. "It's the biggest. I always wanted a huge Christmas tree that would take a ladder to put the star on top."

"What else did you want?"

"So many lights that it was blinding."

He grinned and walked to stand beside her. "White lights or colored?"

"I'm not picky," she declared. "I like your mom's idea. She loves it all, so she does it all. Colored lights on a white tree with purple ornaments. White lights on a green tree with red decorations."

Clayton reached out and touched the ends of her hair. "So, if you had no budget and were set loose in a Christmas store?"

"I'd buy it all," she said with a laugh. "My house would drip Christmas in every room."

"Oh, God," he said in mock astonishment, his head tilted back. "Don't let Mom hear you."

Abby's laugh drew him in. It was warm and welcoming, and when he was with her, it was like he was coming in from the cold. He could smile and laugh and tease—all of the things he hadn't done in months.

But Abby's smile quickly vanished. Clayton studied her, reading the tightening of her shoulders and the frown that meant her thoughts were once more on her brothers.

"I could've let my brothers go into the foster system," she said in a low voice. "Many people suggested that I should. They said that at eighteen, I wasn't capable of taking care of them." Her chest lifted as she inhaled. "I wasn't. I knew that, just as I knew it'd be easier to let them go. I could worry about only me."

"No one would've blamed you."

Her mouth twisted as she lifted one shoulder in a shrug. "I saw what the foster system was. If I could've been guaranteed that my brothers were kept together and were sent to a good, loving home, I might have done it. But it wasn't a chance I could take."

"Because you love them."

She looked at him and nodded, the lights of the trees shining like a thousand stars in her eyes. "For six months after mom left, they slept with me in my bed. There were nights Brice wouldn't close his eyes for fear that I'd be gone when he woke. He kept my gown fisted in his hands all night."

It made Clayton want to track down their mother and give her a piece of his mind. But he also knew the trio was better off without such a woman. Perhaps that's why she'd left them. At least that was what he was going to tell himself—and them, if they ever asked.

"I've taken it one day at a time for these last eight years. Eight years," she repeated with a shake of her head. "I don't know where the time went. I should've planned better. By this time, I should've obtained a better-paying job so we could breathe easier."

"Ninety percent of the population lives paycheck to paycheck, Abby. Don't be so hard on yourself. You've given those boys a stable, loving home."

She looked at him and grinned sheepishly. "I've never said any of this to anyone before."

"I'm glad you told me." And he meant it. He wanted her to trust him, to share details of her life.

Because he wanted to be with her.

And he recognized that, without her, he was an emotional wreck. But Abby centered things, and stabilized him.

Now, it was his turn to share. "I didn't want to come home because I'm not the person I was when I left. I've been in war and have seen death up close. I've killed."

She moved closer, rubbing her hand up and down his arm. "As you said, you were in war."

"Not all of my missions were during war."

"You were a SEAL," she said. "You were the ones sent in to help others because y'all got the job done."

He took her hand and looked at the tree. "I see the men I've killed every time I close my eyes."

"And no one here would understand that."

He nodded and turned his head to her. "It's a weight that I'll carry for the rest of my days. I fought for my country, and I saved people. But I was also sent on missions to take out our enemies."

"The fact that you're here says you're a survivor. Unfortunately, we survivors are always left to carry the burden of what's left. Frankly, I'm glad you're here. You were needed, and I think you needed this place, too."

"I did." But it was more than the ranch that his soul craved.

It was Abby.

# Chapter 16

Clayton was definitely someone she could get used to having around. Abby liked the thought of him, but she also knew better than to hand over her heart so quickly. Not only had she accepted the loneliness she'd tried to hide, which made her yearn for someone—that wasn't true. She didn't long for just anyone. She wanted Clayton.

Then there was the fact that she didn't know if he was staying or not. What good would it do for her to fall for someone only to have him leave?

She'd guarded herself so fiercely for so long, she knew she'd be devastated if Clayton left. So while she ached for more of his kisses, she couldn't let herself think—or dream—of anything more.

That was easier said than done when she sat across from him at the dinner table. With effortless conversation and good food, it was easy to imagine how life might be with him.

Each time she looked up and found his pale green eyes taking her in, it caused her heart to beat faster.

Though he didn't exactly wear a smile, Clayton's demeanor had loosened by several degrees. He was more relaxed, an ease she hadn't seen from him before.

Well, except when they'd kissed.

It wasn't long before Justine and Ben shared stories about Clayton when he was younger. When Landon was mentioned, all three Easts' eyes filled with sadness, but the joy of talking about Landon made up for that.

All too soon, the meal was finished. While Abby helped to clear the table, Ben and Clayton talked to her brothers about what to expect while staying at the bunkhouse.

Brice and Caleb listened raptly, nodding as the men spoke. The way her brothers had taken to Ben and Clayton made Abby all too aware of how much her brothers had needed a stable man in their lives.

She waved to her siblings as they headed out the door to where Shane waited for them. "Be good," she called.

"We will," they answered in unison.

Justine came up beside her, wearing a smile. "You did good with them, Abby."

"I just see all the ways I've screwed up."

Justine chuckled before turning back to wipe off the counters. "There's isn't a handbook for raising kids. We do the best we can. Every parent or guardian tries not to make the same mistakes their parent or parents did, and in the process, we make new ones. It's just the way things work."

"I fear I've screwed them up for life," Abby confessed one of her great worries.

"Oh, honey. That's simply not true."

She turned to Justine. "They have abandonment issues."

"They aren't the only ones," Justine stated, giving her a pointed look. "And it's justified. Abby, your mother didn't just leave your brothers. She left you, as well. You always leave that out."

"I was eighteen."

"Age doesn't matter when a parent leaves. A child will always need that parent. Always."

Abby put the cork in the wine bottle. "Thank you for opening your home to us. I think I'm going to get some work done now."

"Are you sure? Ben and I are headed upstairs, but you and Clayton could watch a movie or something."

That sounded sublime. "I'll wait and see what Clayton wants to do."

"All right, honey. I'm going to get my man into bed. I'll see you in the morning."

"Goodnight."

Abby watched Justine walk from the kitchen to the grand staircase. The love between Clayton's parents was what Abby longed for. She'd never thought she would achieve it. Mostly because it was hard to find a man when she didn't put herself out there, but then there weren't that many men around that she wanted to date.

That is until she'd met Clayton.

On her way to the office, she paused beside a wreath of freshly cut fir and inhaled the aroma. Though she wasn't part of the East family, this was the best Christmas she'd ever had. And if it took her scraping by even more than usual, she would start saving so her brothers could have a proper Christmas tree and maybe even some garland.

Really, all she wanted was the lights. They added magic to any room.

Abby sat behind the desk and took a deep breath before she tucked her hair behind her ears and immersed herself back into the accounting nightmare of the ranch.

She had no idea how long she worked before she pinched the bridge of her nose and lifted her head to stretch her neck. That's when she found Clayton stretched out on the sofa, his hat covering his face.

"I was beginning to think I was invisible," he murmured sleepily.

She grinned despite herself. "How long have you been there?"

"Almost an hour."

Aghast, she said, "Are you serious?"

He pushed his hat up with his thumb and looked at her without moving his head. "Yes, ma'am. When you work, you absorb yourself fully."

"Why didn't you say something?" she asked, mortified.

"I didn't want to disturb you. It looked as if you had found something."

She tossed the pencil on the desk. "I did. Well, I think I did. He could've transposed numbers, but I think it was done on purpose. I want to see how often this occurs before I can say one way or the other."

Clayton sat up and swung his legs over the side of the couch while adjusting his hat. "You think this is how Gilroy began taking money?"

"I do. This is a long process, though. At the rate I'm going, it's going to take months."

"And if you worked at it full-time?"

She shrugged. "I'd say about a month. I'd want to be thorough, and there may be a need to look even farther back than when Nathan took over."

"Then I want to hire you."

Abby was so taken aback she could only stare at him.

"I'm serious," Clayton said. "We need someone we trust to look at the books with a skeptical eye."

"You barely know me."

It was his turn to shrug. "Call it gut instinct. My parents feel the same way."

"But we've discussed this. I'm not licensed."

"You said you do this kind of thing every day in your job."

She nodded woodenly. "I do. With Gloria then checking behind me."

"Every time? Are you sure Gloria checks everything?"

Abby began to reply, but she hesitated because she knew that Gloria had stopped checking her work over a year ago.

"That's what I thought," Clayton said. "Are you fighting this because you don't want to work for me?"

How did she get herself into these situations? "Not at all. You and your parents have been incredible. I just think a ranch this size should be working with someone reputable. Someone with clout."

Clayton leaned back, resting his arms on the back of the sofa. "Gloria wants our business, doesn't she?"

"Yes." Dear God. She'd forgotten that Gloria had asked her to bring in the Easts, which would mean a ten percent bump in pay. It wasn't a lot, but that little bit could do amazing things. It's what she'd told her brothers on the drive over, but she didn't like how she'd felt about Gloria's offer. So she'd also told her brother she wasn't going to do it.

"What did Gloria offer you?"

Seeing Clayton out on the ranch, it was easy to forget that he also knew the business side of things. And was, apparently, shrewd.

"A ten-percent raise."

Clayton raised a pale brow. "That's it? With what the ranch would bring her in revenue, she should double your salary."

"Unfortunately, Gloria doesn't think like you."

"That's her loss. And my gain."

Abby could feel the erratic beat of her heart and the nervousness that tightened her stomach into a ball. "You can't be serious about this."

"You've already said that. And I am."

"But . . ." She racked her brain thinking of other arguments. "You've not spoken to your parents about it."

"You don't know that," he retorted.

That made her pause. "Oh. Have you?"

"A bit." When she started to talk, he dropped his arms and scooted to the edge of the sofa. "Stop, Abby. I hear your arguments, and I'm sure if I gave you time, you'd come up with a hundred more. The simple fact is, you've done more for us in the few hours that you've looked at the finances than the people we paid to do it over the years."

Abby preened at his compliment.

"I'll be honest," he continued. "I placed a call to Gloria when I first got into town and left a message. I've not returned her phone call. And I don't plan to. I want you working here. You're more than qualified. Not only have you worked for Gloria for four years, but you're halfway to your degree."

Obviously, he had spoken to her brothers about how long she'd worked for Gloria. Abby liked that he'd gotten all his facts together. It proved that he had thought this through, and that it wasn't just something off the top of his head.

He rose and walked toward her. "You won't have to work nearly as hard. With the extra time, you'll be able to get your degree quicker. And to sweeten the deal, I'll double whatever salary you make with Gloria."

"You can't say that when you don't know what I make," she said, the shock of his words still reverberating in her mind.

Clayton leaned down and put his hands on the arms of the chair so their eyes were level. "I can. I did. And I'll say it again."

"But the money was stolen."

With one hand, Clayton punched a few keys on the keyboard and the screen filled with banking information. When she saw the sum, her eyes widened.

She jerked her gaze to him. "The money was already replaced?"

"This is my money. I put it in the account until the stolen sum could be found or the bonding paperwork you sent in is completed."

"Oh." Shit. He was as loaded as his parents.

He held her gaze. "I had nothing to spend my money on. So, I invested. Heavily. This is part of the reward."

"Part?" she asked in a soft voice.

"A small slice."

With him being so close, she was reminded of their kiss the night before. There was a ruthless determination in his gaze that she recognized from seeing it both at the sheriff's station and when he wanted her to look over the books. He wouldn't relent until he had what he wanted, and right now, he wanted her working for him.

What kind of fool passed up that kind of opportunity?

It would put her close to him. Daily. She would have to fight the desire that curled through her each time he was near. And if there were more kisses? She couldn't even think about that, because she wanted to taste him on her tongue again, to feel his hard body against her.

To have his hand gripping her hair again.

"I wouldn't be bonded," she said. "I can't since I'm not licensed."

His lips curved into a satisfied smile. "You won't have access to the accounts. At least not until you are licensed. So that's not a worry."

"Don't you want to know what I make with Gloria?"

"No. Wait. Yes, I do. What's your salary?"

Abby shifted uncomfortably. "I'm still hourly. She didn't want to pay for medical insurance."

"Well, that's pretty shitty of her. Does she know she's treating her best employee so horrendously?"

"She doesn't care."

His gaze dropped to her mouth. "I'll say again: Her loss. My gain."

Abby was really beginning to like those words.

"Maybe just pay me hourly until I get my degree and become licensed. That seems fair."

"I'm going to have to teach you how to bargain, because you suck at it."

She laughed until he took her hand and pulled her to her feet—and right into his arms. Her breasts pressed against the sinew of his chest. Every thought vanished as she recalled the way his lips had moved over hers, how he skillfully turned their soft kiss into one that raged uncontrollably, scorching them from the inside out.

Because in his arms, she remembered she was a woman. A woman with needs. A woman who wanted — and needed—to feel desire.

And he was a man who would lead her down that road with the promise of untold pleasure in his eyes— and his kiss.

God help her, she'd readily follow him anywhere.

"No, Abby Harper, I'm going to pay you what you should've been earning all this time. You're worth it."

How could she withstand such words? "You barely know me."

"I know you. I know you have a kind heart, you're fiercely protective of your brothers, and you think of everyone but yourself. I know the intoxicating taste of your kiss and the heavenly way you feel in my arms."

Whatever resistance she had left evaporated before Clayton's lips claimed hers.

# Chapter 17

Clayton watched the sun rise from beside a barn, his thoughts on Abby. It had nearly killed him to stop at just one kiss the night before. But the entire weekend lay before them.

And he intended to make use of it.

Since his parents were early risers, he'd already talked to them about hiring Abby. Both had agreed with his decision. He hadn't been sure what he would've done had even one of them been uncertain. Thankfully, that hadn't been an issue.

"You sure are tying Abby to the ranch nicely," his dad said as he came to stand beside him.

There was a nudge on his arm. Clayton looked down and saw the mug of coffee that he quickly accepted. When he lifted his gaze, his father was staring at the pink sky.

Clayton brought the cup to his lips, but before he drank, he said, "I suppose I am."

"A man does that when he sees something he wants."

"Yep."

"Are you sure?"

Clayton was silent as he contemplated the question. "It's the one thing I am certain of."

"Then don't let her get away." His father turned his head to him then. "Don't think we've not seen the change in you since she began coming here. She's done what we couldn't. We might have brought you back, but she made you whole again."

"What if she doesn't want me?"

His father grinned. "She does, but if you're still worried, my advice is to tell her your darkest secrets. Let her in, son. Show her everything. She'll either accept you or she won't."

"Yeah."

"Damn, but this weather feels good," his father said and closed his eyes as he lifted his face. "After all the cold days, a warm one every now and again is nice."

Clayton could only shake his head. The Texas weather could turn on a dime. Though the temps were in the upper fifties right now and forecasted to be in the sixties mid day, a surprise cold front could move in and drop everything into the forties quickly.

His father opened his eyes. "I guess you'd better sneak me back inside before your mother sees me."

Clayton looked over his shoulder to find his mother standing on the porch with a hand on her hip, glaring at Ben. "Too late."

"Damn," his dad murmured, his face wrinkling in consternation.

"Benjamin East, get your fine ass back here. Your eggs are getting cold."

Clayton watched his father break into a huge smile. He leaned close, and in a conspiratorial voice said, "Apparently, I'm no longer house bound."

"Don't push it, or she'll strap you to the bed," Clayton warned.

"Don't give her any ideas." His father took a couple of steps and paused. "Hm. That might be fun, though."

Clayton shook his head, a smile on his face as he watched his father walk back to his mother before they disappeared—arm in arm—into the house.

His gaze lifted to the window of Abby's room. As if his thoughts summoned her, a slim hand moved aside the curtain before she appeared. She looked over the ranch before her gaze dropped.

The moment their eyes met, it was like being kicked in the stomach. But that's what Abby did to him. She excited him, moved him. She made him yearn and ache once more.

With a soft smile, she vanished behind the curtain again. Clayton sped through his morning chores and returned to the house as Abby entered the kitchen.

"Good morning. How'd you sleep?" he asked as he gave her a once over. He liked the pink plaid flannel button-down she wore, and he really liked how it was tucked into her jeans, allowing him to see her curves.

She smiled. "Very well."

"I have a surprise for you."

"Before or after I work on the books?"

He'd known she was going to say that. "I can't talk you into taking the day off, can I?"

"Afraid not."

"That's too bad," he said as he set his mug down. "I'll give you until lunch. But after that, you're all mine."

Whatever she'd been about to say was interrupted by the arrival of his parents. While his mother insisted on making Abby breakfast, Clayton slipped out. It was either leave then or not at all. And since Abby felt as if she needed to work, he'd only slow her down if he were near.

So, he'd let her work so she didn't feel guilty. But after, he wasn't going to let her anywhere near the office. Not for the rest of the day, and not on Sunday. He didn't intend to tell her that, though. She'd discover it soon enough.

Clayton walked to the barn where Brice and Caleb were following Shane everywhere he went and listening to every word the ranch manager had to say. And Shane loved every minute of it.

By mid-morning, the chores were done, and the workers, along with Shane, Brice, and Caleb, were gathered around a paddock as Clayton led out a horse. He called Brice over first and taught the teen how to put on the saddle blanket, saddle, and bridle. Only then did he allow Brice to climb atop the sorrel gelding for his first lesson in riding.

Caleb could barely contain his excitement when it was his turn. And he'd been paying attention. Clayton didn't have to tell him much as Caleb readied the buckskin mare. Both boys took to horseback riding naturally.

When lunchtime came, they dismounted with great reluctance. It was only the promise of more riding that got them off the horses. The tack was removed and hung up, and the horses brushed and let out to pasture.

Clayton was just as ready to get to the house as the boys, but not for food. He wanted Abby and their afternoon. During the meal, she and his parents listened intently as Brice and Caleb described their first lesson.

The meal seemed to stretch on forever. Clayton couldn't remember ever being so anxious about anything. When lunch was finished and the kitchen cleaned, he took Abby's hand and led her to the barn.

Diamond was already saddled and waiting next to the bay. Abby halted and looked at him, her eyes widening as a smile formed.

"Are we going riding?" she asked.

"Yes."

She was grinning eagerly when she walked to Diamond and stroked the mare's neck in greeting. "In the paddock like my brothers, right?"

"No."

"But, Clayton, I don't know how to ride."

He brushed Diamond's mane from her forehead. "This mare is one of the gentlest horses we own. There's no other one I'd put you on. Diamond will take good care of you. And so will I."

Abby met his gaze. "You only live once, right? I trust you."

That's all he needed to hear.

He helped her get her foot into the stirrup before she threw her other leg over the horse and gently sat down. She reached over and secured her right foot before she sat up. Clayton then taught her how to hold the reins in both hands as well as how to move them in order to get Diamond to turn, stop, and back up.

In less than thirty minutes, they were headed away from the barn on horseback. He glanced over at Abby to find her grinning. She looked at him and laughed merrily.

"I've always wanted to ride," she admitted.

"You can ride Diamond any time you want."

She shook her head. "You're too nice."

"Maybe I just like you."

Abby's gaze slid away, but the smile remained. He took her to one of the best spots on the ranch. It had an amazing view and offered some seclusion.

They stopped and looked down into the ravine. The sound of water reached them even ten feet up. He dismounted, and Abby followed.

"Wow," she said as she looked down at the water and then over the undulating hills. "I didn't think anything could be prettier than the area around the house. I was wrong. This place is. . . ."

"Magical," he supplied.

She turned her head to him and nodded. "Yes. Magical."

Clayton untied the blanket at the back of his saddle and handed it to Abby. Then he loosely secured the horses' reins around the pommels of the saddles and let them graze. They wouldn't go far, and even if they did, they'd return with a whistle.

When he turned around, Abby had spread the blanket and was sitting on it with her hands clasped around her knees. Her eyes were closed, and the sun beamed upon her as if spotlighting her beauty.

Clayton didn't need any help noticing her. He'd seen her loveliness from the beginning. Though he didn't want to interrupt her, he had to get closer. The ride over had been pure torture with their knees brushing occasionally.

"Sit," she murmured.

He lowered himself, stretching his legs out and leaning back on his elbows. He couldn't take his eyes from her.

"This is what I needed." She turned her head to look at him. "How did you know that?"

"I didn't. I wanted to take you to one of my favorite places. And I wanted you alone."

Her lips tilted up in a grin. "Alone?"

"Yeah. To do this," he said as he reached for her, dragging her down on top of him as he plundered her lips.

He groaned as her mouth opened for him. Whatever thoughts he had of going slow vanished at the first taste of her. He rolled her onto her back and settled between her legs while blood rushed to his cock.

The need to be inside her, to connect their bodies was so great that he had to fight not to tear her clothes off. Then, to his shock, she yanked his shirt out of the waist of his jeans and pressed her palm against his side.

A heartbeat later, her hands moved between them as she began unbuttoning his shirt. As soon as it fell open, he yanked it off. She sat up, her eyes devouring him as her hands slowly roamed over his body.

"My God, you're gorgeous," she murmured.

He tensed when her hands ran over one of his many

scars, but she didn't so much as pause at them. She stared hard at his tattoos but said nothing about them either.

"A warrior and a cowboy." She looked up at him, her blue eyes darkened with desire. She then knocked off his hat. "I don't think there's anything you can't do."

He slid a hand around the back of her neck and held her as he lowered his head to kiss her. Their tongues dueled, the desire rising higher with each touch and taste. Before he laid her back, he slowly unbuttoned her top and gently opened the shirt. It was his turn to marvel at the stunning woman before him.

She wore a nude bra with black lace cupping her full breasts. Unable to help himself, he ran a finger from her neck down into her cleavage. Her eyes closed as her chest heaved. He pushed her shirt over her shoulders and watched it fall down her arms. Then he reached around and unhooked her bra.

The moment the glorious mounds were freed, his balls tightened, and his mouth watered. Dusky nipples hardened into tiny pebbles beneath his gaze.

He cupped a breast, testing the weight of it in his hand before he ran his thumb over the tight nub. She moaned, her head dropping back. Seeing her with such a look of pleasure on her face made him desperate to watch her as she came. He wanted to bring her ecstasy, to have her shout his name as she found her release.

She gripped his arm and raised her head to look at him. But he wasn't finished with her breasts yet. He still had the other one that begged for attention.

Their gazes held when he bent and took one nipple into his mouth. When he began to suck, her breathing became erratic. He laid her back on the blanket and set-tled over her, moving from one breast to the other. While his mouth sucked one nipple, his hand pinched and rolled the other. With each swipe of his tongue, her moans grew louder, her hips slightly rocking against him.

He groaned as his cock swelled, eager to be inside her and feel her wetness surround him. To have her body clamp down on him, milking him as they climaxed to-gether.

She sunk her fingers into his hair the same time he reached for the waist of her jeans.

# Chapter 18

Desire raged, and need consumed her. Abby couldn't catch her breath, but she didn't care. The feel of Clayton's hands and mouth on her felt too good.

The sensations rushing through her halted all thought, making her *feel* each swipe of his tongue and caress of his calloused hands. The awareness of his touch and his breathing was incredible.

How had she forgotten desire and passion? The sizzling, inconceivable tightening low in her belly as her need mounted so quickly, she was already on the verge of an orgasm—and he'd only touched her breasts.

With quick fingers, he unbuttoned and lowered the zipper of her jeans. The air that brushed against her hot skin made her suck in her stomach. She began to tremble, but not from the cool breeze. No, it had everything to do with Clayton's hand splayed across her stomach and his fingers inching lower to her sex.

Her breath locked in her lungs when his hand slipped

beneath the waist of her panties and moved lower. When he cupped her, she jerked, the air rushing past her lips as she moaned.

"My God," he murmured huskily and sucked harder on her nipple.

Then, suddenly, Clayton was gone. Abby forced her eyes open while trying to control the tide of desire that bombarded her. It wasn't until he took her foot in hand and unzipped her boot that she realized what he was doing.

While he removed her footwear, she began to push her jeans over her hips and kick them off, along with her panties. Then, she was on her knees, helping him yank off his cowboy boots. Her fingers wouldn't work right as she fumbled, trying to unbutton his jeans. It took him helping her before they finally knelt naked in the sunlight.

She had run her hands over his chiseled chest earlier, taking in the hard sinew and rigid planes. Now, she let herself *see* him—his tattoos and all the scars from his battles.

Her palms had found many of the scars before. Some were small, some large and jagged. She couldn't imagine the pain he'd suffered with each of them. Yet it wasn't what defined him. He didn't allow it.

She glided her fingers across the tribal tattoo that ran over his left shoulder and down his forearm as well as across part of his chest. An oval scar marred the ink slightly. A bullet wound that had been so close to his heart.

Her head tilted to look down. She bit her lip when she

glimpsed his arousal jutting between them, thick and hard. Even more scars were on his thighs. It just proved that he didn't hesitate to do what had to be done, even if it meant putting his life on the line.

When she raised her gaze to his face, it was to find his lips gently curved while he looked at her as if she were the most precious thing in all the world.

It made her heart skip a beat.

"You're the most beautiful thing I've ever seen," he said as he slowly ran his hands up her arms, touching her reverently.

She couldn't think of the words to reply, so she decided on action instead. Abby pulled his head down. The moment their lips met, his hands grasped her hips and brought her against his cock.

Her head dropped back when his lips moved along her jaw and then down the column of her throat. She wrapped her arms around him, holding him tightly even as she sighed when his teeth lightly scraped along the skin of her shoulder.

His muscles moved beneath her hands as he lifted her until she wrapped her legs around his waist. She cried out when it brought his arousal against the sensitive flesh of her sex.

The next thing she knew, she was on her back with Clayton's hands braced on either side of her head as he leaned over her. She wanted him inside her so badly that her brain stopped working.

With his pale green eyes watching her, he circled her nipple with his finger, coming closer and closer, but never touching her before moving on to the other breast.

The torture was exquisite and made her ache for him. When she reached for his cock, he quickly caught her hands and captured them above her head with one hand.

Excitement drummed through her as she impatiently waited for him to touch her.

Abby was like a feast laid out before him, and Clayton couldn't decide where to partake first. But since they had all afternoon, that meant he could have her every way he wanted.

He let his eyes roam over her body. So soft. Her curves were mouth-watering. He'd never liked the girls that were stick figures. He wanted a real woman with all the amazing curves that came with such a beautiful body.

His perusal stopped at the juncture of her thighs. Her legs were still spread as he knelt between them. Her triangle of dark curls beckoned, as did the sight of the swollen, pink flesh of her nether lips.

When he'd cupped her before, her back had arched, and she'd let out a low moan that made his cock jump. What would she do when he teased her clit or sunk a finger inside her? His body shook just thinking about it.

He glanced up at her to find her blue eyes hooded as she watched him. Her lips were parted, and her chest rose rapidly. He glided his hand down her side to the indent of her waist and over the flare of her hip to her thigh.

Her breath hitched when his hand moved across her belly to the triangle of curls at the junction of her thighs. Clayton held her gaze as he slowly caressed downward and lightly swirled a finger around her clit.

She bit her lip, her body tensing. It only took one more swipe before she whispered his name as her eyes rolled back in her head.

The way her hips rocked in time with his finger mesmerized him. He was so focused on bringing her pleasure that he didn't realize she was close to climaxing until her body jerked and she let out a cry.

He didn't relent in his teasing, though. While in the middle of the orgasm, he thrust a finger inside her. And then nearly came himself when he felt her body clamp down on him.

Clayton clenched his teeth and began pumping his hand. Her screams grew louder as he felt another orgasm claim her. The pleasure on her face and the way her body flushed were things he'd never forget.

To see her head thrashing side to side and hear her moans was exactly what he needed. But he also knew he would never get enough of her.

Unable to hold back any longer, Clayton withdrew his fingers and quickly pulled the condom from his pants. Once it was on, he positioned himself at her entrance. Then he pushed inside her. Her tight, wet heat nearly sent him careening toward his own climax.

His touch was ecstasy. Abby barely drew in a breath before the second climax swarmed her. It was more intense than the first, flinging her into a vortex of blinding pleasure.

And then he was inside her.

Her body was more than ready and quickly stretched to accommodate him. He moved slowly, gradually, until all of him was inside.

That's when she opened her eyes. He leaned over her with his eyes squeezed shut and his arms shaking from the effort not to come.

She touched his face, and he stilled instantly. When his green eyes met hers, something solidified between then, bonding not just their bodies but also something deeper.

It scared her, but she didn't pull away. She couldn't. Not with him looking at her so tenderly. Despite the trepidation she felt with whatever was happening between them, his steadfastness kept her from bolting.

"I've fantasized about this moment from the first time I saw you."

She was about to reply when he withdrew and then thrust. All words deserted her. She gripped his arms as he began moving, building his rhythm with each drive of his hips.

Somehow, this man had actually seen her. Not the hot mess of a woman she'd become, the one trying to juggle her life, work, and her brothers. No, he saw the woman beneath.

He refused to let her back down, pushing her in new, frightening directions. He saw her fears and worries and made some of them his own. He recognized her need and woke her desires.

And he appeared to have no intention of stopping anytime soon.

She'd never felt more beautiful or wanted than in that moment. He'd given her pleasure before himself, playing her body as if it were his favorite instrument in the universe. His skilled fingers had flung her over the precipice with ease.

Abby clung to him now as he pounded her body with long, hard strokes that had yet another orgasm building. She let the pleasure take her, welcoming the bliss while his hard body filled her again and again, deeper, harder.

He shifted slightly, causing him to rub against her clit. And just like that, another climax roared through her.

In a daze of ecstasy, she watched Clayton. She caught a glimpse of his pleasure, so pure and unadulterated as it crossed his face that it made her breath catch.

She couldn't look away as he gave one final thrust, his back arching as he came. The sight was glorious. His face pinched, his muscles straining, and a sheen of sweat covering his body.

When his head dropped forward, she pushed his hair back and looked into his eyes. With his breath still coming in gasps, he leaned down and put his lips against hers for a moment.

She liked his weight atop her, so she wrapped her arms around him, holding him close. They remained that way until their breathing evened out. Then he pulled out of her and removed the condom before rolling onto his back. He reached for her, and she eagerly moved against him.

"Damn," he said, a smile in his voice. "That was amazing."

She grinned. "Yeah. It was."

He played with the ends of her hair as they grew quiet. Abby closed her eyes, content to lay upon him, listening to his heart and the birds.

"I want you."

She chuckled without opening her eyes. "Again?"

"Always," he replied in a solemn voice.

Her eyes snapped open when she heard his reply. Then she rose up on her elbow to see him. "What?"

"I've been around the world more times than I can count. I've met a lot of people, but no one has caught my attention like you."

She wanted so badly to believe him, and a part of her did. But she wasn't ready to talk about such things. Perhaps she never would be.

All these years she'd been alone, she'd claimed it was because of her brothers, but Justine had made her see the truth. Abby hadn't let anyone close because of her fear of abandonment. And it reared up now.

As if sensing that she was thinking of returning to the house, Clayton pulled her back down on top of his chest. "I wanted you to know how I felt. There's no need to reply. Just enjoy the afternoon and this fine weather we've been given."

That she could do. It was thinking of the future that gave her hives. No. It was thinking of a future with Clayton. She could see the years stretching before her where she was alone. She always had. Ever since her mother left.

Clayton never stopped touching her. He caressed her back and arm in slow movements that lulled her and eventually allowed her muscles to relax. But his words replayed in her head.

How wonderful it would be if she and Clayton could be together.

But how long would it take him to see all of her flaws? When would the things she did become annoying? Or her brothers? How long could they go without getting into trouble as they always did? The Easts had been forgiving, but everyone had their limits.

It was no great feat to think of all the ways she could drive Clayton away. And she hated herself for it, almost as much as she hated her mother for making her and her brothers so scared of the possibility of everyone leaving them.

# Chapter 19

The day would forever be imprinted in Clayton's memory. He'd had to tell Abby how he felt, but once he saw her begin to retreat, he'd ceased the conversation. She wasn't ready to hear what he had to say.

After another hour in the sun locked in each other's arms, they rose and dressed. He took her down to the water to walk along the edge.

"I can't imagine having all this land as a playground," she said and tossed a rock into the water.

He looked around, thinking back to his younger days. "We did have grand adventures."

"Let me guess, you always won?" she asked cheekily.

He grinned. "Always."

"I'm not buying it." Abby bent and scooped water into her hand before throwing it at him.

Clayton didn't dodge it. Instead, he rushed her, grabbed her from behind when she tried to run, and lifted her against him as he turned. Her laughter rang out, echoing around them. He loved the sound of it. In fact, he basked in it.

He set her on her feet, but he didn't release her, and the way she leaned her head back on his shoulder, she seemed content to be in his arms.

"You're sad here," she said after a moment.

He began to argue until he realized she was right. "It reminds me of Landon. We were here all the time. Sometimes with my parents, sometimes alone."

"That was so dangerous."

"Yes. Very. My parents never knew."

"Is that . . . is this where he died?"

"No." Clayton kissed the side of her head and took her hand as he walked her back up to the top. He whistled to the horses and folded the blanket.

"I'm sorry," she said. "I shouldn't have asked."

He glanced at her and shook his head. "It's okay. It's just not something I've talked about in a very long time."

They didn't speak again as he helped her mount and got onto his own horse. He motioned for her to follow him as he led her through pastures and around herds of cattle. She didn't ask any questions, simply took it all in.

Finally, they reached the spot. Clayton dismounted and walked to the corral. He rested his hands along the wooden fence that showed no signs of the destruction. His mind was instantly transported back to that horrible day.

"Landon always tried new things," Clayton began. "He'd watch someone do something a few times, and then have the ability to mimic it nearly to perfection. It was his gift. That and he was the most likeable per I knew."

Abby came to stand beside him, folding her hands before her on the fence. She turned her head to him and rested her cheek on her hands.

He glanced at her, but his gaze was pulled back to the corral. "It was two weeks after Landon's thirteenth birthday. He'd been begging dad to let him learn to bull ride. We were both able to rope soon after we were in the saddle. And we learned to ride horses before we could even walk.

"Dad said there was a need to learn to rope, that the skill would come in handy on the ranch. He was right. However, he had a disdain for bull riding. He said it was pointless, and too many men died trying to show off. There were few things my father had such an opinion about, so Landon and I knew he wasn't going to change his mind. I thought the matter was closed. For about a week, Landon didn't mention it.

"Then a new bull my father bought arrived. He was enormous. This massive, black beast was in a new place and not at all happy about it. So Dad moved him out here to adjust to things for a few days. The animal terrified me with his snorting and stamping, but, as usual, Dad was right. The bull stopped kicking and head-butting everything after a day or so. He even allowed us to pet him.

"That's where everything changed for Landon. That night, he came into my room to get me. We often snuck out to play in the hayloft or go to the bunkhouse with the men. That's what I thought we were doing that night, but he brought me here."

Clayton had to stop as his throat tightened with emotion. Abby put her hand on his arm. Her touch gave him the strength to continue down the road of memories that had turned the tide of his life in the most vicious way.

He licked his lips and said, "I knew as soon as we arrived what Landon planned. I tried to talk him out of it. I suggested all kinds of other things for us to do, but he wouldn't listen. I knew something bad was going to happen. I should've immediately gone back and gotten Dad or Shane or someone, but I didn't. I couldn't leave. So, I watched in horror as Landon climbed through the fence and walked to the bull."

Abby's fingers tightened on his arm.

Clayton was grateful for her touch. "Can you believe the bull didn't so much as twitch? It was like he didn't care. Even when Landon petted him, the animal didn't move. I honestly thought the night might end all right. Landon was usually so level-headed. He always made the right decisions. But that night, he wouldn't listen to reason. I begged and pleaded with him to return to the house. He looped a rope around the bull's neck then walked to the fence and climbed up before scooting over to the animal's back. Then he climbed on."

He closed his eyes, recalling how his stomach had fallen to his feet when his brother had jumped onto the bull's back. Clayton had been torn on whether to stay with him or run to get someone, because he'd known—an instinct he'd recognized even at a young age—that something horrible was about to happen.

"For a few seconds, the bull did nothing," Clayton said and opened his eyes. "I was screaming at Landon, but we were so far from even the bunkhouse that no one could hear me. I can still see my brother's face, the moonlight shining on him like a spotlight. He was grinning like he always did. He told me everything was going to be all right. Then he kicked the bull. My heart leapt from my chest, but amazingly enough, the bull still did nothing.

"The night would've ended right there, but one of us had made a mistake, one that we'd been taught never to do. When we'd gone through the pastures, we didn't close one of the gates all the way. I don't know if it was Landon or I who did it, but some cows got through. The bull smelled them, and he wanted to get to them. He went nuts, running and bucking. He slammed up against the fence where I stood. The sound of the wood cracking was as loud as a shot.

"Landon began screaming as he desperately tried to hold on. I kept yelling at him to jump off. He was barely hanging on as it was. If the bull got out, Landon could get trampled. Our eyes met. We both knew then if he was going to make it, he had to get off. He tried to jump onto the fence. He was so damn close. He should've made it, but he fell short by a few inches. The bull was already leaning toward the fence, so Landon got caught between it and the animal. A half a foot and the fence was all that stood between my brother and me.

"Landon called my name." Clayton squeezed his eyes shut for a moment. "The terror in his voice was horrific. My blood felt like it was made of ice. I was sweating and scared to death, and everything seemed to move in slow motion. Yet, I couldn't move. I tried to reach for him, but he crumpled to the ground, moaning in pain. The bull didn't even know Landon was there as he ran over him again and again, trying to get out of the corral. All I could do was stand there and watch helplessly until finally the fence broke and the bull ran to the cattle. I rushed into the corral and gathered Landon in my arms."

Clayton dropped his chin to his chest, his stomach heaving at the mental image of his brother. His throat tightened painfully as he fought back tears. "You couldn't even recognize his face. He was broken and bloody. I tried to lift him and carry him back to the house, but I was too weak. So I sat in there and held him until Shane finally found us."

Abby turned him so that he faced her. There were tears rolling down her cheeks as she pulled him against her. Clayton buried his head in her neck and simply held onto her as if she were a lifeline.

And in her arms, some of the pain he'd carried from that night melted away. It didn't matter whether it was from sharing the story or Abby herself, but he felt freer.

"You know it's not your fault, right?" she said, sniffing.

"I should've gotten someone."

"Then you might not have been there when he died."

Clayton leaned back to look at her. "I heard Shane tell my parents that the bull ran right past me. He said it was a miracle I hadn't been trampled, as well."

"All these years, you've carried guilt. I can see it in your eyes."

He glanced away, toward the corral. "Yes."

"It's time to let that go. You were kids, and your brother wasn't going to listen to you. You did all that you could."

He turned from the corral and wrapped an arm around her shoulders. She put her arm around his waist and leaned her head against him as they walked to the horses.

"Thank you for sharing that with me," she said.

He wasn't quite ready to let her go, so he held onto her. "I've not had reason to talk about it in a long time. As long as I can remember, I always knew the ranch was going to be Landon's. My parents said that we could work it together, 50/50, but then I overheard my parents talking one day about what would happen if we fought over something. It had happened to my dad and his sister. She sold him her share after a long, drawn-out fight because she wanted to sell the ranch, and he didn't. I didn't want that, so I told myself then that the ranch was Landon's."

"And then it became yours, which compounded your guilt," Abby said softly. "I know all about carrying guilt."

Curious, he looked down at the top of her, but she gazed off into the distance. "How?"

"The night Mom left, I told her to go."

He was so shocked that he was at a loss for words for a minute. "You can't honestly believe it's your fault your mother left."

"I told her to go." Abby repeated, then dropped her arm and walked to Diamond.

He watched her, recognizing that petting the horse calmed her. "Do you want to talk about it?"

She shrugged half-heartedly. "There isn't much to say. Mom was griping about how I should take more responsibility and look after my brothers so she could have some fun since she'd birthed us and raised me. I was pissed because I was supposed to go on a date that night.

It was two nights after graduation, and she'd been on my ass for months, telling me to get a good-paying job and help her with money.

"I was so tired of hearing the same load of crap that I told her I wasn't going to help. I said that I was now an adult and I planned to get my own place. I said that she was the one who'd had the kids, and it was her responsibility." Abby swallowed hard. "It was all a lie. I wouldn't have left my brothers with her, but I was angry, so I lashed out. I told her she was the mother, not me."

Abby's face crumpled then as she turned her head to him, her blue eyes so full of pain that he ached for her. He wasn't sure whether to go to her or not. She looked on the verge of breaking down, but she had given him comfort during his story.

His decision made, Clayton walked to her. Near enough to touch if she needed it.

"I went out that night," she continued. "I partied with my friends until three the next morning. It felt good to forget the recurring fight and all the troubles with Mom. When I got home, I went straight to bed without checking on my brothers. It was Caleb who got me up the next morning because he was hungry. I told him to go get Mom, and he told me she wasn't there.

"I was instantly awake then. I went to her room, and the drawers were half opened, allowing me to see that they had been emptied. I ran into the kitchen and found the note on the table with the papers she'd already signed giving me guardianship of Brice and Caleb."

A tear rolled down Abby's cheek. "Brice had found the papers first. He was in a corner in the kitchen with his knees drawn up to his chest, rocking back and forth as he silently cried."

Clayton pulled her against him. He could see the picture she painted clearly. A young girl with too many responsibilities given even more, who set aside her own anguish to deal with her brothers' grief.

"Your argument didn't send your mother away," he told her. "The fact that she already had those papers drawn up says that she'd been planning it for a while."

Like right after Abby had graduated high school.

Abby looked up at him with spiked lashes from her tears. "But if I hadn't yelled at her, she might not have left that night."

"Darlin', if it hadn't been that night, it would've been another."

She buried her head against his chest and cried harder. He rested his chin atop her head, feeling her body shaking from her sobs. This wasn't how he planned the day to go, but if this was what Abby needed to heal her soul, then he would hold her for however long it took. Because it was time she finally let her grief out.

# Chapter 20

So this was what happiness felt like. Even with her breakdown of tears and the shared stories, the day was the most amazing she'd ever had. He'd held her gently, soothing her until she'd finally stopped crying.

Abby looked over at Clayton as they walked the horses through pastures. She listened intently as he told her stories about the annual branding or the rounding up of cattle to sell. It was obvious he was trying to lighten her mood, and it was working.

The East cattle were some of the most sought after around. They were known for their hale and hearty stock with bloodlines—apparently, that was very important—that traced back to renowned bulls.

If she'd been impressed before, she was awed now. Knowing the ranch was steeped in history and seeing it firsthand were two completely different things.

Out on the land, looking over vast landscapes of rolling hills with enormous herds of cattle, it was easy to imagine how life might have been two hundred years earlier. To be tied to such a place boggled her mind and made her crave it all at the same time.

While Clayton told her tales of growing up on the ranch, she shared stories of funny times with her brothers. It was easy to talk to him and share things. After exchanging such accounts of heartbreak, they were able to laugh now as if the weight of the past had been removed from them both.

When they traveled to a separated pasture where about thirty horses ran free, she couldn't take her eyes off the beautiful creatures. But the big orange ball slowly lowering in the sky drew her gaze away. She wished she had the power to stop time.

"What is it?" Clayton asked.

She didn't wonder how he knew something was wrong. You couldn't share your deepest hurts with someone and not have them know you. And, somehow, that made her feel good.

"I'm not ready for the day to end," she confessed. It never entered her mind to lie or not speak from her heart.

There was a bond between them now that was as strong as the one they'd developed by sharing their bodies. Because revealing the things that hurt someone the most, created a connection just as strong.

"Neither am I."

Their eyes met. It would be so easy to fall for him. Hell, she was already halfway there. If only she could stop thinking about all the ways he could leave her.

She was the first to look away. She recalled his words after they'd made love.

*Abby, I want you. Always.*

More than anything, she wanted to believe him. Not that she thought he was lying, but people changed their minds. She was sure he did feel something for her. Now. But what about next week or next month? Hell, next year?

Her own mother hadn't even stayed. And wasn't a parent's love supposed to be unconditional? So what was it about her that made even her mother stop loving her?

"You're letting the past in again," Clayton said in a soft voice.

"I know."

Diamond shifted beneath Abby and gave a loud whinny to the other horses. As one, the horses in the pasture turned their heads to them and let out whinnies of their own. And just like that, the past evaporated like smoke.

Abby stroked the mare's neck. "I think I'm in love with her."

"I can see that," Clayton replied with a chuckle. "I do believe she feels the same."

They continued riding. Abby asked about the cattle shoots she saw and learned all she could about ranching. Not that she needed to know any of it in order to take care of the books, but she wanted the knowledge.

Dusk soon settled over them, signaling the day was finished. Or so she thought.

"Want to check in on your brothers?"

Her head snapped to Clayton. "Yes. But, I don't want them to see me."

"Not a problem," he said with a wink.

They veered their horses back toward the house,

riding in silence as they approached the bunkhouse. She pulled back on the reins to halt Diamond when Clayton stopped his horse. It wasn't until she began to dismount that she felt the pull in her leg muscles.

"I got you," Clayton whispered as he came up behind her, a strong arm wrapping around her while he lowered her to the ground.

She winced as she tried to stand. Her legs were Jell-O, muscles she hadn't known she had were tightening and throbbing with pain. "Goodness."

"I should've warned you that you'd be sore."

Sore? She wasn't sore. She could barely move. Yet she smiled because it felt wonderful to be riding. Despite the pain, she wanted back on Diamond.

"It'll pass soon. Promise," he said.

"I didn't think I was riding for very long."

His lips grazed her cheek as he released her. "Just wait until tomorrow."

"You're enjoying this," she said with a smile.

He shot her a wink. "Maybe a little. Come."

His hand enveloped hers as he led her around and then behind the bunkhouse. A fire roared within a circle created by logs of various sizes. There were several men, including Shane, who sat with her brothers around the flames.

One of the men was telling a story that had her brothers listening with rapt attention. To see them like this made her heart full. They were utterly entranced, completely happy. The years of hardship and worry had seemingly melted away, leaving their faces looking youthful and vibrant again.

Whatever they had done that day had exhausted them.

Caleb rubbed his eyes while Brice kept yawning, but neither of them appeared ready to call it a day.

"They'll fall asleep in the middle of dinner," Clayton whispered.

Abby almost wished she could see it. "Do you think they'll sleep through the night?"

She could feel rather than see Clayton's frown. "There's nothing for them to fear out here. Shane and the men will guard them."

"You misunderstand," she said, turning her head to him. There was just enough light from the fire for her to see his face. "Neither of them has slept an entire night since Mom left. They check on each other and me to make sure everyone is still in the house. It's why my brothers don't have friends over or go to friends' houses."

In response, Clayton took her hand and squeezed it. "Should we bring them to the house?"

"They made it through last night. It should be fine."

"Why didn't you say something yesterday?"

She shrugged, shaking her head. "I didn't want to remind them. Besides, they had each other. I don't think they worried last night."

"I wasn't going to tell you, but I saw Shane this morning. The boys refused to go any further than the barn until they saw you this morning. Only then did they set out."

The news wasn't surprising, but it still made her hurt for her brothers. "They're making progress though. They didn't come in the house and look in my room for me."

"I think they know in their hearts that you're not going to leave them."

Nothing but death could take her away from Brice and Caleb. She told them that all the time, hoping to soothe their fears. Maybe one day they would accept her words. She watched her brothers for a few more minutes before she motioned to Clayton that they could leave. When he said they were walking their horses to the barn, she shot him a grateful smile.

"How about you?" Clayton asked. "Do you sleep the night through?"

She shook her head and tucked her hair behind an ear. "I'm so used to waking up for my brothers that it's now a habit."

"You wanted to check on them last night, didn't you?"

She grinned at him. "I did, but I didn't leave the house."

"A good thing since the alarm would've gone off."

"That would've been horrible."

They shared a laugh. And when his hand sought hers again, she was glad to interlace her fingers with his. It wasn't until they reached the barn that he released her.

She followed him, leading Diamond to her stall. But when Clayton began to unsaddle her, she stopped him. "I want to learn."

His eyes crinkled in the corners as he gave a nod. With his instructions, she removed the saddle, saddle blanket, and the bridle. She refused to allow him to carry the saddle back to the tack room, wanting to do it herself. But halfway there, she was regretting her choice as the saddle was heavier than she'd expected—and her legs were killing her.

Still, she got the saddle and the blanket on its rack while Clayton hung up the bridle. Then he showed her where the feed was. She stood, wide-eyed, at all the different feed laid out before her.

Since each horse had different dietary needs, each one got different allocations. She scooped the designated amount into the bucket and carried it to Diamond, who waited with her head over the stall door.

Except Clayton told Abby to wait for the feed. Instead, he led her to the hay where she got an armful and put it in the feed trough. After, Clayton handed her a brush.

"Tell me what to do," she urged him.

He closed the stall, locking her in with Diamond, while he rested his arms on the door. "You groom a horse before and after a ride. Before ensures the horse is clean. After is to remove any dirt or sweat and to check for injuries. Since we didn't do any hard riding and the horses didn't sweat, there isn't a need to hose them off."

She nodded, listening even as she lightly ran the brush along Diamond's neck while the horse munched on the hay. "Got it."

"Now, as you brush her, look for any rubbing or chafing where the saddle, girth, and bridle were. Also, run your hands down Diamond's legs to feel for any cuts or bumps."

Abby followed his instructions, learning more about horses in a few minutes than she thought possible. Riding one was vastly different than taking care of one. By touching the mare, Abby further discovered the animal and strengthened the bond they had already formed.

"Walk to Diamond's back leg. Keep your back to her head and lean against her."

Abby frowned at him, wondering what he was getting her to do now, but she didn't question Clayton. Mostly because she wanted to know everything about horses.

"Lean harder," he advised. "When you feel her shift her weight off that back leg, then you'll know you've pushed enough."

It took a couple of tries, but finally Diamond shifted.

"Great," Clayton said. "Now lift her foot to check her hoof."

She only hesitated a moment before she reached down and lifted the back leg. With Clayton looking over her shoulder, he told her what to look for. After she finished with that foot, she did the other three. And when she looked up, Clayton was gone. She paused and heard him murmuring to his mount.

Abby remained with Diamond, softly brushing the animal with long, sure strokes. When she looked over and saw the horse standing there with her eyes closed, Abby felt a kind of joy that she'd never experienced before.

"It's pretty amazing, isn't it?" Clayton whispered from the stall door.

Abby ducked beneath Diamond's neck and walked to him. "It is. Thank you for this. Words can never fully express what you've given my brothers or me today."

He grinned and opened the stall door to hand her the feed. Abby dumped the grain into the trough and reluctantly walked from the stall. Together, she and Clayton made their way to the house.

As soon as they entered, the smell of food hit Abby,

and her stomach let out a loud rumble. Yet it was nothing compared to Justine and Ben greeting them.

Abby felt a part of something with Clayton and his family. And that was a very dangerous thing.

# Chapter 21

The explosion of an RPG not twenty feet from Clayton shook the ground near his feet. Debris rained down upon him, clunking loudly against his helmet.

He raised his M4 rifle and fired off three quick shots, striking two targets right in their hearts. His ears were ringing, but he could still hear the shouts of his team.

A glance to his right showed Conaway kneeling over Cook while Ramirez and Sanders covered him while he attempted to staunch the flow of blood on Cook's side.

Clayton quickly moved to help them, and along with Price, they formed a circle around Conaway and Cook. In between firing, Clayton looked down at Cook, who began to cough up blood. He clutched at Conaway's arm, his eyes wide.

Sanders was struck in the leg by a bullet. He let out a string of curses and dropped down to his stomach and kept firing.

"They're surrounding us!" Ramirez shouted over the gunfire.

This wasn't the first time Clayton had been overrun by the enemy, and he doubted it'd be the last.

His left shoulder jerked when a bullet tore through it. "Fuck!" he bellowed.

Not because of the pain, but because one of the assholes had gotten a shot off.

Clayton changed out the magazine in his rifle and sprayed bullets in the direction where the shooter was. He saw a man fly backward after being hit.

Behind him, Conaway was calling to command that they had a man down in critical condition. Air support was thirty minutes out. Clayton knew Cook wouldn't last that long. Conaway was administering medical, but Cook needed a doctor if he were going to live.

They had lost so many members of their team in the last year, and Clayton was tired of seeing his friends die while the terrorist numbers continued to grow. It felt like a never-ending battle.

The spray of bullets was interrupted by a grenade that landed five feet from him. The bang deafened him and threw him violently into the air.

Clayton's eyes snapped open as he clutched the sheets. It took a minute before he realized he was safe in his bed at home and not in the middle of battle.

He untangled his legs from the sheets and swung them over the side of the bed before he sat up, covered in sweat. If he didn't see the men he killed in his nightmares, he relived battles.

Every. Fucking. Night.

He rubbed his left shoulder, feeling the pain of the bullet ripping through his muscle and into bone as if it had just happened instead of two years ago.

After squeezing his eyes closed, Clayton looked at the clock. It was two in the morning. Three hours of rest. That's all he'd get this night. He knew better than to try to sleep again. He'd just lay awake, tossing and turning as images of the nightmare replayed in his mind.

He pushed off the bed and stood before making his way into the en suite bathroom and turned on the shower to cold. Clayton stood beneath the icy water until his body finally began to cool down. Only then did he wash the sweat from himself and get out.

After toweling off, he yanked on a pair of jeans but left them unbuttoned. Then he walked from his room. He couldn't stay in there. A stroll through the house, checking doors and windows was his only option.

But he got no farther than Abby's room. He stood outside her door, staring at the knob. It had been hell to sit across from her at dinner and not reach for her hand.

Worse was when they sat outside with his parents drinking coffee around the fire pit as a new cold front moved in. He'd been beside her, all too aware of her scent, her smile, her laughter.

He'd wanted to pull her onto his lap and nuzzle her neck. To yank her up against him and kiss her with all the raging desire within him.

Instead, he somehow managed to keep his hands to himself—even when she had walked sleepily up the stairs after saying goodnight. Not giving in to the rampant yearning for Abby that consumed him had been the hardest thing he'd ever done.

Now that he stood outside her room, he was engaged in that same struggle. And losing.

Epically.

What kind of creep would he be to walk into her room and watch her sleep?

He closed his eyes and saw the battle in his nightmare, felt the heat and sweat of that horrible place—smelled the blood, death, and gunpowder. Clayton put his palm on the door. He needed something, anything to pull his mind from the nightmare.

With his forehead against the door, he tried to talk himself into turning away. Instead, his hand found the doorknob and silently turned.

Unable to help himself, Clayton opened his eyes as the door soundlessly cracked open. The first thing he noticed was that the curtains had been pushed wide open, and the pale blue light of the moon flooded the room.

His gaze went to the bed—only to find it empty.

In the next heartbeat, he found Abby standing against the wall, staring somberly out the window. She wore a short, black satin robe that hung open, and beneath it was a bright pink nightshirt that brushed the tops of her thighs and read, *Single All The Way*.

One leg was bent, her foot braced against the wall with her arms hanging by her sides. He wanted to know what she was thinking and even what she saw when she looked out the window.

Was she reflecting on their day together? How they'd made love under the sun, their bodies finding passion

and pleasure? Because, suddenly, that was the only thing
that was on his mind.

And the longing to claim her again.

He opened the door wider and stepped into the room.
Her head turned to him, their eyes meeting. She held
out her hand to him. It was all the invitation Clayton
needed.

Closing the door softly behind him, he walked to her,
taking her hand. He stood before her, basking in her
beauty. He ached to have her in his arms and feel the
comfort and calm that she gave him.

She put her hand against his cheek. With that one action, she told him that she saw his pain and was there
for him. He was so used to hiding his grief and agony
that it was second nature. But not around Abby.

She'd obliterated those walls without even knowing
it. Hell, *he* hadn't even realized it until it was too late.
Now, he ached for her.

He wished he had the words to describe how lovely
she looked with the moon tinting her skin blue. If only
he had a poet's tongue to let her know how her soul
called to his—and that he willingly answered.

But if he didn't have the words, he could show her.

He moved closer until their bodies were nearly touching while his cock began to harden. With a palm on the
wall near her head, he used his other hand to trail his
fingers over her cheek and down her neck.

The pulse at the base of her throat beat wildly as her
lips parted. Without a doubt, he knew she felt the same
untamed need that consumed him, that same primal
craving that only someone who matched you in every
way could feel.

He continued moving his finger to her shoulder and the edge of her robe. He followed that edge over her breast, right across her nipple. She let out a long breath, her eyes briefly closing.

His fingertip continued downward, over her stomach and her hip to her thigh. When he reached the hem of the robe, he focused on her gown. Sliding his hand beneath the nightshirt, he skimmed his palm up her thigh to her hip.

Her chest was heaving now, desire burning in her eyes. Then he cupped her sex. The moment he found her without panties and wet, his rod grew so hard that it was painful.

While he pushed two fingers inside her, she spread her hands on his chest and moaned. He couldn't stop his hips from rocking as his fingers thrummed her.

Then she unzipped his jeans, dipped her hands into his jeans and wrapped her fingers around him. He hissed in a breath, the contact sublime when she began to slide her hand up and down his length.

He leaned forward to brush his lips against hers before claiming her mouth as they each fondled the other. It was sexy as hell.

But it wasn't enough. He needed to be inside her, to have their bodies connected. He shoved down his jeans before he lifted her, holding her over his cock.

With her hands in his hair and her legs around his waist, their gazes locked and held as he lowered her. Her eyes bulged when the head of his arousal found her entrance and pushed inside her.

"Clayton," she murmured when he thrust once, pushing deep inside her.

He wound his hand in the long length of her hair and brought her head to him for another kiss that was frantic with need as desire burned like an inferno within him.

She shimmied out of her robe. He kicked off his jeans. Then he turned and made his way to the bed. The only movement of his cock within her was when he walked.

The soft cry she gave as she tore her lips from his made his already heated blood burn. She quickly yanked off the nightshirt, baring her gorgeous body to him.

He bent his head and licked a turgid nipple. She rocked her hips as her body tightened around him.

Clayton hissed in a breath because that movement had nearly sent him over the edge. This brave, beautiful woman had somehow stolen his heart while breaking the chains of the past that had held him.

He turned and sat on the bed. She leaned over him until he had no choice but to fall back. He gazed up at her as her mane of dark hair flowed to either side of his face.

With her hands braced on his chest, she began to rotate her hips slowly, moving faster and faster. Even as his body grew taut with the orgasm that begged to be released, he watched as her eyes fell shut.

She sat up straight and let her head fall back. The ends of her hair tickled his balls, and her breasts swayed with her movements. Her hips rocked back and forth as her cries filled the room.

He gripped her hips, urging her faster. Her nails dug into his chest right before her body stiffened. Clayton dug his fingers into her hips as he fought not to come while her body pulsed around his cock.

When it became too much, he pulled out of her and

shifted them so she was on her hands and knees before him. He plunged into her again, grinding deep.

Each time he saw her climax, it satisfied something deeply male within him. A part of him that no one had ever touched before— or ever would again.

She turned her head and looked at him over her shoulder. Her lips were swollen from their kisses, her eyes darkened with desire.

This amazing woman was meant to be his. He knew it with a certainty he couldn't shake. He didn't know how, but he had to make her his, to ensure their hearts and souls were bound forever.

No matter how long it took, no matter what he had to do, he would win her.

Clayton withdrew until only the head of him remained. Then he plunged deep. She moaned loudly as he began thrusting. She moved back against him, meeting each of his movements and taking him deeper—all the while clamping down on his cock.

Each time he drove into her, she wore away his control until he could no longer hold back his orgasm. That's when he realized he wasn't wearing a condom. They'd both been so wrapped up in desire that it had never occurred to either of them.

Clayton pulled out of her and came on her back. Afterward, he stared down at the evidence of their lovemaking and couldn't believe how close they'd come to making a mistake.

Without a word, he rose and walked to the connected bathroom to wet a towel before he returned and cleaned her.

When he turned to put the towel away, she grabbed

his hand. He met her gaze as she pulled him toward her and lifted the covers with her other hand. The towel dropped from his fingers as he crawled in beside her.

With their bodies sated, and her snuggled against him, Clayton found his eyes growing heavy.

# Chapter 22

Happiness had always been something Abby recognized in her daily life. She and her brothers were healthy, they had a roof over their heads, and money to get by. Things were tough, yes, but they had each other.

She focused on the good things and made sure her brothers laughed every day. When you looked for happiness and appreciated the things you had, it was hard to think you had a bad life.

But it wasn't until Clayton had barreled into her life that she really understood the word happiness.

He'd flipped a switch that made her feel as if there were a light on inside her that radiated outward. Then again, waking up in his arms was a heady feeling. As she opened her eyes and looked around the room, everything seemed brighter, and she felt more alive.

Last night, she'd been unable to sleep as her thoughts were filled with Clayton, their lovemaking, and his job offer. As if her very mind had conjured him, she'd found him in her doorway.

And what a sight he'd been, standing there shirtless with his ripped chest on display. She'd never seen a man look so sexy with nothing on but a pair of unbuttoned jeans hanging on his trim hips.

Slowly, she shifted her head on his chest so she could see him. His face was relaxed and turned toward her, his arm holding her tightly—even in sleep. His dark blond locks were disheveled, giving him a boyish look that she found endearing.

Last night, she'd seen so much anguish in his eyes that it had broken her heart. She hadn't asked what it was because there had been no words between them. But she didn't think it was his brother.

There was a shuttered look that came over Clayton whenever he thought about Landon. The previous night had been different. He couldn't hide the pain, almost as if he wore it like armor.

And then she realized it must have to do with his time in the military. He'd said the things he'd witnessed and done changed him. It had shaped him into the man he was today—but it had also left him scarred physically, mentally, and emotionally.

She placed a kiss on his shoulder and gradually moved from the confines of his embrace. Though she was loath to leave him, she wanted to start breakfast for everyone.

Abby dressed and brushed out her hair before she quietly slipped out of the bedroom. It was just before six, and already she saw people moving about outside. While she looked up a recipe online for homemade biscuits that she'd made before, she caught a glimpse of her brothers walking into the barn. She watched them smile at each other as they hurried after Shane.

Forcing her attention back to breakfast, Abby looked through the kitchen cabinets and pantry to find everything she needed. Then she made coffee.

The biscuits were already in the oven, and she was frying bacon and sausage when Justine and Ben came in.

"I knew I smelled something delicious," Ben said with a smile.

Justine finished tying off her braid. "Sweetheart, you didn't need to do this."

"I wanted to. Sit down and enjoy your coffee while someone else cooks for you this morning," Abby said.

Ben's brows rose as he chuckled. "A woman giving orders. She'll fit right in," he said to Justine.

"Have you seen Clayton?" his mother asked.

Abby kept her gaze on the pan. "I was the first one down."

It wasn't a lie, and she didn't have to tell them she knew Clayton was still sleeping. Abby wasn't trying to keep his parents from knowing that they were having sex. She just wasn't quite ready to share that information. With anyone.

Ben grunted. "That's strange."

"Leave him," Justine chided as she poured their coffee.

She was finishing up the eggs when her skin suddenly heated. Lifting her gaze, her eyes clashed with pale green orbs. Her heart missed a beat as she looked at Clayton. For a long minute, he stared at her before a slow smile pulled at his lips. He then walked to her, leaning close. His hand rested on her hip, giving her a light squeeze. The entire time, they never looked away from each other.

"I wanted to wake with you in my arms," he whispered.

Her stomach did a little flutter at his husky words. And she didn't even care that his parents were watching them. "You were sleeping so soundly that I didn't want to disturb you."

"Next time, don't leave the bed," he said with a wink.

*Next time.* He was so sure there was going to be another time. With those two words, something eased within her. Because despite telling herself that it was temporary and that she needed to prepare herself for it to end, she wasn't ready to let go.

It wasn't as if their relationship had been defined yet. Hell, it might never be. This might be all she ever got.

Clayton helped her carry the dishes to the table before he called in his parents to the dining room. Since it was just the four of them, they sat across from each other. While everyone put the food on their plates, Abby suddenly discovered that she wasn't hungry.

Justine's food was delicious. Now, Abby worried that her meal wouldn't be up to snuff. What if she'd overcooked the bacon? Or worse, what if they liked it super crispy and it wasn't done right.

Then there were the eggs. She'd scrambled them. What if they hated those types of eggs? She should've asked. What had she been thinking to want to cook breakfast?

"This is so good," Justine said as she swallowed a bite of eggs.

Ben nodded, grunting in agreement as he shoveled another forkful of sausage and egg into his mouth.

"It's better than good," Clayton said as he spooned more eggs onto his plate before reaching for the bacon. "It's amazing."

Justine held up the biscuit. "I need this recipe."

"Sure," Abby said with a grin.

Their praise allowed the nervous band around her stomach to loosen enough that she was able to eat. After another few minutes, she'd forgotten all about her anxiety as easy conversation filled the room.

When breakfast was finished, she looked forward to what Clayton had in store for them that day. But her excitement was dashed when he and Ben were called out to one of the pastures for something.

Abby tried to help Justine with the dishes, but the matriarch shooed her out to go and "relax."

She didn't know how to relax. Especially not at the ranch. They'd told her to make herself at home, but she wasn't sure they'd really meant it. She was a guest, and that meant she wouldn't go walking about as if she owned the place.

Abby made her way to the office and sat down behind the desk. Now, this was something she knew and understood. Numbers on the page were as familiar to her as cattle and horses were to Clayton.

The numbers were her friends. They told a story, if a person knew how to look. And Abby loved to unravel such tales.

She was following a line item back through months and years when she found a stack of invoices that had never been filed away. Attached to a sheet was a picture of some cattle, all showing the large E branded on their hindquarters.

Abby frowned. There was something about that E that troubled her. It was right on the edge of her mind, but she couldn't recall what it could be or why it would make her apprehensive. She set it aside and moved on, sinking deeply into her work.

But the brand kept bothering her. She kept the invoice within view, hoping it would trigger whatever was just out of reach.

"I think I should put a lock on the door and throw away the key. It's the only way I'll keep you out of here."

She smiled at the sound of Clayton's voice and looked over the computer screen at him. He held his hat in his hands as he grinned at her. "Your mom told me to relax."

"And you couldn't find anything better to do?"

She shrugged, wrinkling her nose. "I didn't want to bother you, so I thought I'd get some work done."

"Well, you're finished for the day," he said and put his hat back on and held out his hand. "Come on."

Abby didn't need to be told twice. She pushed the chair back and rose to go to him. They left the house and walked to where Ben was with her brothers. They stood in front of a few square bales of hay with fake cow horns tied to the front.

"They're learning to lasso," Clayton told her.

"Ah." She wanted to continue watching them, but Clayton kept walking so she followed to see where he'd take her.

They stopped at a fence and looked over a pasture

where Shane and two other men she recognized as ranch workers were on horseback rounding up cattle.

"What are they doing?" she asked.

"Loading them up to sale."

Her gaze turned at the sound of an engine to see a semi pulling to a stop. "Sale?"

"You do know that beef sold in the grocery stores comes from cattle, right?" he teased.

She nodded woodenly. "Yeah. I just . . . well, I didn't think about that."

"We're the largest supplier in the area."

That meant some of the beef she'd bought, cooked, and eaten had most likely come from the East Ranch.

"You're not going to turn into a vegetarian, are you?"

She laughed and shot him a look. "No. I love meat too much."

"Once the calves are born in January, we'll start branding in March. It's a big affair that goes on for a month or two depending on how many calves we have in the different herds."

Branding. Her gaze locked on the E on the hind end of a cow in the pasture. "You mentioned selling cattle to others."

"It's not our biggest market, but we do. People pay a pretty penny for our stock."

"What is done about your brand on the cattle?"

Clayton put an arm on the fence. "There's paperwork involved to prove that the new owner has the right to whatever cattle he's bought from us."

"And the brand?"

A small frown formed. "If it's a small rancher, he

may leave the brand. There are some who rebrand the cattle. Why? Some frown upon rebranding because it harkens back to the days of cattle rustling."

Her heart started thumping as she realized what had been bothering her. The brand she'd seen in the paperwork at Gloria's was similar to the Easts'.

"Abby?"

She forced her gaze to him. Her ears were ringing, her palms sweaty.

"What is it?" Clayton asked with a worried frown as he grabbed her arms.

"The brand."

He swiveled his head to the cattle before looking back at her. "What about it?"

"Everyone knows that brand. It's just an E."

Clayton's frown deepened as he shrugged. "You can't use an elaborate brand, or it won't be clear on the hide."

"No, you don't understand." Her hand was shaking as she brought it to her forehead. "It's easy to manipulate."

He stepped closer to her. "What are you trying to say?"

She swallowed hard. "Last week, I was keying in invoices for one of Gloria's clients. He registered a new brand. 4B."

"People register brands all the time," Clayton said.

Abby pointed to the herd. "You've had cattle stolen. How easy would it be to rebrand over the E with a B?"

Clayton's lips thinned as he stared at the cattle. "Very fucking easy." His head jerked back to her. "Who was the individual?"

"I can't remember. We don't pull up names, only the numbers we assign clients."

He yanked off his hat and shoved a hand through his hair in frustration.

"I'll find out who it is," she declared. "It'll be easy."

"And can get you into serious trouble," he said with a shake of his head.

She lifted her chin. "I'm going to do it. If it is your cattle, they were stolen from you. The person or people responsible should go to jail."

Suddenly, there was a shout behind them. Abby turned to find Brice with his hands in the air, celebrating his having lassoed the horned hay.

# Chapter 23

If anyone was going to be put in a position of danger, it should be him. Clayton tried to tell Abby that, but she wouldn't listen.

When they'd sat down with his parents during lunch Sunday afternoon to tell them her theories, it had been his mother, not his father, who had exploded in rage. The four of them spent the remaining hours coming up with a plan, a strategy that didn't include Clayton doing any of the dirty work he was accustomed to.

All too soon, the weekend had come to an end. It had been pure hell to watch Abby drive away with her brothers. And while he'd actually slept deeply within in her arms, Sunday night, he didn't so much as doze.

He watched the sunrise while fighting with himself about whether to go to Abby's or let her go through with the plan. When he'd lost the battle and decided he needed to see her, he'd discovered every key to every vehicle on the ranch was missing.

And he knew who was to blame—his mother.

"She'll be fine," his father said when he found Clayton standing at the back door where the keys were kept on hooks.

"She won't. I need to do this."

"But you can't, son. You wouldn't know the first thing about what to do or what to look for."

And that's what rubbed Clayton raw. He turned away, stalking outside while looking for something to occupy him. The plan was for Abby to text him around lunchtime with the information. That was hours away though.

He was going to go insane waiting and worrying. Because he thought of the worst possible outcomes—and each of them put Abby, Brice, and Caleb in danger.

It was just another day at the office. Of course, no matter how many times Abby told herself that, it was anything but. Every time she looked at the computer screen, she began shaking.

And she hadn't even begun to look for anything yet.

She was so not cut out for any type of snooping. It felt as if everyone in the office were watching her. What had made her think she could do this?

The answer was simple—Clayton.

She'd wanted to do it for him. After everything he'd done for her, she wanted to repay that by giving him the information he and his family needed. If she wasn't wrong.

That was her worst fear. That she'd watched too many TV shows and had connected the two brands, but in fact, they weren't. But the only way to find out was for her to actually find the name and address and let Clayton check it out.

What little sleep she'd gotten had been peppered with dreams of her getting caught by Gloria or being arrested for some unrelated stupidity. That was her brain working overtime, which didn't help the situation at all.

She kept her head down and worked for about an hour. It was all she could manage before she looked at the stack of files on the corner of her desk that she'd worked on Friday. It wasn't uncommon for her to go back through something, but she was so nervous this time that she kept second-guessing every action she took.

Finally, she sorted through the files and found the one she was looking for. She memorized the client number before taking the files to a desk in the back for the part-time college student who came in and filed everything.

Abby returned to her desk and worked for another two hours before she went to key in the customer number. She was about to hit enter when Gloria shouted her name.

Quickly deleting the number, Abby rose and walked to Gloria's office.

"Well?" her boss said with raised eyebrows. "Do you have something to tell me?"

Abby swallowed hard, her mind going blank, forgetting all the great ideas Clayton and his parents had given her to say if she got caught. "What?"

"The East Ranch?" Gloria stated, her voice rising with agitation.

Abby shifted feet as her hands grew clammy and she began to sweat. "What about them?"

"It must have been one hell of a weekend if you can't remember the deal we made on Friday," Gloria said as she leaned back and crossed her legs. She eyed Abby. "You're usually much sharper than this."

Relief surged so quickly through her that she grew light headed. Abby grabbed hold of the back of the chair before her and smiled. "I'm sorry. I didn't get much sleep last night."

"Something going on with you and Clayton? I heard that he was gorgeous." Gloria raised her shoulders to her ears as she smiled. "I've not caught a glimpse of him yet, so tell me every detail."

Abby was glad she didn't have to lie about whatever it was that she and Clayton were. Gloria moved on so quickly that she was now focused on what Clayton looked like.

"He is as handsome as they say," Abby said.

Gloria gave her a look that said she wasn't buying it. "Come on, Abby. You may lock yourself away from the men, but even you must see that Clayton is a catch."

"He's kind," she admitted. "And good-looking."

"Tell me he's got a cute ass in Wranglers," Gloria pleaded. "I've got a weakness for cowboys."

Abby grinned. "It's not cute. His ass is magnificent."

Gloria clapped her hands together and leaned forward. "I knew it! You aren't as dead as you appear. You were checking him out."

"It's hard not to with someone who looks like that," she confessed.

Gloria issued a loud laugh before she sat back with a wide smile. "Tell me you reeled him into the company, Abby. I'm ready to get your raise going starting today."

Abby hated lying. It didn't matter if it was telling her brothers that Santa Claus was real or fibbing that she hadn't eaten the last slice of chocolate cake. That's when she realized she didn't have to lie.

"We did speak about the firm. Clayton asked me several things in regards to you and the business. I do know they're looking to fill the CPA spot," she said.

Gloria picked up a pen and played with it as she looked shrewdly at her computer. "With the money Gilroy stole, the Easts are going to need someone who can manage things better."

"What about looking to see if Gilroy was bonded?"

Gloria waved her words away. "Only companies like mine are bonded. No way the Gilroys did that."

"But shouldn't you look?"

"If he becomes my client, I will."

No, actually, it was something she'd make Abby do. For some reason, that irked Abby greatly. "Maybe look now and show that you're willing to go the extra mile."

"Oh, sweetie," Gloria said with a fake laugh. "Time is money, and I don't waste time on anyone who isn't a client. It's too bad you didn't get the Easts on board this weekend."

In the past, Abby would've walked out, defeated. But now, she didn't push aside the anger that welled within her. She stared at Gloria. "You make it sound as if I won't get the raise."

"You failed to gain me the Easts."

"There was no time limit on our deal," she stated. "You simply said that I had to bring them in."

Gloria narrowed her black eyes, her lips pinching, showing deep lines around her mouth. "You've found your backbone, I see. You're right. There wasn't a time limit put on my offer. So be sure to get them in. Soon."

Abby nodded and turned on her heel to walk back to her desk. When she looked at the clock, she decided to wait a few more minutes until it was lunch and most everyone had left the office.

She always remained behind, eating at her desk as she worked, so no one would look twice at her. Because they never did. When she was one of three people left in the office at lunch, Abby still found herself shaking when she input the client number and hit enter.

The screen blinked and pulled up the file. It took a few more clicks before she found the name of the business, the owner's name—which she recognized—and the address, all of which she entered into her phone and hit send.

Then she cleared the screen and tried to eat her lunch. She couldn't stomach the sandwich. Instead, she ate her banana. It took another twenty minutes before her nerves calmed.

Her part was finished. She only needed to wait to hear back from Clayton on whether she'd found the person responsible for thieving his cattle. She knew it could take some time before she heard anything, so she promptly got to work.

When five o'clock finally came, she couldn't get to her car fast enough. In no time, she was on her way to the ranch since Brice and Caleb had gone together after school.

When she pulled up, Clayton met her, opening her door before she turned off the engine. "Well?" she asked him.

He gave a shake of his head. "I didn't go on the property, but I took a look around. It's a new owner who doesn't appear to have any stock yet."

She'd gone through all the anxiety for nothing, but at least they had checked it out. Still, she'd been so sure her hunch was right.

The few hours with Clayton were over before they began, and then she and her brothers were back in the car headed home. All three of them were subdued.

She glanced at Caleb, who had called shotgun before looking in the rearview mirror at Brice. Both boys gazed out their windows, lost in thought. Ever since they'd left the ranch Sunday evening, they'd been quiet.

Abby was trying to think of ways to ask them if they were all right without actually saying the words since her brothers clammed up tight when asked that. When she pulled into the driveway, and the beams from the headlights landed on the open front door, she gasped.

"What the hell?" Brice stated as he reached for the door handle.

"Wait!" Abby yelled, but he and Caleb were already out of the car.

She threw the car into park and turned off the ignition but left the lights on before she jumped out of the vehicle while fumbling for her phone. She was trying to dial 911, but the call wouldn't connect. That's when she saw that her battery was dead.

"Dammit," she murmured and walked to her brothers, who stood looking at the door.

The porch light was out, leaving only the car to illuminate the area. The front door had been kicked open by the looks of the shattered remains where the deadbolt had been. It made her blood turn to ice to think that the lock she counted on every night to keep them safe had been no more help than if it were a piece of tape.

Caleb tried to push her away when Brice slipped inside the house. She shook her head and followed them. The bright beams of the car lights through the front window allowed her to see that the house had been ransacked.

She gasped at the destruction and the way their few meager things had been ripped, torn, slashed, or smashed as if the items were nothing but trash. Tears welled in her eyes. Why would someone do this? They had nothing of value that a thief would want.

There was a shout from Caleb. Abby jerked her head up at the sound, but all she saw were shadows. Then she saw Caleb as he swung something—a baseball bat—at someone before there was a loud bang and a flash in the dark.

The next thing she knew, Brice had joined Caleb in attacking someone, but the intruder wasn't alone. Abby screamed when the gun discharged again. She tried to get to her brothers but kept tripping over things.

"Abby!" Brice yelled.

She looked up and found a gun pointed at her face not five feet in front of her. Something slammed into her side the same time the gun went off.

Abby grunted when she fell on something hard that rammed into her kidney. She began fighting whoever was on top of her before she heard Caleb say her name.

She then pulled him down for a hug. There were sounds of footsteps and yelling, and then Brice came to kneel beside her. Something clicked, and she put her hand over her face to shield her eyes from the bright beam of the flashlight.

"Abby?" Brice said, his voice shaking.

She smiled up at him. "I'm fine. Are you two?"

Caleb sat up as Brice turned the light on him. The blood covering his shirt made Abby's heart drop to her feet. But her brother said, "It's not mine."

That's when Brice turned the light to her and said, "It's yours, Abby."

# Chapter 24

Clayton sped through the streets, his clammy hands gripping the steering wheel of the truck as his stomach knotted. Ever since Danny's call, the world had moved in slow motion with Clayton feeling as if he were bogged down in tar.

And all he wanted to do was get to Abby.

"You won't do her or the boys any good if you wreck," his father said from beside him.

Clayton didn't bother with a response. He wasn't able to put together any words, not when his mind kept tumbling over the fact that someone had broken into the Harpers' home.

Someone was hurt. Clayton knew it. He'd heard it in Danny's voice. After years of delivering such news, Clayton recognized the tone. What pissed him off was that Danny wouldn't tell him anything. Just told Clayton to get there ASAP.

Clayton would've walked out in his briefs had his

mother not shoved clothes into his arms and ordered him to dress. He was the one used to being in the middle of peril, of knowing that every breath could be his last.

He knew what conflict looked like, tasted like. Smelled like. It wasn't supposed to be here in Clearview. Especially not in Abby's home.

The sight of red and white flashing lights could be seen seconds before the sirens sounded as an ambulance whizzed by, headed toward the hospital. Clayton jerked his head around to stare at it before being forced to use his rearview mirror.

His father put a hand on his shoulder. This wasn't a time for words, because there was nothing anyone could say that would make it better.

Seconds later, the red, blue, and white lights of patrol cars came into view. A deputy was on site, moving rubberneckers along. Clayton pulled off the road behind a squad car and threw the truck into park. In one smooth motion, he turned off the engine and exited the truck.

"Sir, you can't—" a deputy started.

"Danny!" Clayton yelled, looking around the man currently blocking him.

Danny came out from the house and hurried toward them. He said something to his fellow deputy, and soon, Clayton and his father were let through the line of policemen.

Clayton's feet grew heavy the closer he came to the front door of the house. He'd seen so many dead during his time as a SEAL, but this was different. This was Abby. He wasn't sure he'd be able to handle it.

". . . get away. It was Brice who ran to a neighbors and had them call 911," Danny said.

Clayton looked at him, his throat closing painfully. He didn't understand why Brice hadn't used Abby's cell phone. And he was too afraid to ask the question—even if he could've gotten the words out.

When Clayton stepped into the house, he saw the destruction of every piece of furniture, picture, and item in the living room and into the kitchen. Walls had holes in them, cushions had been cut open, and shards of glass littered the floor.

But it was the blood that pulled his gaze. He'd smelled it the instant he walked through the door. The familiar, metallic odor hung heavy in the air.

"Holy shit," his father murmured.

Danny wiped a hand over his face. "Yeah. Someone was making a statement here."

"Where are they?" Clayton asked in a low voice.

Danny jerked his chin. Clayton looked through the living room toward the kitchen to find both Brice and Caleb sitting at the table staring off into space as deputies stood near them.

Clayton didn't have to ask to know that Abby had been the one in the ambulance.

"She's going to be fine," Danny said. "The wound is minor."

Clayton fisted his hands, squeezing his eyes closed. A wound. Abby was wounded. "Gun or knife?" he demanded. He knew what both felt like, and he hadn't wanted Abby to ever know that kind of pain.

Danny hesitated. "Gun."

Clayton dropped his chin to his chest and fought the red haze of fury that ripped through him.

"The boys are going to need you," his father said. "You have to hold it together for them."

His dad was right. Clayton took a deep breath and lifted his head the same time he opened his eyes, pinning Danny with a look. "What happened?"

Danny pursed his lips together before putting his hands on his hips. "The door was busted open when they arrived. Brice and Caleb came into the house with Abby trailing behind them. They didn't realize anyone was inside until one of them hit Brice."

"And?" Clayton urged when Danny went quiet.

Danny blew out a breath and gave a shake of his head. "Caleb managed to grab his baseball bat that was near the door. He said he got a couple of good swings that connected with someone because he heard the grunts. That's when another of them pulled a gun and fired two warning shots. For whatever reason, they turned the weapon on Abby. Caleb managed to knock her out of the way, but not before the bullet grazed her shoulder."

"Is that her only injury?" Ben asked.

Danny shrugged his shoulders. "She landed in a lot of glass, as well."

Clayton walked past his friend and headed toward the kitchen. As he entered, the boys turned their heads to him. To his surprise, they rose and walked to him. He spread his arms and pulled them near.

Though neither made a sound, he felt the tears they cried by the shuddering of their bodies. He held them for several minutes before Caleb pulled back.

"I want to see Abby," he declared.

Brice stepped away but refused to meet Clayton's eyes. "Me, too."

"Gather some clothes," he told them. "We're going to the hospital, but you'll be staying at the ranch until we get this sorted out."

When Clayton turned to watch them pick their way to their rooms, he found his father and Danny behind him. "This wasn't an accident."

"I agree," Ben said.

Danny's brow snapped together. "What do you mean?"

"The Harpers had nothing of value, Danny, and you know it," Clayton said. "Look around. I bet every room looks like the living room and kitchen. Hell, they smashed every plate. That's rage."

His father blew out a long breath. "This destruction could've extended to someone's life."

"What do you know?" Danny demanded.

"Abby gave us a name of a new ranch. The brand they registered made her think how easy it would be to re-brand over our E."

Danny briefly closed his eyes. "The stolen cattle."

"Yep. And Clayton went to take a look at the ranch today," Ben said.

Clayton gave a frustrated shake of his head. "I saw nothing, nor did I speak to anyone. Yet, it's mere hours after I make that drive that someone does this?"

"I agree," Danny said. "This isn't a coincidence. What's the name of the ranch? I can do some digging on my own."

It wasn't that Clayton didn't trust Danny, but he was

in protection mode. And he was used to doing things another way. Thankfully, he didn't have to lie to Danny as Brice and Caleb came out with their bags in hand.

Clayton watched as his father led the boys from the house. He remained behind until the brothers were out of earshot, then he turned to Danny. "I'll tell you who it is, but not tonight."

"Clayton, you're not in the Navy anymore. You can't go after this person on your own," Danny cautioned.

He grinned, but there was no mirth in it. "I may not be in the military, but I'll always be a SEAL. And everything I learned is going to come in handy."

"Please, don't go after this person on your own."

Clayton stopped as he started to walk away. He turned back to look at Danny. "Give me a few hours. Once you know the name, you'll swarm the place and possibly ruin any chance I have of discovering who all is involved."

"What makes you think it's more than one person?"

"It took skill to steal the herd and bull from us. And it took several men and trailers. One person might be running this, but I want everyone involved."

Danny raised a brow. "And Brice? He's part of it, and he refused to give us anything."

"I think he may change his mind now. Either way, the sheriff's department can't go barreling in."

"Dammit," Danny muttered as he ran a hand through his hair. He glared at Clayton. "I'll give you some time, but don't make me regret it. SEAL or not, I'll still arrest your ass."

Clayton gave a nod. "Understood."

He left the house and got in the truck. The boys were

in the backseat, silent as death. Clayton glanced at his father before he started the truck and backed up before turning the vehicle around.

While he felt better knowing that Abby wasn't in mortal danger, the fact remained that someone shot her. He was going to find out who that was.

And he would make the person pay.

Painfully.

By the time he parked the truck in the hospital parking lot, he'd thought of twelve different ways he could take out the people who had hurt Abby and her brothers—each one more satisfying than the last.

Clayton led the way into the hospital and was directed to the ER where they had Abby. His steps slowed when he saw her lying so still on the bed with the IV bag and monitors beeping. Blue curtains hung, sectioning off Abby's bed from others.

"She was awake earlier," Caleb said in a voice strained with worry.

Clayton put his hand on the teen's shoulder. "It's most likely the pain medicine," he explained.

His dad motioned for the boys to follow him. "Come. You'll see that she'll wake soon."

Clayton slowly followed the three of them to the bed. Brice took one side and Caleb the other. They stared down at their sister for a long moment before they grabbed her hands.

He saw a tear roll down Brice's face. Clayton couldn't press him for information on the cattle rustlers. Now wasn't the time. But soon. After what those people had done to the Harpers' house and to Abby, surely Brice would talk.

"I'm going to call your mother," his dad whispered before walking away.

Clayton stood at the foot of the bed noting how pale Abby looked. The bright white bandage that peeked out from her hospital gown was a reminder of how close she'd come to death.

"I hit one of them," Caleb said. "I hit him so hard I heard him cuss. And my bat cracked."

Clayton looked at the youngest Harper. "You did good."

"I should've aimed higher. Or lower. The lights were out," he said, his breathing becoming harsh. "Only the headlights coming through the living room gave us light. I tried a switch, but the lights didn't come on. That's when we heard them."

Brice stood silently as another tear rolled down his cheek.

Caleb drew in a ragged breath. "If I'd hit lower, I might have taken one of them out and moved on to the other. Hell, I don't even know how many there were."

"Hey," Clayton said, drawing Caleb's gaze. "I want you to listen to me. You did a good job hurting them. No matter how much you could've done, it's never enough when someone is harmed. Trust me. I know this."

"I almost threw up when I saw her blood," Caleb confessed.

Clayton looked from Caleb to Brice, waiting until both boys had their eyes on him. "No one is going to hurt either of you or your sister again. I'm going to make sure of it."

# Chapter 25

Even in a drug-induced sleep, Abby still heard the sounds of gunshots in her dreams, still felt the impact of Caleb's body against hers.

She hadn't wanted to leave Caleb and Brice, but the paramedics hadn't given her a choice. So as she pushed through the fog of the painkillers, her mind was focused on them.

When she came to, she felt something in each hand. Her eyes opened, and she saw Brice first. He was slumped in the chair next to the bed with his neck at an awkward angle while he held her hand.

She turned her head to the other side and found Caleb with his head resting on his arm on her bed as he, too, held her hand. She smiled, her heart full, knowing that her brothers were safe and unharmed after such a horrific incident.

Abby looked at the end of the bed as she felt a pull. That's when she spotted Clayton. A rush of emotion filled her, causing her to blink back tears. He nodded, his own face tight with emotion. She knew without asking that he was the one who had brought her brothers to the hospital.

"They wouldn't leave," he whispered.

She pressed her lips together, fighting back the rush of tears. Once she realized she'd been shot, she'd put on a brave face for her brothers, and now that they weren't looking, she could let her fear show.

"Thank you," she mouthed.

He briefly looked down at the bed. Just as his lips parted as if he were going to say something, Brice stirred. She watched as her brother's eyes parted, glancing her way before they shut again. A moment later, he jerked upright, his eyes open once more.

"Abby," he said.

Caleb grunted before he lifted his head and blinked several times at her. The tears she thought she had under control filled her eyes when her brothers both hugged her. She held them tightly while looking at Clayton, uncaring that her wounded arm began to throb painfully.

"I'm fine," she told them. "But you two need to rest."

Caleb rubbed his stiff neck. "Clayton said we're staying at the ranch."

"That's very kind," she said to Clayton.

He shrugged. "Your sister's right. You should rest. Dad was here earlier, but Mom came to get him. I've already texted her to come get the two of you now. She's been cooking all night, and she expects you to gorge yourselves when you get there."

"Soooooo, no school?" Caleb asked her hopefully.

Abby squeezed his hand. "I think we all deserve the next few days off."

"Someone needs to stay with you," Brice said.

"I'll be doing that," Clayton announced.

Abby watched her brother consider Clayton's words. Finally, Brice gave a nod of acceptance. They had a few more minutes together, which allowed Abby to look over her brothers to make sure neither had been physically harmed. And then Clayton walked them to the exit where Justine waited to drive them home.

A nurse came in to check Abby's vitals and bandage while Clayton was gone. She had Abby sit on the side of the bed while she went about her examination.

Abby hated the smells of hospitals almost as much as she hated the sight of one. It reminded her of her father suffering through months of tests before they discovered that he had some rare disease. She couldn't even recall what it was, only that it had eaten away at him slowly, extending his misery until he was so full of painkillers that he no longer remembered her.

"How is she?" Clayton asked the nurse as he walked up holding a small bag.

The nurse smiled in greeting. "It's a graze, which is good, but it doesn't hurt any less."

"I know," he said.

Abby had seen the scars on his body. If anyone knew what kind of pain she felt, it was Clayton. She started to reach out to him but thought better of it. However, he had other ideas. He set the bag down and then came to sit beside her, folding her right hand in both of his large ones. His touch reassured her, comforted her.

Eased her.

"You're going to be in some pain for a few days," the nurse said as she removed the IV from Abby's left arm. "The doctor has sent in a prescription for pain meds to the pharmacy for you to take as needed. Don't move around too much. You need to give your body time to heal."

Abby frowned when the nurse signed something on the chart she carried. The removal of the IV was good news, or so she hoped. "Does that mean I can go?"

"It does. I'm getting your paperwork started now. Give me a few minutes. Until then, you can get dressed."

Abby couldn't leave the hospital quickly enough. She and Clayton didn't talk about what had happened, but he kept a hold of her hand.

"There's some clean clothes," Clayton said as he jerked his chin to the bag near a chair.

She didn't know who had gotten them for her, but she was thankful since she didn't relish putting on her shirt that was covered in blood. In fact, she wasn't even sure where her clothes were.

It was midmorning when Clayton helped her into his truck before he pulled her against him. She drew in a deep breath, letting his scent of man, leather, and strength fill her. His hand rubbed up and down her back. He didn't say a word, just held her. And that's all it took for the tears to start.

She'd been terrified of dying, of her brothers getting hurt, of so many things. In his arms, she could let down her walls and allow him to shoulder her worries and fears for a few minutes. And once she began crying, she couldn't seem to stop.

She didn't know how long they sat there before her tears dried and she lifted her head to look at him. "I'm so glad you're here."

"I've never been so scared as when Danny called to tell me something had happened. He wouldn't tell me more than that."

She ran a hand down his face. "Why did Danny call you?"

"Brice told him to."

She would have to thank Brice later for that. While they had known the Easts for only a few days, it felt like years. "I need to see what was stolen from the house."

Clayton shook his head as his face hardened. "You're not going back there. You don't need to see that."

"I have to. It's our home. I have to get it cleaned up."

But he kept shaking his head. "We'll hire someone to do it. You don't want to go back. Trust me."

"What don't you want me to see?" she asked.

He blew out a breath, his head turning away for a moment. "The people who broke into your house weren't thieves."

"How do you know that?"

"They destroyed everything. They even busted walls."

She frowned, not comprehending what she was hearing. "But . . . why?"

"I think this is about the stolen cattle. And the 4B ranch I went to check out yesterday."

Her stomach clenched in dread. "I didn't think you saw anything."

"I didn't. But someone must have seen me."

She leaned back in the seat, her stomach churning in fear. "Then you did find the right place."

"Yes," he replied with a single nod.

"And the people think Brice told you."

Clayton drew in a breath and released it before he nodded once more.

She put a hand to her forehead as she looked out the windshield. "Which means that they were there to carry out their threat against him."

"I don't think he was the target."

Her gaze jerked to him as her arm fell to her side. "You think it was me? You're wrong. They fired two shots before aiming at me."

"Maybe. Maybe not. Maybe I'm reaching in thinking that they threatened to do you or Caleb harm if Brice told."

She wasn't sure what to think anymore. All she knew was that people had broken into their home, wrecked their things, and shot her. Did it really matter who those people had threatened?

"What are you going to do?" she asked.

He slid a hand around to her neck and pulled her toward him for a long, lingering kiss that made her melt and forget about all the horror of the night before. Her body became languid, and it had nothing to do with the pain medicine and everything to do with the wonderful, hot man holding her.

His touch, the taste of him, had the ability to wipe away all the horror of the past few hours and replace it with a burning desire only he could quench. She didn't question her feelings or allow herself to think of anything other than Clayton. Because for the first time, she not only felt safe, she knew she—and her brothers—was completely protected by him.

And that did wonders for her state of mind.

Clayton ended the kiss and pressed his forehead to hers. "I'm going to take you home and get you settled."

She smiled when he said "home," and didn't correct him. The ranch did feel like home, but she cautioned herself about getting attached. For her brothers' sakes, as well as her own, she needed to keep things in perspective.

Clayton had asked her to work for him. He was giving Brice a second chance. And they'd had sex. Twice. That didn't mean they were in a relationship.

While her heart argued that no man would've gone to get her brothers and stayed at the hospital if he didn't care, she admitted to herself that she did want a relationship with him. She wanted . . . everything with him.

"Then," Clayton continued, "I'm going to dig deeper into the name you gave me."

Ronald Baxter. "I know him. Well, I knew *of* him. He was ahead of me in school."

Clayton held her gaze and promised, "He won't hurt you."

She put her hand over his heart, felt it beating beneath her palm. "I know."

They drove back to the ranch with the sound of the radio in the background. Every time she blinked, she saw the shadows of the night before and the flash of the gun. She'd slept in the hospital thanks to the pain-killers, but she wasn't sure about later that night. What if someone had come to her house not to just wreck everything, but to hurt one of them? Worse, what if one of her brothers had been shot? Or killed?

Abby turned her head to Clayton. "What if you're wrong about it being Baxter who came to the house?"

"That's why I'm going to do a little digging."

"I don't want you hurt."

The smile he gave her was cold and full of lethal intent. "Oh, I hope they do come for me. I'll show those assholes a thing or two."

"Clayton, please."

"Abby, they shot you and fired two more rounds into the house from a gun that could have been pointed at Brice or Caleb. They destroyed your home. And they could be the same people who stole our cattle. I'm not going to sit back and do nothing."

She licked her lips. "The police would think differently."

"Yeah. I know," he murmured as he slowed the truck before turning into the ranch.

"Brice could give you the answers."

Clayton glanced at her. "Yes, he could. I watched him for hours before he fell asleep in that chair at the hospital. He's scared, yes, but he's more worried about you and Caleb. It's how I know whoever he's working with threatened the two of you and not him."

"I can get him to tell you."

"He needs to come to me on his own."

"I'm not so sure he will," she said.

Clayton pulled in to the garage and turned off the truck. "He knows what he has to do. He's working through it. Give him some time."

"You make it sound as if you don't think whoever those people are will come here."

"I don't think they will. You were an easy target. And if they'd wanted you dead, you would be. Last night was a warning."

She couldn't stop the shiver that ran down her spine. "For Brice to keep his mouth shut."

"I drove around the address you gave me yesterday, but I didn't look too hard. That could be the only thing that kept you alive."

"That's stupid," she said with a roll of her eyes. "If they threatened me to keep Brice quiet, wouldn't killing me do the opposite?"

Clayton's lips twisted as he gave her a rueful look. "I think they have the cattle somewhere that can't be easily found, otherwise, why warn Brice? But I think if they planned to hurt anyone, it would be Caleb. That way, you're still there to take care of Brice."

She covered her mouth, sick to her stomach at how easily some people could think of taking a life.

"Abby," Clayton said to get her attention. Once she looked at him, he said, "I'm going to do some snooping on my own. I'm hoping during that time, Brice will figure out that the best option is to tell me the truth. Either way, I'm going to find out everything. It'll go quicker and easier with your brother, but it will get done regardless."

"You won't take these people on by yourself, will you?"

He hesitated before shaking his head. "I promised Danny I'd inform him of what I knew."

It was a small concession. And it was all she was going to get.

# Chapter 26

"He knows."

Gus Lewis slammed his can of beer down on the granite island, uncaring that the alcohol splashed on him. He glared across at Terry Perez. "Enough, goddammit!"

Terry's hazel eyes narrowed. "Deny it all you want, but you're as scared as I am."

"What can one man do?" Berny asked from the couch as he lifted the bottle of tequila to his lips.

Gus glanced at Berny, who had bags of frozen peas on his left arm and ribs. "Clayton East was a SEAL, you dumb fuck."

"So?" Berny said before issuing a loud burp.

"He's drunk," Terry stated.

Gus grunted. If he'd received the whooping the kid had given Berny with the bat, he probably would've gotten drunk, too. "I think he has a broken arm."

"We'll wait until he passes out before we set it."

Gus downed the last of the beer even though it was now flat. It was supposed to have been a simple job. Steal some cattle from the largest ranch around. The Easts had so many, they wouldn't miss a hundred or so.

Fuck. Had they ever been wrong.

Then the kid had to get caught.

Gus dropped his chin to his chest and raked a hand through his hair. He was in way over his head. He'd known it as soon as Ronald Baxter asked for his help. But Gus had never been able to tell Ronnie no.

And Ronnie knew it.

"Why did you shoot Abby? Weren't you supposed to go after the other kid? Caleb?"

Gus lifted his head to meet Terry's gaze. "We told Brice there would be consequences if he told anyone. I gave Brice a warning."

"So you think he told?"

"We don't know that he didn't. Need I remind you that Clayton drove around the ranch yesterday?"

Terry's already thin lips disappeared as he pressed them together. "I'm the one who told you and Ronnie, asshole. So, no, I don't need reminding. All East did was drive around."

"But he came to the ranch, Terry. He was *here*." Gus jabbed the tip of his finger against the counter a couple of time.

"He didn't find the cattle. Nor will he."

Gus blew out a breath that was filled with frustration and irritation. And fear. "We were lucky."

"Ronnie isn't going to let anything happen to us," Terry said as he leaned his elbows on the island counter.

Gus didn't reply. What could he say? Terry and Berny

had never seen Ronnie at his worst. But Gus had. Twice. And he never wanted that kind of anger directed his way.

Gus crushed the empty can in his hands and tossed it in the garbage before he walked to the fridge to get another one. Standing with the refrigerator door wide, he opened the can and guzzled half the beer before he closed the door with his elbow.

"You should've shot at the youngest Harper. That's what Ronnie wanted," Terry said.

Gus didn't bother to reply. He'd barely been able to shoot at Abby. He'd fired the first two shots wide in hopes that it would scare all three Harpers out of the house. Instead, both Brice and Caleb had gone nuts.

There was no way he'd be able to kill the youngster. Hell, Caleb was his nephew's age. It also didn't help that he knew Abby.

"Christ," he murmured and downed the rest of the beer.

But there was no amount of alcohol that could numb him enough to continue on the path Ronnie had set them on.

He blamed Ronnie, but ultimately, Gus knew it was his fault. He could've said no to his friend. He *should've* said no. It didn't matter that Ronnie could talk green off a leaf. Everything about this operation was wrong.

And Gus had known it from the beginning.

Since the fourth grade, when he and Ronnie had become friends, he followed Ronnie into whatever trouble awaited them. Smashing the things inside the Harper house had been easy. They were just things that could be replaced. He'd do that all day long rather than point a gun at someone again. It didn't matter that he was a dead shot with any gun or rifle he picked up. That didn't mean he had the right to take a life.

And neither did Ronnie.

If only Gus had the balls to tell his friend that.

Actually, if he was the man his father had wanted him to be—the man his sister thought he was—then he'd go to the sheriff right then.

Gus tossed aside the empty can and stalked from the house, slamming the door behind him. But when he got in his truck, he couldn't start the engine.

Ronald Baxter. There was something about that name that sounded familiar to Clayton. He searched his mind, hoping he'd make some kind of connection. Finally, he went into his closet and pulled out the box from high school.

In the middle of his floor, he sat and opened the box. Crushed homecoming boutonnieres were set aside, as well as his cap and gown and other memorabilia from his senior year. Finally, Clayton came to the bottom of the box where his four yearbooks rested.

He began with his freshman year, thinking that maybe Ronald was older. It wasn't until he was looking through his junior yearbook that Clayton found Ronald Baxter—a freshman.

Clayton stared at the smiling kid with his black hair and vivid blue eyes. He remembered Ronald—Ronnie—as being rather popular. Ronnie had been on the football and baseball teams as well as track.

His good looks propelled him to be the "It" man of his grade. The girls all wanted to date him, and the guys all wanted to be him. Clayton had only known Ronnie because they played sports together. While he hadn't had an issue with Ronnie, there were others who did.

Now that Clayton had a face to go with the name, he was ready to dig deeper into Ronnie's life and find out why the bastard had stolen his cattle. He put everything back into the box and then returned it to the shelf in his closet. Clayton was descending the stairs when he heard his mother's voice from the living room, followed by Abby's.

"Brice hasn't said much," his mother said.

There was a slight pause before Abby spoke. "He's always tried to be the man of the family. He struggles because he can't do the things he feels he should be doing."

"You and the boys are welcome to stay here for as long as you need."

"That's very sweet of you, but I don't want to impose."

His mother tsked. "You could never do that."

Clayton walked toward the living room and peered inside. Both women were on a sofa looking out the windows where Brice sat atop the paddock fence as Caleb aimlessly walked around the barn.

"I'm worried about them," Abby said after a moment of silence.

"They'll talk when they want to," his mother said. "You can't push them. I know from experience. And, sometimes, they never talk."

Clayton realized his mother was thinking about Landon's death and how Clayton had refused to discuss it after he'd explained what had happened. His mother had wanted him to share his feelings and how much he hurt.

But he couldn't. Not then. Hell, not even now.

Clayton wasn't sure how he'd managed to tell Abby the story. There were just some things that could never be put into words—and watching his brother die right before his eyes had been one of them.

"I'll talk to them," Clayton said.

His mother's head jerked around to him. Abby moved slower, but the smile on her face was all he needed to see.

"If either of them will talk to you, it'll be Caleb," Abby said.

He walked to her, fighting not to touch her. Then he stopped struggling against it. He stopped beside the sofa and touched her shoulder. "How are you feeling? Is there much pain?"

"It's manageable," she confessed.

His mother set down her coffee cup on the table beside her. "I can get your pain meds."

"No, please," Abby hurried to say. "I don't like how I feel when I take them. I'll handle things until it gets too bad. Then I'll take another."

His mother smiled and patted Abby's leg. "Just let me know, dear."

Clayton looked at his mother to find her knowing gaze on him. He shot his mother a wink and turned his attention back to Abby. "I don't want you in the office. Take it easy today and rest."

"Oh my God," she cried out, her blue eyes widening. "I didn't call Gloria."

His mother pushed from the sofa and rose to get the

phone. "I'm sure she already knows, but I'll call and fill her in."

"I can do it," Abby said.

But it was too late. His mother had already begun dialing. "She likes to dote on others," Clayton told Abby.

"I'm not used to that."

"If it gets to be too much, just let her know."

Abby looked at him askance. "I'd never do that. She's so kind. I would never want to hurt her feelings."

He squatted down beside her. "Are you really okay?"

"No," she admitted, resting her good hand on the arm of the couch.

Clayton covered her hand with his and squeezed. "Remember what I said. No one is going to harm you here. You and your brothers are safe."

"I know," she replied softly.

He glanced out the window and cleared his throat. "You never accepted the job I offered you."

Her eyes crinkled in the corners as she grinned. "I wasn't sure after we . . . ."

She trailed off, but he knew exactly what she was referring to. "I'm not going to lie. I want you here all the time, and if giving you a job gets me that, then I don't see a problem."

"What if things go . . . sour?" she asked in a hushed voice, her face pinched with worry.

"I could give you a lot of promises, and I could tell you that regardless of what happens with us, you'll always have a job here. But you won't believe them. Actions are what you need."

She swallowed and licked her lips. "People say a lot of things that end up being lies."

"I can have a contract drawn up that will protect you as well as my family."

"I'd feel better about that."

He nodded. "And the two of us? I'd likc to talk about that."

"I—"

She was cut off by the return of his mother. Clayton stood while he listened to his mother explain the conversation that she had had with Gloria. Somehow, his mother had negotiated the next week off for Abby—with pay.

Clayton inwardly grinned. There were few who could stand against the force of Justine East. With Abby in capable hands, he gave her another squeeze and stood. She held his hand tightly before he walked away. Clayton stopped at the back door and put on his coat and hat. Then he walked outside toward Caleb.

He was taking Abby's advice, but Clayton also knew it was going to take longer for Brice to sort through everything going on in his head. Because if the teen was anything like him, Brice was trying to come up with a way that he could've said or done something different that would've prevented his sister from being shot.

Once he accepted that nothing would've changed the outcome, he would open up. And Clayton would be there when he did.

# Chapter 27

It would be so easy to think she was part of something. Abby sighed. How often had she wished her father were still alive? Or that her mom had been able to actually be a mother?

Now that she'd been around Justine and Ben, the longing she'd had for parents all but knocked the breath out of her. With Clayton swooping in to help her and looking after her brothers, and then Justine and Ben doting on her as if she were their daughter, Abby realized just what she and her brothers had been missing all these years.

She hadn't exactly had the best example as a mother, so Abby had taken her cues from what she'd seen on TV or read in books. And she knew that made her a poor substitute, but she hadn't given up.

Nor would she ever.

She might not remember her father's love, and she

had never had her mother's, but she'd made damn sure
her brothers were loved.

As Abby watched Clayton walk to Caleb, she was
once again thankful that he'd come into their lives. He
was a good man, despite the demons that hounded him.
Clayton didn't let them take control, though. If only she
knew that trick.

She looked over at Justine to find the woman's gaze
locked on her son, tears in her eyes. Abby tried to move
her left arm to comfort Justine, but the pain stopped her.

"I'm so sorry about Landon," she said.

Justine smiled and picked at some imagined piece of
lint from her sweater. "I always wondered why they
don't have a word for a parent who loses a child. If I'd
lost Ben, I'd be a widow."

"I think it's because there's nothing that can fill the
hole after loving a child."

Justine turned her head and smiled through her tears
that gathered but didn't spill over. "Maybe. A parent
never gets over the loss of a child."

Abby found her own tears beginning. It was hard to
watch someone suffer so and not feel the heartache. "I
don't want to bring up old memories."

"Oh, sweetheart, you aren't," Justine hurried to say,
a frown furrowing her brow. "Ben and I talk about
Landon all the time. It makes Clayton uncomfortable,
and we understand that. Please don't take it the wrong
way if he doesn't speak of his brother."

"He told me what happened."

Justine's face went slack. "He did?" she asked in a
shocked whisper.

Abby nodded, hoping she was doing the right thing

by relaying the information. "Clayton took me to the spot and told me everything that happened."

The tears finally fell. Justine wiped them away, sniffing. "As far as I know, he's not spoken about it since he told us and the police. He's held it in all these years."

The sob that filled the living room made Abby blink to keep her own tears at bay. She shifted on the sofa to face Justine. "Just like you, he'll always carry that with him."

"I'm so relieved that he spoke of it." Justine reached for a tissue and wiped at her face. "I lost two sons that night. One to death, and the other to darkness. I think maybe Clayton is finally stepping into the light again."

The way Justine looked at her let Abby know in no uncertain terms that Justine believed she was the cause. Abby wasn't so sure. But she wanted to be. She really did.

Justine grinned, her eyes red from crying. "I know there's something developing between you and Clayton. Ben and I approve, by the way."

"Um . . ." Abby began, unsure how to reply.

Justine waved away her words. "I wasn't looking for a response. I just wanted to let you know. And even though I don't know about your past, I realize that you've shouldered a tremendous amount of responsibility over the years. You should be proud of yourself."

Abby looked away. "Thank you."

"I used to tell Clayton not to let the past define him. It might shape you in some ways, but you can't let it hold onto you and prevent you from enjoying the present or looking forward to a future."

She made it sound so easy, but it wasn't. The past had its claws dug too deep to ever let go.

Abby swung her gaze back to Justine. "I wish you would've told me that eight years ago."

"It's not too late to let the past go. You just have to want your present and the future." Justine hesitated as her brows briefly drew together. "I don't mean to make the past seem inconsequential. It is important. You and your brothers learned a hard lesson."

"One I wish they'd never known."

Justine chuckled softly. "That's something a mother would say. You became one the moment you started raising them. Being a sister and a mother can't be easy, but you make it look that way. But I'd like for you to look at the past in another way instead of negatively."

"How?"

"Another lesson you and your brothers learned was that you have each other. No matter what the situation, the bond between the three of you is tighter and stronger than most people will ever know. You're lucky in some regards."

Lucky? No one had ever called her lucky, and yet what Justine said made a lot of sense.

But the older woman wasn't finished imparting her wisdom. "Then there's the lesson of unconditional love. You three give it to each other in such heavy doses that it's amazing to watch. But it doesn't stop there. You've shown Brice and Caleb how to carry on, how to be strong, how to love, and how to keep fighting and hoping."

"Hoping?" she said, choking on the emotion welling within her.

"Yes," Justine said with a nod of her head. "You may think you're drowning in the past, but I can see the hope in your eyes. It's in your words, in your actions, and in the way you smile. Your brothers see it, too. When you take all of that and compare it to one event, doesn't it outweigh the bad?"

"I never used to think so. I used to believe that there was nothing in this life that could ever make up for the bad."

Justine tilted her head to the side, her long braid falling over her shoulder. "See? There was hope in those words. Did you hear them?"

"Yes," Abby confessed.

"Life dealt you and your brothers a horrible blow early on. It would've devastated most people, but the three of you are strong. Otherwise, you wouldn't be standing here—together, I might add—now."

Abby had to admit, Justine was right. But there were still lingering worries. She licked her lips. "Both of my brothers have abandonment fears. I worry that the issue will plague them forever."

"Honey, I wish I could tell you that no one will leave any of y'all ever again, but I can't. It'd be a lie. Death will take us all eventually. Sometimes you have to trust your heart and pray for the best. How will you ever know love if you don't try? Will there be heartache? Yes. But there will also be love so bright and full that it completes you. That's what you tell your brothers." Justine paused. "And yourself."

Abby looked down at the cushion. "What if I can't? What if I can't trust my heart?"

"Then you'll miss out on life. Part of living is feeling the hurts and the joys and all the spaces in between. Living a full life isn't about keeping yourself safe and tucked away so nothing and no one can hurt you. You'll end up alone and lonely. Life is about putting yourself out there to see what's coming. You might get knocked down, but then you pick your ass back up and lift your chin, waiting for whatever's next."

Abby let loose a shaky breath as she lifted her gaze to Justine. "You're an amazing woman. Your family is lucky to have you."

"Damn straight they are, sweetheart. And I tell them that every chance I get," Justine said with a smile and a wink.

"Thank you for the talk."

"I hope you take my advice."

Abby wanted to. "I'll do my best."

"Well, that's better than telling me you can't." Justine laughed and tucked a leg beneath her. "So, tell me. When are you going to quit working for Gloria and start here? Oh, yes, don't look surprised. Clayton told us he offered you the job."

Abby shook her head in amazement. If there was ever a woman who could do wonders to help her, it was Justine.

Some things would never change. And Clayton was okay with that. He looked in the mirror at the bunkhouse and spread the black paint over his face.

There was an ominous feel to the coming night. Dusk settled over the land with heavy clouds on the horizon and the sound of distant thunder. The horses were agitated, stomping in their stalls, while others in the pasture stared off into the distance.

Clayton put away the paint and pulled the black beanie on his head to cover his hair. With his black shirt and pants, he'd be near impossible to see in the dark. He slid a pistol into the holster on his hip and tucked the knife into his boot. Then he looked at the scope that would help him see across the distance.

"You should bring the rifle that goes with that," Shane said from behind him.

Clayton looked at him in the mirror and turned around to face him. "I do this alone."

"Because I'm too old to keep up?"

"Because I can be in and out without any of them knowing I was even there."

Shane leaned against the doorway as he blew out a breath. "They're expecting you."

"They expect me to come in with the authorities."

"No." Shane jerked his chin to him. "They're expecting this. They know you're a SEAL, though I doubt they know all you can do. Shit, I don't even know everything you can do."

Clayton shrugged. "Nor will you."

"The point I'm trying to make is that they're on the lookout for you."

"I can promise you, Shane, they'll never see me coming."

"You don't know how many there are."

Clayton grabbed the scope he'd taken off a rifle and put it into his thigh pocket. "Which is why I'll be scouting the area. And I need you here," he said before Shane could give another argument. "We talked about this. The security system is not yet online. I need someone to watch over my parents, Abby, and the boys."

"You know the men and I will. Everyone else is in place. I just don't like you going in alone."

Clayton normally had his team with him, but he wasn't worried about being on his own. Not against Ronnie and the men he'd hired.

"Ben and Justine can't lose another child," Shane said. "And Abby can't lose you."

"They won't. I'm not going out there to hurt anyone." Even if that's what he wanted to do. "I'm going to find our cattle. Then I'm going to call in Danny."

Shane pushed his cowboy hat back on his head and nodded. "It's a good plan."

"I'm still convincing Abby to be mine," Clayton said as he walked to Shane and briefly clamped a hand on his shoulder. "I'm not going to do anything to jeopardize that."

The ranch manager grinned as he pushed away from the door. "You've got it bad, huh?"

"Yeah. I believe I do."

The smile faded. "Be careful, Clayton."

He gave a nod and walked into the darkness, jogging toward the northwest. It was going to be several miles of running over his own family's land and through others' property before he ever reached Ronnie's, but this was just a walk in the park compared to some of his previous missions.

And yet, this one hit too close to home.

# Chapter 28

It was easy to become one with the night. It was ingrained so deeply within him, that Clayton could do it in his sleep. Though it had been months since he'd run such a distance, it only fatigued him a little. But it still irritated him. He'd gone soft since leaving his team, and that was evident now. If he were still in fighting shape, he wouldn't be winded.

Clayton paused, leaning against a tree long enough to survey the area around him and make sure no one was near. Then he ran across the open field in front of him.

He'd left East land two miles back, and that meant that he had to be more cautious. The pasture before him was owned by someone he didn't know, and though he'd rather go around, time was of the essence.

The thunder from earlier was moving closer, becoming more frequent. Staying low and moving from cover to cover, Clayton made his way to the fence and deftly vaulted over it. Then he was running for cover once more.

It took Clayton twice as long to get to Baxter's land than it had to cross his own. At least while on his property, Clayton had been able to run full out without worry of being seen. When he finally made it to the border of Ronnie's land, Clayton dropped down onto his stomach beside some bushes. He pulled out the scope and used it to get a better look at the house.

He noted the best places for anyone to lay in wait for him and checked to make sure no one was there. Bit by bit, he progressed around the house, noting the two trucks and the lights on within the residence. Finally, he moved closer to the house and checked inside. He saw a man on the sofa, an empty bottle of tequila loosely held in his grip with bags of frozen peas on his arm and side.

That had to be the asshole Caleb had beaten with the bat. The teen hadn't thought he'd done much damage, but obviously, he had. Though Clayton couldn't see in all the windows of the house, it looked as if the man passed out on the couch was the only one inside.

Clayton looked toward the back of the property where the barn was as it began to rain. The others were out there. Most likely with his cattle. He kept low and made his way to the barn. There were no horses in the stalls. A check showed him that three mares were in a connected pasture.

When he'd discovered that Ronnie had taken his cattle, Clayton had pulled up the land on his computer to study it and the terrain. The 4B ranch was just under twelve hundred acres. It was tiny compared to the East

Ranch, but there was lots of land around Ronnie's that could be bought so the 4B could grow.

As the minutes ticked by, Clayton moved through the pastures, thankful for the cover of night and the clouds that kept the moon hidden. The rain came down harder. While the weather hid him, it also made it more difficult for him to see. With the thunder and the distant flare of lightning, the cattle would be on edge.

Clayton's search of the 4B ranch was a bust. There was nothing there other than a small herd of forty cattle that weren't his.

But where were the other men? And where was his herd? He thought back to the map he'd seen of the land surrounding the 4B. There were a hundred acres for sale toward the west that had been vacant for some time since it had been foreclosed on.

Clayton turned and headed in that direction. He moved swiftly over the land, pushing himself hard. Tonight was just reconnaissance, but he had to find the missing cows. When he finally jumped the barrier that separated 4B land from the foreclosed property, Clayton hunkered down by the fence and looked around.

His senses told him someone was near. He scanned the area through the rain. Though his eyes saw nothing, he trusted his gut. It had saved him many times. He pulled out the scope again and looked through it. That's when he saw an elbow sticking out from behind a tree.

Clayton lowered himself to the ground and military crawled. He'd only gone about thirty feet when he heard the first string of curses. He paused, listening. A moment later, he heard it again. He looked to his right and then shifted in that direction. After a few minutes, he found the man leaning against a tree, huddled in a rain jacket while holding a rifle. His continued grumbling as he looked farther out across the vacant land while trying to stay warm and dry confirmed what Clayton had suspected.

With the guard's attention more on the rain and the fact that he was on duty out in the cold, it was easy for Clayton to go around him without the man even noticing him. Once past the guard, he flattened himself against a tree and scanned the area again. The roar of the rain was loud. It would drown out most anything.

While some might think the rain would keep others from searching, that wasn't the case with Clayton. He was used to going on missions in all kinds of weather. However, his targets weren't SEALs. They were ordinary citizens who knew ranching and hunting. They were the type who would believe the weather would keep him at home. Which meant they wouldn't be too concerned with looking for him since their attention would be on the cattle stirred up by the lightning and thunder.

Still, Clayton kept to cover as he headed in the direction the guard had been glancing. A quarter of a mile later, he heard the moos. He blew out a breath, and it formed a cloud before him. Clayton crept closer until he came to the pasture where his cattle were being held. As soon as he saw the E brand, the fury that he'd kept at bay filled him.

It would be so easy for him to find the men guarding the herd and disable them so he could take his cattle back. But that meant moving the herd over miles of land that wasn't his. He would have to come back with reinforcements now that he knew where the cattle were. Just as he was moving away, something out of the corner of his eye caught his attention. He looked over to find Brice.

The teen was on his stomach, a rifle pointed at something. Clayton shifted positions and saw the man on horseback. His cowboy hat was pulled low, shadowing his face while the collar of his raincoat was pulled up.

He watched as Brice sighted down the barrel. Clayton couldn't let the kid kill anyone. He started crawling toward him when lightning crackled through the sky, lighting up everything like daylight, a second before there was a loud boom.

The cattle, already spooked, began to shift, looking for a way to run. And that was right in Brice's direction. There was no way Clayton could get to him in time. He shouted Brice's name, but the rain and the thunder drowned out his voice.

Clayton caught sight of the teen rolling out of the way before the herd started toward him. In the next second, Clayton was up against a tree to stay clear.

The man guarding the cattle leaned low over his horse as he raced to get ahead of the herd to halt them before this turned into a stampede. Clayton watched the man for a long time and noted that he slowly and steadily calmed the herd.

By the time that was done, Clayton no longer spotted Brice. He glanced at the man to make sure his attention was still on the cattle before Clayton went after Brice.

But there was no sign of the boy.

Finally, Clayton started back to the ranch, hoping that Brice was headed there himself.

\* \* \*

Just as Abby predicted, she wasn't able to sleep. She paced her room before finally going to Clayton's. Except he wasn't there. And that sent her into a tailspin of worry.

She went downstairs, hoping he was in the barn. With the lights out, she sat in the living room and stared at the barns and pastures for hours, but there was no sign of Clayton.

It was an hour before dawn when she saw him walking toward the back door. He stopped on the porch and began to remove his sodden clothes. She jumped up and rushed to the downstairs bath for a towel.

She met him at the door when he walked inside, naked. Their gazes met. She spotted the remnants of black paint on his face and held the towel out to him. He dried off and scrubbed the paint from his face, then wrapped the towel around his waist and held out his hand. Wordlessly, they walked up the stairs to her room.

There was so much she wanted to ask him, but he dropped the towel, lifted the covers, and waited for her to climb into bed before he followed her. As he pulled her against him, she felt his cool skin.

He stared at the ceiling, seemingly content with just holding her, though he was careful not to touch her injured arm. After several minutes, she found her eyes closing. She must have dozed off because when she opened her eyes, the room was lighter.

"Sleep," he murmured and kissed her forehead.

He was warm to the touch now. Solid and reassuring, she began to drift back to sleep when she remembered how she'd found him. "What happened?"

"I found the herd."

She let her mind contemplate just what he had done. "Ronald Baxter?"

"Yep. I didn't do anything. I just wanted to locate them."

"And?"

Clayton blew out a breath. "I do know him, though I've not seen him since I graduated. What's his reputation?"

"I haven't heard anyone talk about him in ages," she said. "Then again, I don't hang around those I graduated with. Not that I was in the popular crowd anyway. Besides, he was a senior when I was a sophomore."

While Clayton played with her hair, he nodded. "I need to know more about Ronnie."

"Why? Why not just go get your cattle now that you know who has them?"

"They're not on his land."

"Oh." She frowned, still not understanding. "But you know Ronald took them?"

Clayton put his other hand beneath his head. "I suspect. I never saw him. It'll be hard to prove it's him unless the herd is on his land, or he's with them."

"There's also Brice."

"Yeah," he murmured.

She frowned as she shifted her head to look at him. "Is there something you aren't telling me?"

"I'm still sorting through things."

"Which means there's something you aren't telling me."

He cut his eyes to her. "I don't want to worry you."

"Well, too late. I'm there now. And if you don't tell me what it is, my mind will spin all sorts of scenarios.

Trust me when I say, it'll be worse for everyone. I'll bug you, I'll go to Brice, I'll—"

"I get it," Clayton said with a small laugh. He kissed her forehead, his grin fading. "You know I talked to both of your brothers yesterday."

She nodded her head, her stomach in knots. Her worry for her brothers mixed with her own fear and had her so on edge that she couldn't shut off her mind and stop imagining all the things that could have happened.

"Caleb wishes he could've done more. He's upset that he didn't stop you from being hurt."

Abby shook her head in disbelief. "It's because of Caleb that the bullet didn't do more damage."

"I've told him that. He's talking about things, and he's willing to listen. It'll take him some time, but he'll be okay."

"And Brice?"

Clayton's lips flattened for a moment. "He wouldn't talk to me. He'd closed himself off. Just as I suspected, he's trying to sort through things to find an outcome where he wins."

"And?" she pressed.

"He wants to fix things on his own."

She frowned in confusion. "How do you know that if he didn't talk to you?"

"Because I saw him tonight with a gun pointed at one of the men guarding the herd."

# Chapter 29

It only took a few words to turn a world upside down. Abby knew this from experience, and yet Clayton's words sent her spiraling.

"He didn't do anything," Clayton quickly added.

Abby rolled onto her back and tried to get her breathing under control. "He was going to shoot somebody."

"I don't know what was going through Brice's head," Clayton said as he pushed up on an elbow to look down at her. "I told you what I saw."

She turned her gaze to him. "I didn't even know he knew how to handle a gun."

"Don't go down that road. Focus on the fact that he didn't fire the weapon. You can talk to him later about it."

"Where is he?" she asked, sitting up.

"Back at the bunkhouse."

"Oh, my God," she said and scooted to the other side of the bed where she got up, wincing as she accidentally used her bad arm. She walked to her bag of clothes that her brothers had packed for her. "I need to go see him."

"Abby," Clayton said, suddenly beside her.

She jerked in surprise. "How the hell do you move so fast?"

One side of his lips lifted in a grin. "Habit. Listen, please calm down."

"I can't calm down. These people broke into my house, shot at my brothers, and then shot at me. Now you tell me Brice was there with a gun!"

Clayton began to grab her shoulders then dropped his hands. "I looked for him before I returned last night. He didn't do anything. Now he's back."

She lifted her gaze to the ceiling, praying for patience. "Once Brice sets his mind to something, he'll continue on whatever path that is until he succeeds."

"That's different than taking another person's life," he argued.

"Unless those people attacked his family."

Clayton's brow furrowed in a frown. "Dammit," he muttered before turning on his heel. "Stay here. I'm going to talk to him."

"I'm coming."

She'd only gotten two steps when he whirled around. "Abby, do you think he'll talk to you about it?"

"No," she replied. Her brother liked to keep things bottled up.

"And if he's gone back?" Clayton asked.

She nodded in understanding. "You'll take off to go find him, and I won't be able to keep up."

"Exactly."

"But I have to know either way," she insisted.

Clayton hesitated, a muscle in his jaw working. "Can you be dressed in five minutes?"

"Give me two."

He gave a nod and was gone. Abby hurried to her clothes, discarded her nightshirt, and found a pair of jeans. She bit her lip when her arm began to pound, but she had no choice but to use it because there was no getting up a pair of jeans with one hand.

She chose an oversized sweatshirt that was the easiest thing she had to put on but it left her covered in sweat and shaking from the agony. Then she decided against socks as she pushed her feet into her slightly used gray Ugg boots she'd gotten at Goodwill.

When she reached the door, Clayton was walking from his room completely dressed. He looked at her, his lips thinning. "You've hurt yourself."

"I'll survive."

They walked side by side down the stairs to the back door. Clayton paused and helped her into his mother's rain jacket before he put on his coat and hat. As they left the house, Abby pulled up the hood of the jacket in an effort to keep the rain off her.

It wasn't the precipitation she didn't like. It was the cold *and* the rain. The temperatures had plummeted overnight, leaving her chilled to her very bones. She clamped her teeth together and practically had to jog to keep up with Clayton's long strides.

He directed them to the UTV. She climbed into the passenger side and closed the door, grateful to be out of the rain. He started the engine and pointed the vehicle toward the bunkhouse while she held her arm, trying to will the pain to lessen.

When they pulled up to the side of the building, Clayton shut off the engine and turned his head to her. "Stay here. I'm going to check to see if he's in there."

Clayton had no sooner opened the door than a figure stepped from behind the bunkhouse. When Abby saw it was Brice dripping wet with a rifle slung over his shoulder, she started to get out of the SxS. But Clayton's hand on her leg stopped her.

"Let me," he whispered.

Somehow, she stayed put, wishing that she'd made her brothers stay in the main house last night. But before dinner, Caleb had asked her if he and Brice could sleep in the bunkhouse. She hadn't had the heart to deny them.

Her gaze moved from Brice to Clayton and back to Brice when her brother walked beside the UTV before climbing into the bed. Clayton got into the vehicle and started the engine.

As he drove off, Clayton said, "He won't talk to me. But I did convince him to come back to the house with us."

She slumped in the seat. But no sooner had her mind grasped that he was fine than Abby knew she had to think of something to say. The problem was that she didn't know how to handle this situation or even what to say to Brice.

Back at the house, the three of them filed inside. Clayton walked Brice upstairs for a hot shower and a change of clothes. Needing something to do, Abby went to the kitchen, but she could barely move her arm.

As she stood there with tears clouding her vision,

wondering what to do, a soothing arm came around her. Justine pulled her close and held her.

"It's all right. Why don't you sit down while I get breakfast going? My goodness, Abby, you're shaking. Sit, sit," she ordered as she removed the raincoat. "I'm going to get a blanket for you and start some coffee."

Abby numbly sat at the bar while Justine draped a thick blanket around her. Within minutes, a cup of coffee with steam wafting up from the liquid was placed before her. She wrapped her hands around the mug, letting the heat seep through her palms.

She stared at the quartz counter as Justine moved about the kitchen. Every sip of the coffee helped to warm her. Then, finally, Clayton returned. He took one look at her and went to the bottle of pain meds. She shook her head when he lifted it. The pills clouded her mind and put her to sleep. Right now, she needed to think. Later, she'd take one.

Clayton blew out a breath but relented. He returned, holding a cup of coffee for himself. "The gun hasn't been fired."

"At least there's that," she murmured.

Justine stirred the pancake batter, holding the bowl against her. "Clayton told me what happened. I'm not condoning what Brice almost did, but you are his world, Abby. He felt helpless when you were shot."

"And he's afraid of telling me anything in case Ronnie and his men get to you before I get to them," Clayton said.

Justine shot her a sad smile. "So he tried to take matters into his own hands."

"I don't know what to say to him," she admitted.

Clayton put his hand atop hers. "Just be there for him. Listen if he wants to talk."

"And don't push him if he doesn't," Justine added.

Mother and son shared a look that spoke volumes about the past. If they could get through Landon's death, then she would make sure she, Brice, and Caleb got through this.

Another fifteen minutes passed before Ben walked into the kitchen beside Brice. Her brother's dark brown locks were still wet, but he was no longer shivering. The too big clothes he wore were most likely Clayton's.

Abby turned to Brice and opened her arms. He rushed to her, clasping her tight. She didn't even care that he was hurting her arm.

"I almost did something stupid," he said.

The last time Brice cried was when their mother left, but this was the second time in two days that she heard the tears in his voice. "But you didn't. That's all that matters."

He pulled back, sniffing. "Damn, Abby. Your shoulder. I forgot."

"I don't feel it," she lied.

He gave her a flat look, telling her he didn't believe her. "I'm ready to tell y'all everything."

"First, we eat," Justine said and motioned for Brice to get the plates.

Clayton leaned close and said, "Mom always thinks things are dealt with better on a full stomach."

"Don't come between my wife and food," Ben said with brows raised. "You don't want to see what happens."

To her surprise, Abby found herself smiling. She slid from the stool and carried her coffee into the dining room. Clayton held out her chair for her before taking his seat across from her.

Brice was silent as he put out the plates and utensils while Justine set the stack of pancakes and the syrup in the middle of the table. After the blessing, the food was passed around.

Once everyone had taken a few bites, Ben look to Brice, "You can begin your story whenever you're ready, son."

Brice set down his fork and swallowed the bite in his mouth. Then he turned his head to Abby, his pale blue eyes meeting hers. "I'm sorry. All of this is because of my idiotic mistake."

"You owned up to what happened," she said with a smile. "That makes me proud."

He glanced away. "I met Ronnie at the feed store after school one day when I was trying to find a job. He hired me to help clean up the place he'd just bought. The pay wasn't much, but it was something."

"I had no idea you had a job. I thought you were staying after school for basketball practice."

Brice shook his head, his shoulders drooping. "I was thrown off the team for my attitude and slipping grades. I was going to wait until Christmas to tell you about that and the job when I surprised you with the money."

Abby set down her fork, no longer able to eat. "I don't care about basketball or why you aren't on the team. All I want is honesty between us."

"I know. I hated lying to you," he said softly. Brice then blew out a breath. "At first, I thought the job with

Ronnie was a stroke of luck. It didn't take me long to realize that he'd heard about the crowd I used to hang with and my brush with the cops."

"So he went looking for you," Ben said.

Brice nodded slowly before meeting Abby's gaze. "Ronnie came to me with a plan. He said if I joined them, he'd give me five thousand dollars. All I had to do was help them steal some cattle. When I asked if it would hurt whoever we stole from, he told me ranches have insurance for such things."

Her brother's face crumpled as he struggled to get out the next words. "I know you've always told me that the easy way out of things is rarely ever the right way, but I was tired of seeing you struggle to pay the bills and buy us food. You were working yourself to death, and I wanted to give us all a cushion in the bank to get caught up on past-due bills. And I really wanted to go to the grocery store and buy whatever we wanted."

Abby didn't even try to stop the tears. She put her hand on his face. "Your heart was in the right place. I can't fault you for that."

"No," Brice bit out. "But I made another stupid decision."

Clayton shook his head. "Someone took advantage of you, Brice. That's completely different."

Her brother swallowed and swiped at his cheeks that were wet with his tears. "Ronnie told me if I said anything to anyone they'd kill Caleb and then come after Abby. I couldn't take the chance of something happening to my family. Then they came, and I hadn't said a word to anyone."

"That's on me," Abby said. "I found something at

work and pieced it together. I'm the one who gave Ronnie's address to Clayton."

"And I found the cattle last night. When I saw you," Clayton said.

Brice looked between them, resolve forming in his eyes. "So we can take them down now?"

"Yep. Want to help?" Abby asked.

Her brother sat up straighter. "Please."

# Chapter 30

The need for action, to take back what had been stolen and set right what had been broken burned through Clayton. For the first time, his mission assisted both himself and his family.

While serving in the military, he'd gone on hundreds of operations that protected his country—and therefore his family. But this was different. This served no one but those he cared about.

Christmas music played, and the Christmas lights on the tree and in the garland were turned on as if his mother wanted to remind him that there was more going on than hunting down a thief. Clayton stood in the doorway and watched Abby with Brice and Caleb as they sat before the giant Christmas tree in the living room. Over the last week, more presents had been put under the tree. Clayton knew his mother had bought things for the Harpers, and he whole-heartedly approved.

Since Brice relayed his story, the teen looked as if the

weight of the world had been removed from his shoulders. He laughed and smiled with ease now.

When Clayton thought about how close he'd come to losing Abby, his stomach churned viciously. He'd known upon meeting her that she was different than anyone else. The more he got to know her, the more he liked what he learned.

It hadn't taken him long to fall for her, and to fall hard. He'd wanted her to know that his feelings were growing fast and deep, because he didn't want her to think she was just a passing fancy. Not when she meant so much more.

He saw a future with Abby. That was special since he hadn't seen his future in years. With her, he felt as if he'd finally found the other half of his soul.

Without a doubt, he knew he loved Abby. He'd suspected it before the shooting, but it was after he discovered that she'd been hurt that he knew for sure he couldn't live without her.

It was just a little over a week until Christmas. The holiday had never meant that much to him, but that was before Abby. Now, he couldn't wait to spend it with her. He wanted to wake up that morning and walk with her downstairs to watch Caleb and Brice open their presents.

He wanted to watch her open her own presents.

"When are you going to tell her?" his father asked as he came up beside him.

Clayton looked at him with a frown.

His dad smiled. "It's obvious you're in love with her, son. You should tell her."

"What if she doesn't feel the same?" That had been

weighing on his mind ever since she'd shut down when he tried to tell her of his feelings after they had made love the first time.

"How will you know if you don't give her a chance to answer?"

The doorbell rang, interrupting their conversation. Clayton met Abby's gaze before he opened the door to Danny and two other sheriff's deputies. When Clayton stepped aside to let them in, Brice was beside him. The teen stood tall with his chin lifted and resolve in his blue eyes.

"I'm glad you finally came around," Danny said to Brice as he and the others filed in.

Clayton closed the door and started toward the office when he saw Abby standing in the foyer with Caleb. He walked to her and pulled her against him for a long, slow kiss. Desire heated his blood, making him yearn to take her upstairs to his bed and make love to her all day.

He pulled away and smiled at her before he made his way to his father's office to begin planning how they would take down Ronnie Baxter. Clayton closed the office doors behind him and found the three deputies, his father, Brice, and Shane looking at him. It had only been two hours since Brice told his story, but in that time, Clayton had already done most of the work.

"We should have more men," Danny said as he crossed his arms over his chest.

Ben nodded in agreement. "We will. Shane will take another ten from here."

"I'm not sure if that'll be enough," Danny argued.

Clayton walked to the map of the area that he'd hung on the wall. "It probably won't be. I'm just not sure who we can trust. I don't want Baxter tipped off before we get there."

Danny's arms dropped to his sides. "Are you telling me that you think there's someone working with Baxter in the department?"

"Shane placed the call about the stolen cattle, but no one came. It was by sheer accident that you were on that back road and saw what was going on. I've not investigated if Ronnie does have someone at the sheriff's department in his pocket, but right now, I don't want to chance it."

A muscle ticked in Danny's jaw. "Point taken. And before you get started, I have some good news. Nathan Gilroy has been caught in Galveston on a ship headed to Cuba. It seems he had a bit of a gambling problem, and debts he couldn't pay."

"So he used our money to pay off the debts?" Ben asked.

Danny shook his head. "No, Nathan just wanted to get out."

"And the money?" Clayton asked.

The deputy shook his head before removing his cowboy hat. "He spent a lot, but I suspect by the time the FBI is through with him, he'll have given up the bank accounts he's used."

"Well," Ben said as he looked at Clayton. "One problem nearly solved."

Clayton nodded and then focused on the map. He pointed out Baxter's land and the adjacent parcel that they were using to hold the cattle. "They're antsy," Clayton said. "They're expecting something, so we need to come in undetected. I've already scouted spots where they'll likely set up guards." He circled the sections with a red marker as everyone stared at the map. "There's a road on two sides of Baxter's property, which makes it easy for them to know if someone's coming."

Danny snorted. "Yeah, because the other option is to walk across miles of land in order to reach it."

"That's what I did," Clayton said.

Brice added, "Me, too."

Abby stood at the window looking out the back of the house to the horses that were being saddled as she thought about Clayton's kiss. He'd never shown that kind of affection in front of others before, especially not her brothers.

"I like him, you know," Caleb said.

She looked over her shoulder at her youngest brother and smiled. "I do, too."

Caleb walked to her side. "It's not the ranch or this house, although both are amazing. His folks are good people. But really, it's the way Clayton looks at you."

"How does he look at me?" she asked, wanting to know.

Needing to know.

Caleb grinned, his brown eyes crinkling at the corners. "Like you're a buffet, and he wants to dive in."

Abby couldn't help but laugh at her brother's analogy. "Is that so?"

"Just like you look at him like he's the gold at the end of a rainbow and you're expecting it to disappear."

"Because I am," she admitted.

Caleb bumped his shoulder into her good one. "Don't be, sis. Clayton isn't the leaving kind."

"It's not that simple. Sometimes, things happen, and people drift apart."

"But wouldn't you rather see where this takes you than to always wonder?"

If Abby thought Justine's words were wise, then she was bowled over at her fourteen-year-old brother's wisdom. "Yes."

"Then stop holding back. You like him. I can see that. Go for it, Abby. Me and Brice will always have your back no matter what."

She rested her head on his shoulder. "It's scary."

"I'm sure it is, but you can't let life continue to pass you by. You've done enough for us."

"It'll never be enough."

He wrapped an arm around her. "And that's why we love you so much."

"You're going to make some girl a wonderful husband. Or guy. You know. If you're into that sort of thing."

Caleb laughed softly. "I'm all about the girls, sis. It's the boobs. I love them."

"Okay, okay," she hurried to say as she wrinkled her nose. "I get it. You don't have to say more. And I don't need to know more."

"I don't care if I ever find someone or not. If I do, great. If I don't, it's not the end of the world. Just look at Shane."

Abby lifted her head to look at Caleb. She didn't share Shane's story with him, but she would someday. Shane had loved, and loved hard, though he didn't have his woman with him. Abby prayed the same didn't happen to Caleb or Brice.

She smiled, wondering what the future held for her

brothers. "You're too young to be thinking about mar-
riage anyway. You've got plenty of time."

"Exactly," Caleb said with a wink.

The conversation moved on to other things, safe
things like school and baseball. Two hours later, when
the rain was nothing more than a fine mist, the men
exited the office. Abby stood from the sofa and walked
to the back door and the waiting horses. Ben stopped
beside Justine as they watched the others.

Brice came to her, and Abby saw that the boy she
knew was falling away as he became a man right before her eyes. She'd never been more proud of him.

"I'm going to make this right," Brice said.

She pulled him forward to kiss his cheek. "Be safe
and come home to us."

"I will. Love you, Abby."

"Love you, too," she replied.

Caleb walked out with Brice. When Abby looked
past Clayton, his parents had disappeared. Leaving them
alone.

"The same goes for you," she told Clayton as she
closed the distance between them. "I need you to be safe
and come home."

He tenderly touched her face before his lips were
on hers. There was no denying the depth of emotion that
he poured into the kiss. It curled her toes and made her
knees weak. She forgot all about the pain of her wound
as she clung to him with her right arm. His hand cupped
the back of her head while his other splayed on her back.

Abby bit back a groan when he ended the kiss. Then
his pale green eyes gazed at her as if memorizing her
face.

"I'll always come back to you," he said. "Always."

She was so shocked at his words that she couldn't form a reply. Then he stepped back and pivoted, walking out of the house to the others. Her gaze was riveted on him as he swung up onto the bay gelding. He, Brice, Shane, one of the deputies, and ten ranch hands rode out. And she didn't miss the rifle strapped to Clayton's saddle.

Caleb came back into the house, looking longingly at the group. "Mr. Ben and I will be guarding the ranch," Caleb stated.

"Where are Danny and the other deputy?" she asked.

"They're going a different route in their cars."

Abby returned her gaze to Clayton. She stared at him and Brice until they were no longer visible. Everything should go smoothly. Then again, Clayton was going after the men who had shot her.

"Don't worry," Caleb said. "Clayton will take care of everything."

But at what cost? "Yeah."

"He was a SEAL," Caleb stated.

"I know."

He rolled his eyes. "A *SEAL*, Abby. Do you know what kind of shit they can do?"

"Watch your language. And, yes. Well, sort of."

His eyes went wide. "They are badasses. Like true badasses. I wish I could see him in action."

"I don't. It's bad enough that Brice is in the thick of it."

Caleb glanced out the window. "Clayton won't let anything happen to him. He promised me and Brice that he'd always look out for us."

"When did he say that?"

"Yesterday after he brought you home from the hospital. I believe him, Abby. Like I said, he's not the leaving kind."

No, she was beginning to think that Clayton was the forever kind.

# Chapter 31

It all had to go according to plan. Clayton knew if one thing got messed up, then Baxter could get away with cattle rustling. Clayton wanted to catch him instead of putting Brice in the position of testifying—though it would likely come down to having the teen's cooperation anyway.

The fourteen of them reached the edge of East land. There were still miles of property to cover, however. Luckily, they could do that atop the horses.

Thanks to the deputy with him, who was there in case any homeowners got ornery, they were able to eat up the miles. Clayton kept them hidden as much as possible, but sometimes, they didn't have that option.

The closer he got to Baxter's ranch, the more focused Clayton became. It had always been that way during a mission. Though the men with him weren't SEALs, he trusted each of them to do their parts.

Most of the men from the East Ranch were there simply to keep the cattle from being driven off by Baxter's men, but that didn't mean the East men wouldn't step in if needed.

"Danny and Pete are in place," Roger, the sheriff deputy with them, said as he put away his cell phone.

Clayton nodded. His group was just a few miles from 4B land. He grew antsy. He was ready for this showdown with Ronnie. The only thing Clayton was concerned about was whether Baxter would be there.

"What the fuck, Gus!"

Gus ignored Terry as he stared at Berny. "You should get to a doctor."

"I'll be fine," Berny stated, his skin a sickly green shade.

"You look like shit. You're drunk, and your arm is broken. Hell, for all we know, your ribs are, too."

Berny shook his head of red hair. "My ribs are only bruised. I've had a broken rib before so I know the pain."

Gus fought to keep his cool. "Whatever. The point is, you'll be of no use to me."

"You mean *us*," said a deep voice behind him.

Gus turned to see Ronnie walk up. His old friend wore his favorite black Stetson hat and the large belt buckle pronouncing him as Steer Wrestling Champion from the previous year.

"You don't look happy to see me," Ronnie said.

The problem Gus always had was figuring out when Ronnie was joking. And when he wasn't. Because thinking Ronnie was teasing when he was really angry resulted in pain for whoever was that stupid.

"You know I am," Gus answered neutrally, just to be safe.

Ronnie flashed a wide smile and slapped him on the arm. "I'm just fucking with you. Damn, Gus. You'd think after knowing me for over twenty years, you'd recognize the difference."

"I'm on edge."

"I can see that." Ronnie looked over his shoulder to Terry and Berny. "Why didn't you take care of the dead weight?"

Gus didn't need to ask what Ronnie was referring to. Though Gus might be many things, he wasn't a killer. Nor would he turn into one. "He's hurt, but Berny swears he can do the job."

"You'd better hope he can," Ronnie threatened in a low voice. "Because you just vouched for him. If Berny slips up, it's your ass on the line."

Gus looked into Ronnie's blue orbs. "No."

"Excuse me?" Ronnie said, surprise flickering briefly in his eyes before they narrowed on Gus.

"You chose these two. I told you my reservations about them, but you ignored me. If anyone's ass is on the line, it's yours."

Ronnie stared at him a long time before he gave a snort, his lips curling into a grin that didn't show an ounce of humor. "One of the reasons we remained friends this long was because you were a spineless follower. Don't go find courage now, Gus. You won't like the outcome."

"You're right," Gus said. "I've always followed you, but I've saved your ass several times as well. Perhaps you need to remember that. Because right now, you need friends."

Ronnie looked away and drew in a deep breath. "Fuck. I always hate when you're right." He swiveled his gaze back to Gus. "Keep your courage then."

He walked to his horse and mounted, leaving Gus to draw in a shaky breath. After a few seconds, he, too, climbed atop his horse. Gus looked over at Berny, who still looked a bit green, whether it was from the hangover or the pain, Gus didn't care, as long as Berny stayed in the saddle and did his job.

"Let's get the cattle moved," Ronnie said and spurred his horse into a gallop.

Terry quickly followed and then Berny. Gus hesitated. Apparently, he was the only one worried about Clayton. Terry had thought the SEAL would show up last night, and when he hadn't, Terry believed they were free and clear. But Terry didn't know Clayton. Gus did.

Gus recalled how single-minded Clayton could be back in high school. That had more than likely been magnified ten times over after Clayton joined the military. There was no doubt in Gus's mind that the Easts knew who had their cattle.

If Brice hadn't ratted them out, then that meant Clayton had put things together on his own. Which meant that they were royally fucked.

Gus nudged his horse forward and caught up with the others. He looked back over his shoulder as the hairs on the back of his neck rose.

\* \* \*

"Easy," Clayton told the others. "They can't see us. He's just checking to see if anyone is following."

Shane adjusted his seat in the saddle. "We can't follow them."

"No, but I know where they're headed," Clayton said as he waited for the four men, including Baxter, to disappear over the hill before he turned his horse. "Single file."

The others fell in behind him as they moved like ghosts over the land.


"Aren't they the most beautiful things you've ever seen?" Ronnie asked.

Gus looked out over the seventy head of cattle, his gaze going to the E brand. "They're fine stock. It's why the Easts do so well."

"It's time for some competition."

But was it really competition if Ronnie stole the very animals he intended to go up against the Easts with? Gus kept his thoughts to himself, though. It would do no good to share them with Ronnie.

"You're worrying me, Gus."

He turned his head to look at Ronnie. "You shouldn't be."

"I'm not so sure. Before the shooting with Abby, your head was on straight. Now, your mind seems everywhere but with me."

"If that were true, I wouldn't be here now."

Ronnie's blue eyes narrowed. "You're scared."

"You're damn right I am. It's not a matter of *if* Clayton East comes. It's a matter of *when*."

Ronnie laughed while shaking his head. He turned

his gaze back to the cattle. "Clayton is just a man. He's nothing more, and I've got a bullet with his name on it to prove it."

"Since when do you talk so easily about taking someone's life?"

"Since I set my sights on becoming the biggest ranch in a hundred-mile radius." Ronnie's head swiveled to him. "I told you I was prepared to do whatever was needed to get what I want."

Gus was so taken aback that it took him a moment to find words. "Stealing cattle, yes. Helping Gilroy get out of town with the Easts' money after he told you the easiest place to find the cattle, of course. Using Gloria and her CPA firm to help you, definitely. You never said anything about killing anyone."

"Things change," Ronnie said with a shrug. "If you're going to ride with me, you have to be ready for anything. And that means taking someone's life if I order it."

During his years as Ronnie's friend, Gus had done a lot of illegal things. He'd become a master thief, as well. They'd partied hard, gone up against drug dealers, and evaded police on numerous occasions. Gus had been prepared to go to jail for any of it.

But he drew the line at murder. Even if it was Ronnie telling him to do it.

"You're with me, right, Gus?" Ronnie asked in a low, deadly tone.

Gus gave a single nod. "Always."

After several tense minutes where Ronnie stared at him, Gus was already planning on how he would sneak away when the time was right. He wasn't stupid enough

to go to the cops, but he would get as far from Texas—
and Ronnie—as he could.

"I knew I could count on you," Ronnie said finally.

Gus looked behind him. He couldn't shake the feeling that they were being watched. Was it his fear of
Clayton East that manifested this false sensation?

Or was the SEAL out there even now?

"They're about to move them," Shane whispered.

Clayton nodded, his lips flattening. "It's time to end
this."

Shane turned and signaled a group of three of their
men who quickly did the same to the other standing with
the horses. Clayton counted out the two minutes until
he was sure everyone in their group was ready to move.
He assumed everyone was in position. If they weren't,
then everything could go to Hell in a handbasket pretty
damn quickly.

"We'll be ready," Shane said.

Clayton gave a nod and stood before walking from
the brush he'd been hiding behind to stand on a small
hill. Just as he expected, Baxter's gaze found him seconds later.

"Well, I'll be damned," Ronnie said with a cocky
smile. "If it isn't Clayton East in the flesh. I'd heard ru-
mors you were back in town. Real sad about your dad,
by the way."

Clayton didn't respond. He'd dealt with men like
Baxter numerous times, and he knew Ronnie wanted a
discussion. He wanted to show Clayton that he wasn't
scared—that he was smarter.

But Clayton wasn't going to engage the bastard. Instead, he planned to piss Ronnie off. And if he were really lucky, Baxter might feel a fraction of the rage that was boiling within Clayton.

Gus hastily looked around before he told Ronnie, "I think he's alone."

"Of course he's alone," Ronnie stated with a laugh. "What's brought you out here, East?"

Clayton focused on his breathing. It was either that or attack Ronnie.

"Clayton?" Gus called.

He glanced at Gus before returning his attention to Ronnie. Already, Clayton could see how his silence was getting underneath Ronnie's skin.

It helped to calm some of the primal need for revenge that churned through Clayton. But it was a temporary fix. Baxter hadn't just stolen part of the ranch's livelihood, he'd knowingly colluded with a minor, putting Brice in danger. And he'd ordered Abby shot.

Ronnie leaned forward in his saddle and propped his left forearm on the saddle horn. "You better run along home, Clayton. You're out of your depth here. And SEAL or not, you're outgunned."

As soon as Baxter said the words, two other men pulled guns on Clayton. He kept his gaze on Ronnie, though he noticed that Gus didn't reach for his weapon— and neither did Ronnie.

"I'm not going anywhere without my cattle," Clayton stated.

As one, Brice, Shane, the ten ranch hands, Danny, and the two other sheriff's deputies all stepped from their hiding places, guns trained on the four rustlers.

# Chapter 32

It should've ended there. Clayton had hoped it would end there. Then he saw that wild look in Ronnie's eyes, and he had known bloodshed was coming.

The first bullet ricocheted off the tree to his left. Bark splintered and slammed into him. Clayton dove to the ground, rolling to the right as Gus turned his horse around and attempted to flee.

He didn't get far because Ronnie shot him in the back.

Clayton held out his hand for Shane to toss him his rifle. Shane stayed close to Brice to ensure the teen wouldn't get hurt. Knowing Brice was safe, Clayton turned his attention to Ronnie. It would be so easy to shoot the bastard and end it all, but Clayton was tired of the killing. It was one of the reasons he'd left the Navy. And he wasn't going to bring that home with him now.

The sound of gunfire erupted as Baxter and his two

other men opened fire while the cattle began to shift, looking to get away from the noise. In short order, the two other rustlers were tossing aside their weapons and dismounting. Ronnie targeted a few shots at Danny before turning his gun on Clayton.

Clayton took aim, and with one pull of the trigger, shot the gun from Ronnie's hand. Baxter let out a yelp as the herd broke through a fence and started running away. Several of the ranch hands ran to the horses and raced to contain the cattle. Clayton knew they would get the animals back, so he kept his attention on Baxter.

He walked to Ronnie who pulled a knife from the scabbard attached to his saddle and jumped from his horse. Clayton looked at the long blade of the weapon as he tossed Shane the rifle. Then he calmly reached down and pulled the knife from his boot.

"I'm not scared of you," Baxter said.

Clayton began circling him. "Good."

"You think you're something special, don't you," Ronnie sneered as he flung away his hat. "All that money and good looks got you a lot. Then you became a hero. All that's going to change soon."

All around Clayton, he could hear Danny and the deputies handcuffing Ronnie's two other men. "It's going to be pretty hard for you to do that behind bars."

"Oh, I'm not going to jail." Ronnie lobbed his blade back and forth between his hands.

"Are you going to play with that thing or do something with it?" Clayton challenged.

Ronnie's face mottled red with rage as he attacked.

Clayton backed up, evading the slicing movements. Baxter was better than he'd expected. Ronnie ducked one of Clayton's jabs before lunging at him, knocking his hat off. Clayton jerked back, sucking in his stomach and hunching over as the knife came close to slicing him.

Again and again, they each attacked, both coming close to drawing blood on the other numerous times.

Baxter laughed as he kicked Clayton in the chest, shoving him backward. "You thought you'd take me down easily, but you don't know me."

"And you don't know me," Clayton said.

They came together in a clash of strength. Clayton blocked Baxter's downward arc. They stood face to-face, each trying to overpower the other. Ronnie was using brute strength, while Clayton was trained to look for an opponent's weakness and exploit it.

Clayton swung his leg wide before wrapping it around Baxter's and leaning into him. The force of his momentum knocked Ronnie onto his back where Clayton quickly divested him of the weapon and had his knife at Baxter's throat.

Ronnie looked up at him and scoffed. "You'll never win."

"I did today, and that's what matters."

"I knew that little shit would tell you."

Clayton pushed the blade harder against Ronnie's throat, drawing blood. "Brice didn't tell us anything. You thought you were a great mastermind, when in fact, you left a paper trail, Baxter. It was Abby who figured it out."

"Gus should've killed her."

It would be so simple to slit his throat. All Clayton had to do was pull his arm away while applying pressure. Then he could watch Ronnie bleed out right there.

"Clayton."

It was Brice's voice that got through Clayton's red haze of fury. He leaned down close to Ronnie. "Know that I'm giving you your life today, but if you harm my family or the Harpers or I even *think* you sent someone to hurt them, I'll come for you. And I will kill you."

Clayton rose to his feet and turned his back to Ronnie. He heard Danny reading Baxter his rights while cuffing him. Clayton looked down at Brice, who stood beside him holding his hat.

"We did it," Brice said.

Clayton took his hat and set it on his head. "We certainly did."

Danny came to stand beside them. "Gus is dead."

Shane removed his hat to run his hands through his hair. "Shot in the back by a coward."

"I can't believe I thought I could learn anything from these men," Brice said.

Danny blew out a breath and looked at the approaching herd of cattle. "Lessons, son. That's what life is all about."

"Come on, Brice," Shane said. "Let's help the others get the cattle into pens so we can get them loaded into trailers and back onto East land." Shane paused and looked at Clayton. "By the way, Cochise has been found as well."

They really had done it. Clayton watched Shane and

Brice mount their horses and ride away. Somehow, it had all worked out, but he knew more than anyone just how close he'd come to killing Ronnie.

"I suppose you'll come to the station and file charges," Danny said.

He nodded. "Definitely."

"You did good here today, Clayton. And if you had killed Baxter, it would've been in self-defense."

He looked at Danny and smiled. "I'll always be a SEAL, but that part of my life is behind me. I've got something else to look forward to."

"You mean some*one* else," Danny said with a wink.

"Yeah. I do."

Danny slapped him on the back. "Good for you. Now, let's get you home so you can get moving on that. I suppose there'll be a wedding soon."

A wedding. Clayton stood there as a slow smile spread across his face.

"I take that to mean yes," Danny said with a chuckle. His laugh grew louder as he walked to the patrol car.

The waiting was the worst. Abby could practically feel years being taken from her as she anxiously waited for some type of word.

Each time she thought of Clayton getting hurt, she felt sick inside. In a short amount of time, he'd come to mean so very much to her. She'd tried to ignore it and even attempted to run from it. But there was no getting away from someone like Clayton—and she didn't want to.

That's when she knew what her brothers had apparently already seen—she was in love with Clayton

East. It terrified her, but worse was the thought of him not being with her, of them not sharing their lives together.

When she and Justine saw Ben jump into his truck, Abby opened the door to ask Caleb what was going on. Before she could get a word out, her youngest brother ran to the vehicle.

"Caleb!" she yelled as he got into the truck and it sped off.

Justine sighed loudly. "It must be good news. Ben was grinning."

"I just wish I knew," Abby said as she walked back into the house and closed the door.

"You should take one of your pain pills. I can see you're hurting."

Abby shook her head. "I can't. Not yet."

"You've been saying that since dawn."

"I'm good," she insisted.

Frankly, she was. Being so worried about Brice and Clayton, she didn't feel the ache in her arm as much. That would probably come back to bite her later, but for now, she was grateful.

To pass the time, she helped decorate another batch of cookies. Abby then went into the office. There was no way she could stare out the window, letting all sorts of scenarios run through her mind.

One way to take her mind off everything was to immerse herself in the ranch's books. So she took a deep breath and pulled up the form she'd been working from as well as the papers. Then she got to work.

To her surprise, while working, she found three instances where it looked as if Gilroy had purposefully transposed numbers. A thousand dollars here, two thousand there, and so on, and it added up quickly.

Now that she knew what to look for, Abby was able to quickly scan through each month and locate the easiest places where the CPA had begun taking the money. But one question remained. Why? The Easts were paying him a very nice salary, so why would he need to take more? That had her picking up the phone and calling the bank.

Because she still technically worked for Gloria, the bank was used to her calling to see about certain clients and how many accounts they had open. Within minutes, she learned that Nathan Gilroy had opened another account at the branch three years earlier.

Abby quickly added up a few months of sums that had gone missing and asked if those exact deposits had been made in each of those months. Once the banker confirmed it, Abby knew for sure how Gilroy had begun embezzling money. But something must have happened that made him need a much larger sum. Or he just got greedy.

She hung up the phone and sat back in the chair. She lifted her eyes, her gaze clashing with Clayton's. Her heart missed a beat as she jerked upright. His hair was stuck to his head with sweat, and he was covered in dust, but he was smiling and safe. He pushed away from the door and started toward her. Abby rushed around the desk and threw her arm around him.

He pressed his lips against the top of her head and kissed her. "It's over. Baxter and his men are in jail, the cattle are back in our pasture, and there's no longer a threat hanging over your family."

She leaned back to look up at him. "I've been so worried."

"I told you everything would be all right, and I always keep my word."

Abby nodded and hugged him again. "God, it's so good to have you back in my arms."

His hands came to either side of her face as he tilted her head up to look at him. "You and I need to talk. There are things I need to say to you."

"And there are things I need to say to you," she said.

A brow quirked up. "Do you now?"

"Yes," she whispered.

His pale green eyes grew laden with desire as his head lowered to hers. Just before their lips touched, Brice and Caleb began shouting her name.

They barreled into the office, both talking at once.

"Abby, you should've seen Clayton fight. It was amazing."

"I got to herd cattle, Abby. On top of a horse. I want a horse. Can I have a horse?"

"I really want to work on the ranch. I'll even do it for free."

"Me, too. Free."

She had trouble listening to both of them talk over each other, so she just nodded and smiled. Beside her, Clayton kept his arm around her while looking between the two teens.

"I think I need a shot of tequila now," he said when they finally quieted.

But all he did was turn her brothers' attention to him. They began talking again, this time bombarding him with questions about the ranch. As Abby watched the three most important men in her life, she was finally able to admit to herself that she was happy and that this was the life she wanted.

# Chapter 33

The talk Clayton had wanted to have with her, and she with him, didn't happen. Not that there weren't chances, but Abby always chickened out. Besides, she wasn't exactly sure what to say. And since he didn't bring it up, she was afraid to.

For the next week, leading up to Christmas, she and her brothers remained at the ranch. Brice and Caleb had rooms at the house, but they continued to sleep with Shane and the other ranch hands in the bunkhouse. Yet, they were up and ready on time each morning for school.

As for Abby, she had officially resigned her position with Gloria and had registered for a full load of classes starting the upcoming spring semester. And she continued to work as the ranch's bookkeeper—she refused to use "CPA" until she had the degree and the certification.

With the extra money she earned at the ranch, she declined Clayton's offer and paid a crew to go in and clean up the house herself. It had taken them several days, and unfortunately, they were finishing that very day. Which meant she had no reason to remain at the ranch after Christmas.

She saved the spreadsheet she'd been working on and thought about the days—and nights—at the ranch. They had all settled into a routine.

Justine made breakfast where they all gathered in the morning. The boys downed as much food as they could after going so long with so little. Clayton ate almost as much as they did, but she wasn't much for food in the mornings, so Abby was content with a cup of coffee.

Ben drove the boys to school while Justine cleaned the kitchen. Clayton would give Abby a lingering kiss and a wink before walking out to meet Shane. And she would make her way to the office.

Doing the books for the ranch was a full-time position. There was so much to keep her occupied until lunch, and then again until her brothers came home from school and she helped Justine with dinner.

Most nights, Ben and Justine would disappear somewhere together, and her brothers would head off with Shane, doing whatever they could to spend time with the horses. That left her and Clayton with a lot of time together that they made use of by making love.

Abby pushed back from the desk and stood. Her arm was much better, though she still had some pain. She walked to a closet in the office to take out the bags of presents she'd bought her brothers.

It was a sad fact that she was spoiling them fiercely this year. The extra money she brought in had gone to get them caught up with most of the bills, but she kept some out to give her brothers a Christmas the likes of which they'd never had.

She had wrapped the gifts earlier that morning, and she needed to move them to the trunk of her car so her brothers wouldn't see them. Because she didn't plan on putting anything out until Christmas morning.

Yet when she opened the door, the packages were gone. Abby's heart fell to her stomach. She turned and walked from the office to find Justine.

"Hello, dear," Justine said when she looked up from frosting a cake.

"Hi. I'm . . . ah . . . did you happen to find some bags full of presents that I kept in the office closet? I put them in there this morning."

Justine smiled and rotated the cake, bending to see it better. "I did. They're under the living room tree."

"Oh." Well, what did she say to that? "I was actually going to put those under our tree." Never mind that she hadn't actually bought a new tree or ornaments yet. That was something she'd stay up until dawn doing if need be.

Justine looked at her over the cake. "You mean you're leaving?"

"Well, the house is ready."

"So?"

Abby swallowed, racking her brain for what to say. "There's no reason for us to stay now, and I—"

"No reason to stay?" Justine repeated, raising an eyebrow as she straightened. "Are you sure of that?"

She looked away. There was every incentive to stay, but Clayton hadn't asked her. And to be fair, she hadn't had the guts to talk to him about it.

Yet, in her mind, it was his family, his house. It should be up to him to ask her to stay. And he hadn't. In fact, he hadn't mentioned anything about a relationship or his feelings toward her at all. She knew he cared for her. He showed her every day in so many ways.

"Don't go," Justine said. "You promised to stay for dinner tonight anyway. So why not remain so we can have Christmas together?"

That was two days from now. There was nothing she wanted more than to wake up Christmas morning in Clayton's arms. Actually, she wanted to do that every morning.

If Ben or Justine knew that they were sharing a bed, neither of them let it show. Abby had gone to great pains so that they didn't know, and Clayton went along with her, smiling and shaking his head.

"You're family now, Abby," Justine said.

She lowered her gaze to the countertop. "Y'all have been so good to us."

"Then let us continue."

There was no way Abby could refuse, and Justine knew it. Besides, Abby wanted to stay. This gave her the excuse. Clayton knew the progress on her house. What if he expected her to leave tonight? What if her fears had come true and his feelings had changed?

"Okay," Abby said, even as her stomach knotted with all her uncertainties and terrors.

She somehow got through the rest of the afternoon until dinner. Clayton walked in the back door and greeted her with a smile and a kiss before he went upstairs for his shower.

Abby had searched his face for any sign that he wasn't

happy to see her, but she didn't decipher anything. She even thought to go up after him so they could talk. But her doubts held her back.

If he did want to end their time together, why would she want to know that before Christmas? Why not wait until after so at least she, Caleb, and Brice could have a wonderful holiday?

She backed off the stairs and went to the office to do more work until it was time to eat. And when dinner came, she found herself looking around, trying to remember every detail.

Just in case.

"You need to be careful," Justine said the next morning.

Clayton glanced behind him to look for Abby. He frowned at his mother. "Shhh."

"She wanted to leave yesterday."

He paused with the coffee halfway to his mouth. Clayton pinned his mother with a look. "Why didn't you tell me last night?"

"Couldn't you see something was different about her?"

"Yeah. When I asked, she told me she was tired."

His mother rolled her eyes. "Lord, give me strength." Then she looked at him. "Your plan isn't going to work."

"It will."

"She's pulling away, Clayton. Look around," Justine said, spreading her arms. "She never misses a breakfast, but she's not here. She's in the office."

Clayton set his mug down and blew out a breath. "Damn."

"Uh, yeah," his mother snapped.

"I've given her no indication that I wanted her to leave."

His mother shot him a flat look. "You've not told her you want her to stay either."

"I plan on it."

"Son, you should've already told her instead of waiting. I warned you this might happen."

She had, but Clayton had felt sure Abby would take his actions over his words. And he'd made a point of doing everything he could to let her know that he not only wanted her to stay but that he loved her—short of actually saying the words.

He stood from the bar stool and walked to the office, ignoring his mother, who tried to call him back. He walked into the room and found Abby standing at the window watching Caleb and Brice.

"You feeling okay?" he asked as he came to stand beside her.

She looked at him and smiled. "Yeah, I just wanted an early start today. Then I saw my brothers. Do you know that it used to take an act of God every morning to get them out of bed and into the shower? After their shower, they'd go back to sleep. I had to get them up twice. Every morning," she said with a grin. But it faded softly. "And look at them now."

"It upsets you?"

"Just thinking of the future."

"Which upsets you," he guessed.

She gave a light snort with a half grin that followed. "I have so much to thank you and your family for. I don't believe I'll ever be able to repay any of it."

"Who says we want you to repay it?" he asked and wrapped an arm around her.

She rested her head on his shoulder. "We struggled for so long, clawing for every little scrap we could get our hands on. This is such a different world."

"If the money is the issue, I can stop paying you." He smiled when he heard her laugh.

He wanted to make her laugh every day, because the sound warmed his heart just as her smile touched his soul. She'd healed parts of him he hadn't known were broken.

"I have a habit of assuming you know what I want," he told her. "It's why I didn't ask you to stay for Christmas. I thought you knew."

She looked up at him and gave him a genuine smile. "I'll stay. To be honest, I don't think I'll ever get my brothers to leave."

"I'm fine with that. As long as you stay with them."

She searched his face. Clayton almost told her everything right then and there, but he'd been planning for a week now and everything was almost complete.

"My house is done," she said.

He shrugged. "It's clean. It isn't furnished. In case you forgot, they broke and tore up the bed and mattresses. I've been working you pretty hard here, so unless you bought replacements online, you don't have a place to sleep."

"It wouldn't be the first time we slept on the floor."

Those words broke his heart. He held her tighter. "You'll never sleep on the floor again if I have anything to say about it."

"Living here, working here is like a dream. It's hard not to wonder when the nightmare will start."

He kissed her temple. "I could tell you that it won't, but I don't think you'd believe me."

"Look at my brothers," she said. "Their time here has wiped away the past."

He turned her to look at him. "They wanted to let go. Do you?"

"Yes. Very much so," she said with a nod.

"Then let go."

"It's not that easy."

He smoothed back her dark hair and looked into her beautiful, blue eyes. "It is when you have someone to catch you." Clayton wanted to shoot Shane when he called his name from the kitchen. "I've got to go. You going to be okay?"

"Of course," she stated. "Why wouldn't I be?"

He decided not to reply to that question. "I'll see you later."

Clayton kissed her deeply, stirring the fires of desire between them. When he pulled back, her eyes were glossy and her lips swollen.

If he couldn't tell her what he wanted—yet—he could leave her thinking about him.

"Until later," he whispered.

She nodded, grinning. "I'll hold you to that."

"You won't have to." He gave her a wink and went to start his day.

# Chapter 34

*Christmas Eve*

He'd never been more nervous in his life. Clayton tugged at the sleeves of his red button-down. As planned, his mother kept Abby occupied all day so she wouldn't see him.

A knock on his door had him glancing at the clock before he bade them entry. He turned as Brice and Caleb entered the room. Clayton noted that both were wearing the new cowboy boots his parents had gotten them. Unable to wait until tomorrow, his mother had the gifts waiting at breakfast. The boys had been wearing the boots ever since.

"You wanted to see us," Brice said.

Caleb closed the door behind him. "We didn't do anything wrong, did we?"

"No," Clayton said with a smile. "I wanted to ask both of you something. I should've done it earlier in the week, but I didn't want your sister to know anything."

Brice nodded. "And you didn't think we could keep a secret."

"I didn't want to chance it," Clayton said. He cleared his throat. "The thing is, I like all of you living here. I want the three of you to continue living at the ranch. And I want to make it official. I love Abby, and I'd like both of your consents for me to ask her to be my wife."

Brice merely stared at him, but Caleb broke out into a wide grin. "Hot damn. I knew it! I'm all for it, Clayton, and not just because I love the ranch and want to stay here forever. You make Abby happy, and that's enough for me."

Clayton swung his gaze to Brice. "What about you?"

"Abby always denied it, but I used to hear her crying in her room at night. She was stressed about everything, and she was lonely. Everything changed when you came into our lives. I've seen a real smile on my sister's face these last few weeks, and I've watched all the worries slowly melt away." Brice hooked a finger in the belt loop of his jeans. "You don't just make her happy, you protect her. As long as you keep doing that, then I'll give you my blessing."

Clayton bowed his head to Brice. The unspoken threat hung between them, and Clayton had no doubt that if he ever stepped out of line, Brice would be more than happy to not just call him on it, but to take action, as well.

"When are you popping the question?" Caleb asked.

Clayton put his hand on the front pocket of his jeans where the ring rested. "Tonight."

"That's why you hung up the lights," Brice said with a grin. "Shane said it was for the annual party."

Caleb smiled as he shook his head. "I wish I could be there. Make it special for her. Abby deserves the best."

"That she does," Clayton agreed.

Brice elbowed Caleb. "If we go down and help Mrs. Justine now, she'll let us into the sweets."

"Good. I'm starving," his brother answered.

Brice rolled his eyes. "You're always hungry."

"So are you."

That's when the elder of the brothers grinned. "Yeah. I know."

The two walked to the door, but they paused and looked back at Clayton.

"Good luck," Brice said.

Caleb met Clayton's gaze. "I'll be proud to call you brother."

Clayton was taken aback at Caleb's words. He saw a glimpse of the man the youngest Harper would become.

Both of the brothers had shown courage, tenacity, and persistence over the last few weeks, alluding to the men they were becoming. It was a bit daunting to know that he'd had a hand in it, and while he was terrified of screwing up, he was proud of the changes he saw in the teens.

Once they were gone, Clayton looked in the mirror again. He raked his hands through his hair, trying to get it to behave. Then he gave up and grabbed his hat.

When he walked down the stairs, he heard Abby's voice. Just hearing her made him smile. Whether she and her brothers knew it or not, they had become a part of the East family. His parents adored all three of the Harpers, and Clayton was very fond of the boys, as well.

But he was utterly and completely in love with Abby.

He reached the bottom of the stairs and made his way into the kitchen. It was the hub of the house, the place where everyone gathered at all hours of the day. And that was because of his mother and her amazing cooking.

Yet it wasn't his mother he was looking at now, it was Abby. The woman who held his heart had her beautiful, long, dark locks flowing freely down her back. He gazed appreciatively over her mouth-watering curves in the body-hugging, long-sleeved hunter green velvet dress that stopped a few inches shy of her ankles. She wore strappy black heels that added to her sexy look.

Abby leaned to the side, revealing a slit that traveled up her right leg to her thigh. He went hard instantly. It was all Clayton could do not to throw her over his shoulder and take her upstairs.

Then she turned and saw him. The smile that lit up her face made his heart catch. How in the world had a woman like her found her way into his life? When he thought about everything that had occurred just for them to meet, he couldn't help but feel it was fated.

She mouthed, "Hi."

He walked to her and put his hands on her hips. "You look too beautiful for words."

She beamed up at him. "And you look incredibly handsome."

"Mom, do you have everything covered?" he asked without looking away from Abby.

"I do," his mother replied.

"Yep," his father said around a mouthful of chocolate chip cookie.

As one, Caleb and Brice popped meatballs into their mouths and said, "Mhm."

"Good," Clayton said.

Abby raised a brow. "Why do I think you did that on purpose?"

"Because we're going for a walk."

Her brows snapped into a frown. "Now? Aren't there guests arriving?"

Justine smiled and said, "Oh, I think I forgot to tell you we cancelled the party."

"Come on. Just for a little while," Clayton coaxed.

Abby smiled and playfully rolled her eyes. "As if I can say no to you."

He put his hand on Abby's back and led her away. He glanced behind him, giving the others a wink before he helped Abby into her coat. He slipped his jacket on and took her hand as he walked her outside.

"It's freezing," she mumbled.

He chuckled. "Not for long. Trust me."

She followed when he tugged her hand. Clayton led her around to the back of the barn where Shane had hitched one of the horses to a small carriage.

"Oh, my God," she said with a delighted laugh.

"It belonged to my great-grandparents."

Abby walked around it, touching and inspecting the carriage. "Are you taking me for a ride?"

"I am," he said and held out his hand.

She bit her lip as he helped her up inside the carriage before joining her and covering her with the blanket.

Then he gathered the reins, and with a little flick, set the horse into motion.

"This is amazing," she said, looking up at the stars.

It was a clear, beautiful night. Clayton glanced at the half moon and nodded.

They rode in silence for a spell. Abby then leaned her head on his shoulder. "There's nothing in the world that can top the day I've had."

"Is that so?" he asked, hiding his grin.

Her head jerked up as she looked at him with wide eyes. "It's like I stepped into a movie or book. The house with all the decorations, the Christmas music, the presents—that seem to multiply overnight under all the trees, I might add—and let's not forget the amazing smells that constantly come from the kitchen. And now this. It's been magical."

"There's more to come."

She shook her head. "This is all I need. Being surrounded by friends and having my brothers experiencing such a delightful Christmas."

He looked at her and smiled before giving her a quick kiss. "I'm glad you're enjoying it."

She was about to reply when she looked ahead and narrowed her eyes. "Are those lights?"

"Yep."

"Way out here?"

"Yep."

She swiveled her head to him and stared at him a moment. "Are we going there?"

"We sure are."

Abby didn't say anything else as the distance closed. She kept her gaze straight ahead, looking at the lights, but Clayton was dying to know what was going through her head.

He hoped she said yes to his proposal, but he was prepared for her to decline. There was no doubt in his mind that she cared for him, and he was willing to give her as much time as she needed to realize that he wasn't going anywhere. He'd ask her a million times if that was what it took.

When they finally reached the area, he pulled back on the reins to halt the horse and looked over his handiwork. He had to admit, the area did have an enchanted look about it.

Strung between three trees were dozens of Christmas lights. In a circle around the trees were four cordless heaters he'd bought specifically for this. And in the middle of it all was a wool blanket laid out on the ground with several pillows of various sizes. There was a bucket of champagne and two glasses.

"Clayton," she said in a whisper as she gazed at the setting.

"It's all for you, darlin'."

When she turned her gaze to him, there were tears shining in her eyes. "It's stunning."

He wrapped the reins around the brake and jumped down before holding out a hand to her. "Come see."

She didn't need to be told twice. He helped her down, and they walked to the blanket. Abby looked up, smiling at the lights. He watched her, awed by how the little things meant so much to her. He was thankful the heaters were putting off enough warmth so she wouldn't be shivering. His woman had a distinct dislike for the cold.

"The lights would've been enough," she said as she faced him. "But the heaters, too?"

"I couldn't have your teeth chattering."

"You're amazing," she said and threw her arms around him.

He caught her, holding her close. "Only because of you."

They remained locked in each other's arms for another minute before he pulled back and tugged her down onto the blanket.

"Even the blanket is warm," she said with a laugh.

He shrugged but was smiling inside. "Heated."

She threw back her head and laughed as she tucked her legs against her and leaned on one hand. "How long have you been working on this?"

"All week."

"Sneaky, but I heartily approve. No one has ever done anything like this for me."

"I'd like the chance to do it often," he said.

She looked at him. "Is this your way of telling me you want to date me?"

"It's my way of saying I love you, and I want you in my life." He rose up on one knee, but it took him two tries to get the ring from his pocket because his hand was shaking. With his heart beating a million times a second, he held the ring out to her. "Abby Harper, I didn't know how much my life would change after meeting you, but I thank God that it did. I'm a better man with you by my side, and I can't imagine life without you. Will you marry me?"

# Chapter 35

Was this really happening? Abby pinched herself to make sure it wasn't a dream.

Her blood was rushing so loudly, she could barely hear. And that's when Clayton rose up on one knee. She gasped, her stomach aflutter when she watched him fish the ring out of his pocket. As she listened to his declaration and words of love, all she could think about was how she felt with Clayton.

Safe. Needed. Beautiful.

Loved.

"You love me?" she asked.

He smiled, laughing softly. "Very much. Did you hear the rest?"

"I didn't know you loved me. I mean, I know I love you, but you never said anything," she replied.

His green eyes crinkled at the corners. "Neither did you."

"I was scared."

"Me, too. I thought you might run off."

She shook her head. "I couldn't."

"And the rest of what I said?" he asked hopefully. "Will you marry me?"

Abby was mortified as she realized he'd been on his knee, holding the ring during their conversation. She shifted onto her knees and touched his face. At that moment, it was like she was cocooned in love, Clayton's love.

"Yes," she answered.

He yanked her against him, his mouth taking hers in a savage kiss full of desire, need, and hope. She clung to him as he shifted them until she was on her back. Despite her trying to keep kissing him, he pulled back.

"Ah, woman, what you do to me."

"Then why did you stop?" she asked breathlessly.

"For this." He leaned to the side and took her left hand before slipping the band onto her finger.

Abby held up her left hand and gazed at the ring with the lights above her.

"It belonged to my grandmother and her grandmother before her," he said.

She stared in wonder at the ring. It was as if it had been made just for her. The delicate rose gold eternity band had graceful diamond-set scrolls that gave it a timeless, elegant look she loved.

"If you'd rather a new diamond, I can get that for you," Clayton said.

Abby shook her head. "It's perfect. Absolutely perfect."

"Just as you are."

She pulled him back down atop her. "You were meant for me. And I for you."

"Yes. I know that no matter what the future holds for us, we'll get through it together. And I'll reassure you every day that I'm not going to leave you."

That made her smile. He wasn't angry about her fears. He acknowledged them and was willing to work with her. Few men would have done such a thing.

"The abandonment issues I once had don't have such a strong hold over me anymore," she told him. "I don't even know when they stopped having control, only that the fear is like a tiny voice now instead of the roar it once was."

Clayton ran his hand along her cheek as he looked down at her with love shining in his eyes. "I'm going to love you forever, Abby Harper. I'm going to love you so fiercely and so hard that you'll never doubt us for one instant."

"You stole my heart, but you gave me a love so pure and wonderful that you mended everything that was broken inside me. With you, I can do anything."

He leaned down and kissed her. "Merry Christmas, darlin'."

"Merry Christmas."

Abby was near to bursting she was so full of joy. And this was just the beginning of a life of love and wonder before her. A life with the man who was her warrior and hero—Clayton East.

# Epilogue

*Four months later . . .*

"It's time, Abby," Brice said.

She turned from the mirror and smiled at him and Caleb, who stood in the doorway. "You two look so handsome."

At her words, Caleb beamed and tipped his cowboy hat at her while Brice fidgeted with the buttoned collar of his shirt. The three of them had never left the East ranch. Once she and Clayton had returned on Christmas Eve, there had been a huge celebration for their engagement.

Her brothers became quite the cowboys over the next few months. Both rode a horse like they'd been born to it, and their happiness extended to other parts of their lives. Their grades were great, and they both had begun to hang with different friends, but their attention was on the ranch. They willingly did their chores every day without having to be told.

"Abby, you look beautiful," Caleb said as he walked into the room.

She looked down at her wedding dress. Though she hadn't cared about having one, Clayton and Justine had insisted that she get something. Surprisingly, she'd found the perfect one. The vintage lace dress matched perfectly with the ambiance of the wedding set at the ranch.

The gown had long, lace sleeves and a bodice that hugged her figure before the lace dropped in an A-line skirt to the ground. The veil was actually Justine's from her wedding. Never before had Abby felt so beautiful or special.

With a brother on each arm, Abby walked from her room, down the stairs, and out the back of the house just as the sun was setting. The yard had been turned into a scene right out of a fairytale. Flowers dripped from everywhere.

There was a huge tent that had tiny lights strung across the top to mimic the spot where Clayton had proposed. But that was for the reception. Now, her brothers walked her toward an archway of flowers and more tiny lights where Clayton waited.

His blond hair was still long at her request, and his pale green eyes were locked on her. His smile was sexy as he gave a nod of approval when he saw her. His black suit fit him to perfection. She would have to find other reasons for him to wear it, because it looked stunning on him.

And then she was standing before him. Her brothers handed her off, each of them kissing her cheek before going to their seats. Clayton took her hand in his as he gave her a little squeeze.

"My God, woman. You put the stars to shame, you shine so brightly," he whispered.

"You're wearing that suit again. I can't stop staring."

"I'll wear it every damn day then," he said with a wink.

She never took her eyes off Clayton as they exchanged vows and wedding rings. Before she knew it, Clayton was kissing her. The loud cheer that went up had both of them smiling—and remembering that they weren't alone.

"You're mine now," Clayton said as he pressed his forehead to hers.

"I've been yours."

His crooked grin made her stomach flutter. "Let's get out of here and start our honeymoon."

"We can't," she said with a laugh. "And we need to walk down the aisle to the reception."

"You've got an hour, Mrs. East. Then I'll throw you over my shoulder and carry you out of here."

She was smiling when they turned to face their guests. Hand-in-hand, they walked down the aisle to start their new lives. Abby didn't know what the future held, but she knew whatever came, it would be worth it being loved by—and loving—Clayton East.

Her hero.

Her cowboy.